国家社科基金项目“中越跨境民族民间歌谣比较研究
广西一流学科（培育）建设项目：百色学院马克思主义理论一流学科（培育）资助
广西“桂西民族语言文化与译介研究基地”研究成果
百色学院“桂西民族典籍译介研究团队”研究成果

那坡壮族民歌

（汉英对照）

Zhuang's Folk Songs of Napo

(Chinese-English Version)

主　编／覃　丹
副主编／苏虎典　曾湘云　李　涵　祝远德

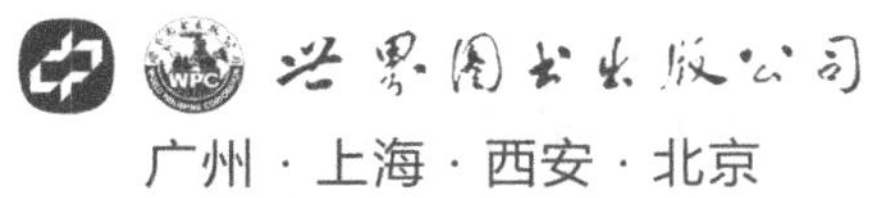

广州 · 上海 · 西安 · 北京

图书在版编目（CIP）数据

那坡壮族民歌：汉英对照 / 覃丹主编 . —广州：世界图书出版广东有限公司，2020.6（2025.1重印）

ISBN 978-7-5192-7522-8

Ⅰ. ①那… Ⅱ. ①覃… Ⅲ. ①壮族—民歌—作品集—那坡县—汉、英 Ⅳ. ① I277.291.8

中国版本图书馆 CIP 数据核字（2020）第 089066 号

书　　名　那坡壮族民歌（汉英对照）
　　　　　NAPO ZHUANGZU MINGE（HANYING DUIZHAO）
主　　编　覃　丹
副 主 编　苏虎典　曾湘云　李　涵　祝远德
责任编辑　魏志华
装帧设计　苏　婷
责任技编　刘上锦
出版发行　世界图书出版广东有限公司
地　　址　广州市海珠区新港西路大江冲 25 号
邮　　编　510300
电　　话　020-84451969　84453623　84184026　84459579
网　　址　http://www.gdst.com.cn
邮　　箱　wpc_gdst@163.com
经　　销　各地新华书店
印　　刷　悦读天下（山东）印务有限公司
开　　本　787mm×1092mm　1/16
印　　张　22.75
字　　数　422 千
版　　次　2020 年 6 月第 1 版　　2025 年 1 月第 3 次印刷
国际书号　ISBN 978-7-5192-7522-8
定　　价　98.00 元

咨询、投稿：020-34201910　weilai21@126.com

国家级非物质文化遗产保护名录

《那坡壮族民歌》

主　编：梁必政

《名花风情歌》

收　集：岑隆恩／汉　译：黄　峰

《浪花歌》

收　集：方国弟／汉　译：黄建忠　方国弟

英译组

覃　丹　苏虎典　曾湘云　李　涵　祝远德

前言

中越边境线上的边陲小城广西壮族自治区百色市那坡县生活着壮族的一个特殊群体。他们以黑为美，以全黑的服饰作为族群的标志，因此，人们习惯以“黑衣壮”来称呼他们。他们保留着原始的生活方式和习俗以及古朴而独特的传统文化，被誉为壮族的“活化石”。

在历史的发展长河中，那坡壮族祖先创造了非常丰富灿烂的民族文化，尤其是他们那远古而精彩的歌谣艺术，可谓是壮族文化宝库里一颗璀璨的明珠，中华民族民间文学园圃里一朵奇丽的花朵，值得当今的人们去挖掘、收集、整理、研究、传承、保护和推介。2006 年，由那坡县人民政府申报，那坡壮族民歌被列入第一批国家非物质文化遗产名录。2015 年，那坡县文化和体育广电局在编撰《那坡县民族文化丛书》时把《那坡壮族民歌》排在丛书之首。2016 年 5 月，《那坡壮族民歌（第一、二卷）》由广西人民出版社正式出版发行。也正是在《那坡壮族民歌（第一、二卷）》出版之际，我们与那坡县文化馆签订了《那坡壮族民歌》英译的合作协议书。

本书选取了《那坡壮族民歌（第一、二卷）》中最精彩、最能体现那坡壮族民歌特色的两套长歌《名花风情歌》和《浪花歌》进行英文翻译。《名花风情歌》通过男女对唱的形式，贯穿以青年男女别致的恋情彩线，围绕买花种、求雨、育种、砍树围园、种花、养花、赏花、修花、收花的对唱，既对种花的劳动过程和相关习俗风情进行了详细的描述，又以花为载体暗喻了爱情的发展过程。歌词中的各种比喻往往令人忍俊不禁、拍案叫绝又回味无穷。《浪花歌》是走亲访友时必唱的歌，整套歌由邀请歌、对浪花歌、请宵夜、禁鸡鸣歌、瞌睡歌、褒家里歌、吩咐歌、送下楼梯歌、分别歌、叮咛歌等组成，既再现了壮族通宵达旦、难舍难分的对歌场景，也是壮乡待客礼仪的生动教材。这两套长歌都是直接采自民间、活态的民歌，风格各异，都是那坡壮族“以歌代言、以歌取乐、以歌会友、以歌传情”的真实表达。

需要特别说明的是，第一，本书是国家社科基金项目“中越跨境民族民间歌谣比较研究”（项目编号：17XZW016）的阶段性研究成果之一，也是广西高校人文社科重点研究基地“桂西民族语言文化与译介研究基地”和百色学院特色研究团队“桂西民族典籍译介研究团队”的研究成果。第二，本书得到了广西一流学科（培育）建设项目（桂教科研〔2018〕12号）：百色学院马克思主义理论一流学科（培育）资助。第三，本英文翻译团队的四名成员中，覃丹和李涵负责翻译《浪花歌》，苏虎典和曾湘云负责翻译《名花风情歌》。在长达三年的翻译过程中，四人始终同心同德，为那坡壮族民歌的英译和传播竭尽全力。两次闭关集中翻译，数次集中研讨，几易其稿，使译稿得到了一步步完善。第四，为了便于读者赏析，我们征得了《那坡壮族民歌》主编梁必政的同意，把《那坡壮族民歌（第一、二卷）》中《名花风情歌》和《浪花歌》两套歌的汉语原版也编排进来，进行汉英对照，使读者能够更好地感受那坡壮族民歌的魅力。

在付梓之际，我们首先要感谢广西大学外国语学院原院长祝远德教授。本英文译稿自始至终都得到了他的指导，并由他帮我们进行了最后的修改和审稿，从每个文化负载词的翻译、英译策略的选择到翻译风格的确定，无不浸润着他的心血。祝教授严谨的治学态度、敏锐的学术眼光、独到的学术视角、厚实的翻译功底是我们学习的榜样，也是我们努力的方向。

我们还要感谢那坡县文化和体育广电局局长梁必政，正是他的远见卓识和对那坡壮族民歌的热爱使得《那坡壮族民歌》得以面世，也是在他的大力支持和帮助下，我们对《那坡壮族民歌》的英译研究才成为可能。感谢那坡县文化馆馆长李冲、副馆长黄克日的大力协助，感谢《那坡壮族民歌》编辑部，特别是执行主编黄峰老师、编者之一方国弟老师，他们总能在我们需要的时候提供及时、无私的帮助，使我们能够更好、更深入地理解民歌。他们几十年如一日地热爱、保护和传承那坡壮族民歌的精神使我们由衷钦佩。

感谢百色学院校领导，我们的翻译工作自始至终得到了他们的支持和帮助。感谢外国语学院的同人们，他们的关注和鼓励给予了我们莫大的鼓舞。最后，还要感谢我们的家人，这三年中，他们一直支持我们、鼓励我们，任劳任怨，无怨无悔，为我们解除了后顾之忧。

翻译没有最好，只有更好。我们的译文从初稿到终稿，几经修改，但由于才疏学浅，倘有需要完善的地方，敬请各位专家、学者和广大读者批评指正。

译 者
2019 年 6 月 30 日

Preface

There is a special group of Zhuang people living in Napo County, Guangxi, a border county between China and Vietnam. They regard black as beauty and black clothing as the symbol of their ethnic group, therefore, people usually call them "Black Clothing Zhuang"; and for their primitive way of life and customs and unique traditional culture, they are also known as the "Living Fossils" of Zhuang people.

In the long history of development, the ancestors of Zhuang in Napo created very rich and splendid national culture, especially their ancient and wonderful art of ballads, which is a shining pearl in the treasure house of the Zhuang culture, and a magnificent flower in the garden of Chinese folk literature. They are worth digging, collecting, sorting, researching, inheriting, protecting and promoting. In 2006, thanks to the application by Napo County People's Government to related authorities, Zhuang's Folk Songs of Napo were approved in the first list of the national intangible cultural heritage. In 2015, Napo County Bureau of Culture, Sports, Radio and Television listed Zhuang's Folk Songs of Napo in the first part when compiling the Napo county Ethnic Culture Series. In May 2016, *Zhuang's Folk Songs of Napo* (Volumes I and II) were formally published by Guangxi People's Publishing House. Just at the same time, we have signed a cooperation agreement with Napo County Cultural Center to translate *Zhuang's Folk Songs of Napo* into English.

This translated text is a selection of two chief songs from *Zhuang's Folk Songs of Napo* (Volumes I and II), namely, *Song of Love Flowers* and *Romantic Lyrics*, which are the most exciting parts and can best reflect the characteristics of Napo Zhuang's folk songs. *Song of Love Flowers* is a form of male and female antiphonal singing, the unique love between young men and women are embodied in the detailed description of the labor process and related customs such as in buying flower seeds, praying for rain, breeding seeds, chopping trees, planting flowers, cultivating flowers, enjoying flowers, trimming flowers, and collecting flowers. With flowers as the carrier metaphor for the development of love, the various lyrics often make people laugh, feel amazed and memorable. *Romantic Lyrics* are the songs that must be sung when visiting relatives and friends, which are composed of Songs of Invitation, Song of Romance, Inviting for Night Snacks, *Alternative Songs*, Overwhelming Cock's Crow, Farewell to Sleepiness, Song of Household Affairs, Song of Lingering, Down the Stairs, Song for Departure, Wish and Response, etc. These songs not only reproduce the scene of Zhuang people singing songs all night long, but also vividly describe the hospitality etiquette of Zhuang people. Though the two songs directly collected from the folk life are of different styles, they are the real expressions of the Napo Zhuang people that "singing for endorsement, singing for fun, singing for friends and singing for love".

What needs to be specially stated is that, firstly, this translation is one of the phased research results of the national social science fund project "Comparative Study of Cross-Bordered Ethnic Ballads between China and Vietnam" (project number: 17XZW016). Secondly, it receives publication funding from "The Construction (Cultivation) Project of First-class Discipline in Guangxi Province (Project Number: GuiJiao Keyan No. [2018]12): The Project of First-class Discipline of Marxist Theory of Baise University". Thirdly, in our four-membered translation group, Ms. Qin Dan and Ms. Li Han are responsible for translating *Romantic Lyrics*, while Mr. Su Hudian and Ms. Zeng Xiangyun are translators of *Song of Love Flowers*. During the three-year translation periods, we have been working hard together for the translation and dissemination of Napo Zhuang's folk songs, with twice closed-door concentrated translation and several times discussions, many drafts were made and the translation was improved. Fourthly, in order to make the reader comprehend the songs better, we had gained the permission of Mr. Liang Bizheng, the chief editor of *Zhuang's Folk Songs of Napo*, to put the Chinese version of *Song of Love Flowers* and *Romantic Lyrics* together with our English translation.

At the time of publishing, we must first thank Professor Zhu Yuande, former Dean of the School of Foreign Languages in Guangxi University, for his guidance from the very beginning to the end. He helped us with the review and final proof of the manuscript. The translation of culturally-loaded words, the choice of translation strategies, and the determination of translation style all witness his painstaking efforts. Professor Zhu's rigorous academic attitude, keen and unique academic perspective, and solid translation skills are examples of our learning and the direction of our efforts.

We also wish to thank Mr. Liang Bizheng, Director of Napo County Bureau of Culture, Sports, Radio and Television and the chief editor of *Zhuang's Folk Songs of Napo*. It is his vision and dedications to the folk songs that make "Zhuang's Folk Songs of Napo" come into being. It is also due to his strong support and help that make this English translation possible. We would like to thank Mr. Li Chong and Mr. Huang Keri, the Directors of Napo County Cultural Center. We should also thank Editorial Department of Zhuang's Folk Songs of Napo, in particular, the executive editor Mr. Huang Feng and one members of the editors Mr. Fang Guodi, for their timely and selfless help so that we can better understand the songs. We highly appreciate their spirit of loving, protecting and inheriting Napo Zhuagn's folk songs for decades.

Our thanks would also go to the leaders of Baise University for their support and help during the entire translation publication process. We also wish to thank the colleagues of Foreign Languages School for their attention and encouragement. Finally, we also want to thank our family members who have been supporting us for the past three years, they have always supported us and encouraged us to work hard without complaint or regret, thus relieving us of worries.

There is no best translation, only better translation. This version has been revised several times from the first draft to the final. However, due to our limited knowledge, there are still rooms to be improved. We would highly appreciate criticism and suggestion from experts, scholars and readers.

Translators

June 30th, 2019

目 录 Contents

名花风情歌

Song of Love Flowers

目　录　Contents

浪花歌

Romantic Lyrics

名花风情歌

Song of Love Flowers

收集：岑隆恩
汉译：黄　峰
英译：苏虎典　曾湘云

一、赶圩买花种

Ⅰ Buying Flower Seeds in Village Fair

1

男：
来啊，妹，来啊，
既然得相会。

M:
Come on, come with me,
Since here we meet.

女：
随哥一起来，
既然得相会。

F:
I'll go with you,
As by chance I meet you.

2

男：
既然我俩得相见，
人情难接拢。

M:
Though we meet together,
I still dare not to venture.

女：
既然来接异地哥，
既然接上一枝花。

F:
I come to meet you from afar,
A flower ideal to my heart.

3

男：
心想栽朵名贵花，
不知合意不合意。

M:
I want to grow a rare flower,
Desirable or not I wonder.

女：
若哥有意就起步，
妹也好心随哥行。

F:
Go forward if you are sincere,
So I can be the follower.

4 男：
可惜墙脚四方木，
欲来流连栽花朵。

M:
As clumsy as a square timber,
How could I grow the flower?

女：
可惜墙角四方木，
若哥念起就栽花。

F:
As clumsy as a square timber,
You can grow it if you desire.

5 男：
哥命属柑树，
哥属恩桃木。

M:
I am orange tree,
I am cherry tree.

女：
妹命属橙树，
妹属柠檬木。

F:
I am lemon tree,
We're trees of the same family.

6 男：
栽花不吐芽，
哪天长出苗？

M:
No bud is yet to show,
When can the shoots grow?

女：
栽花要吐芽，
哪天长也得。

F:
Buds will sprout if you grow,
Soon enough they will show.

7 男：
栽花不吐芽，
哪天长出苗？

M:
No bud is yet to show,
When can the shoots grow?

女：
哥属路上金樱花，
来往人爱瞧。

F:
You're Cherokee rose by the road,
Attracting the people come and go.

8

男：
栽花不乱生，
种花不乱长。

M:
So hard to grow flowers that can live,
So hard to grow flowers that can flourish.

女：
哥命去栽花才生，
郎命去种花才长。

F:
You're to grow flowers that can live,
You're to grow flowers that can flourish.

9

男：
正月降寒霜，
腊月降雪花，
我俩怎么办？

M:
There would be frosts in January,
In December there'd be snow,
What should we do with the flower?

女：
正月不乱降寒霜，
腊月不乱有大雪，
郎哥会盘算。

F:
It doesn't have frosts in January,
It doesn't snow in December,
You'll always be reliable.

10

男：
正月天风沙，
二月天多旱，
种花很难长。

M:
It's windy and dusty in January,
And it's draught in February,
Flowers can't grow easily.

女：
正月立春送吉利，
二月树木吐苗多，
种花长得乖。

F:
Spring comes with good fortune,
Trees sprout out in February,
Flowers can grow lively.

11 男：
栽花还缺种，
到哪天得栽？

M:
I wanna plant but no seeds,
When can I grow the flowers?

女：
花种共去寻，
花种共去买。

F:
We'll look for the seeds together,
We'll buy the seeds together.

12 男：
若妹有种去撒播，
若娘有种想去育。

M:
If you have seeds you can sow,
If you have seeds you can grow.

女：
没种一起找，
没种一起寻。

F:
We'll look for the seeds together,
We'll seek the seeds together.

13 男：
想撒没有种，
想栽没有苗。

M:
I wanna sow but no seeds,
I wanna plant but no seedlings.

女：
花种汉人处有卖，
花种摆摊有很多。

F:
Han people sell flower seeds,
The seeds on stalls are plenty.

14

男：
花种在远方，
晓妹是否能前去？

女：
大凡买得好花种，
路程多远妹也愿。

M:
Flowers seeds are far away,
Would you come along all the way?

F:
If good seeds can be obtained,
No matter how far is the way.

15

男：
指望妹愿行，
我俩讲好一起赶。

女：
唯重花朵愿前行，
路途多远愿启步。

M:
Thanks for coming along,
Together we'll go on.

F:
I wanna go for flowers,
No matter how far is the road.

16

男：
京城路途遥，
闹市路途远。

女：
京城本路遥，
好花在平川。

M:
It's far away to the fair,
It's far away to downtown.

F:
It's so far to the fair,
Good flowers are in the plains.

17

男：
一路没有中午饭，
随身携带晌午饭。

女：
一路没有中午餐，
随身携带晌午饭。

M:
No lunch on our trip,
We take some food along to eat.

F:
No lunch on our trip,
We need to take some food to eat.

18 男:
俩童来听道,
俩丁来听讲,
我们有话说。

M:
You kids please come over,
I have errands for you both,
I'm telling you what to do.

女:
俩童听哥唤,
俩丁来听讲,
蠢仔听哥说。

F:
Two kids thus come over,
Listen carefully together,
And run away for the errands.

19 男:
一丁去找柴,
一伊去找水。

M:
The boy may go for firewood,
The girl may go for some water.

女:
一丁去路上找柴,
一伊去泉井取水。

F:
He gets firewood on the way,
She fetches water from the well.

20 男:
一丁去取水也来,
一伊去找柴也到。

M:
The boy brings back the water,
The girl returns with firewood.

女:
孩童去取水也来,
俩伊去找柴也到。

F:
They bring back the water,
They return with the firewood.

21

男：
细柴来引火，
栗木来架上，
柑橘木来烧。

M:
Twigs are used to start fire,
Chestnut wood to enlarge the fire,
And citrus wood as the main fuel.

女：
一丁灶上架顶锅，
一伊锅底来烧火。

F:
The boy places the pot on stove,
The girl fires the wood under the pot.

22

男：
一丁舀水装下来，
一伊淘米放下锅。

M:
The boy scoops the water,
The girl washes the rice.

女：
米要煮几多？
午饭煮几筒？

F:
How much rice shall we cook?
How many tubes of rice do we need?

23

男：
米煮一筒多，
午饭煮筒半。

M:
Over one tube of rice to cook,
One and a half tube for lunch.

女：
煮筒米够吃，
煮筒多够餐。

F:
One tube is enough to eat,
Over one tube is plenty for lunch.

24

男：
饭锅灶上滚[1]，
用什么来搅。

M:
Rice is boiling in the pot,
What shall I use to stir?

女：
饭锅火上滚，
拿饭牌来搅。

F:
Rice is boiling in the pot,
Spatula serves as stirring lot.

25

男：
什么来搅饭才松？
什么来捞饭柔软？

M:
What to stir makes fluffy rice?
What to stir gets soft rice?

女：
饭牌来搅饭才松，
饭牌来捞饭才软。

F:
Stirring with spatula makes fluffy rice,
Stirring with spatula gets soft rice.

26

男：
丁端锅下三脚卯，
又把菜锅架顶上。

M:
The boy takes the pot from tripod,
And put the wok over to heat.

女：
丁端锅下三脚卯，
又把菜锅架顶上。

F:
The boy takes the pot from tripod,
And put the wok over to heat.

---

①滚，即锅里米饭开始沸腾。

27

男：	**M:**
菜是什么菜？	What are you cooking?
午餐是何食？	What do we have for lunch?
女：	**F:**
一起煮瓜苗，	We're cooking pumpkin sticks,
没有像人肉和鱼。	We have no meat and fish.

28

男：	**M:**
没有佳肴敬姑娘，	No excellent cuisine to serve you,
没有好食敬阿妹。	No good dishes to entertain you.
女：	**F:**
芥菜也是鱼，	Leaf mustard is fish to me,
瓜苗也是肉。	Pumpkin stick is meat to me.

29

男：	**M:**
菜锅火上滚，	Food is boiling on the fire,
放下什么它柔软？	What to make it soft?
女：	**F:**
菜锅火上滚，	Food is boiling on the fire,
放下油盐它柔软。	Oil and salt make it soft.

30

男：	**M:**
一丁提锅下火灶，	The boy takes the pot out of the range,
找个大盆来装菜。	With a big basin as dish plate.
女：	**F:**
提锅下火灶，	Taking the pot out of the range,
大盆来装菜。	A big basin as dish plate.

31	男： 童丁快下桌， 下桌先要什么摆？	**M:** I ask the kids to lay the table, What to place first?
	女： 童丁下饭桌， 摆桌要酱碟先下。	**F:** They are laying the table now, Sauce plate should be first.
32	男： 下桌丁下桌， 摆桌要什么摆下？	**M:** The kids are laying the table now, What to be set on the table?
	女： 下桌丁下桌， 下桌要碗筷摆下。	**F:** They're laying the table now, Bowls and chopsticks should be laid.
33	男： 童丁下饭桌， 下桌接着摆酒杯。	**M:** Now the kids are laying the table, They're placing wine cups on the table.
	女： 童丁下饭桌， 下桌再添套酒杯。	**F:** The kids are laying the table now, One more wine cup is enough.
34	男： 样样摆齐了， 一伊请师公入座。	**M:** All are well prepared , The girl invites the priest to the table.
	女： 样样摆齐了， 请道师入座。	**F:** Everything is prepared, The priest is invited to the table.

35

男：
丁请道公来午餐，
伊请师公来入席。

M:
The boy invites the priest to lunch,
The girl invites the master to the table.

女：
丁请道公坐上席，
我俩单身坐下方。

F:
Seat of honor is for the priest,
We have an inferior seat.

36

男：
请妹陪道公上座，
哥做仆人来打饭。

M:
With the priest you have an honor seat,
I'm willing to serve you I promise.

女：
吃饭吃得香，
吃饭漱口咱抽烟，
我俩流连欲赶路。

F:
The meal I really enjoy,
After lunch and smoke,
We will go on our way.

37

男：
晓妹吃罢了没有？
晓娘吃饱了未曾？

M:
Have you finished your meal?
Did you eat your fill?

女：
妹已就餐吃罢了，
娘也吃饱这餐饭。

F:
I've finished my meal,
I really ate my fill.

38

男：
妹说吃罢就收桌，
收桌收什么在先？

M:
You'll clear the table then,
What to clear first?

女：
吃罢同收桌，
收桌收碗盆在先。

F:
We'll clear the table together,
Bowls and basins first.

39

男：
后包晌午饭，
要粽叶来包。

M:
Then packing some food as reserve,
They should be packed with reed leaves.

女：
饭菜包下袋多点，
我俩安排欲赶路。

F:
Taking more food with you,
The food is taken in the bags.

40

男：
拿担找扁担挑，
带饭装口袋。

M:
The load needs a shoulder pole,
The food is taken in the bags.

女：
装担梢头固好钉，
包好午饭放口袋。

F:
Fixing nails on ends of the pole.
Packing the food into the bags.

41

男：
丁牵灰马出槽外，
伊备船舟放外头。

M:
The boy leads a gray horse out,
The girl prepares the boat outside.

女：
丁牵灰马出槽外，
伊备船舟放外头。

F:
The boy leads a gray horse out,
The girl prepares the boat outside.

42

男：	M:
请道公画符，	We invite the priest to draw magic figures,
请麽师画法。	And the master to cast the spell.
女：	F:
道公来画符，	The priest draws magic figures,
麽公来画法。	The master casts the spells.

43

男：	M:
画符下担头，	Magic figures are drawn on the load,
画法下扁担，	Spells are cast on the shoulder pole,
咱来安排欲赶路。	We get ready to take the road.
女：	F:
画符放担梢，	Magic figures are drawn on the load,
画法放担头，	Spells are cast on the shoulder pole,
儿孙安排欲赶路。	We're ready to take the road.

44

男：	M:
画法在船头，	Spells are on the head of the boat,
画符马鞍上。	Magic figures are on the saddle of the horse.
女：	F:
画法在船头，	Spells are on the head of the boat,
画符马鞍上。	Magic figures are on the saddle of the horse.

45

男：
公马驾紫鞍，
花鞍配母马，
哪匹顺妹骑。

M:
The stallion is fitted with a purple saddle,
The mare matches a colored one,
You choose the horse fits you well.

女：
公马配紫鞍，
花鞍配母马，
哪匹顺哥骑。

F:
The stallion is fitted with a purple saddle,
The mare matches a colored one,
You chose the horse matches you well.

46

男：
俩童来吾道，
俩丁来吾讲，
俩伊来吾说。

M:
You kids please come over,
I have errands for you all,
What to do are in my words.

女：
俩童听哥道，
俩丁听哥讲，
俩伊给哥说。

F:
The kids have come over,
You have errands for them all,
What to do are in yours words.

47

男：
一丁为娘牵马口，
一伊为妹驶船舟。

M:
The boy holds the horse for you,
The girl paddles the boat for you.

女：
一丁为郎牵马口，
一伊为哥驶船舟。

F:
The boy holds the horse for you,
The girl paddles the boat for you.

48

男：
慢在堂上列祖师，
慢在神台曾祖父。

M:
Farewell to ancestors at the ancestral tablets in the hall,
And the grand-father behind the altar.

女：
慢在堂上列祖师，
慢在神台曾祖父。

F:
Farewell to ancestors at the ancestral tablets in the hall,
And the grand-father behind the altar.

49

男：
慢在右台列祖宗，
慢在左台圣花婆。

M:
Farewell to forefathers on the right,
And the grandmothers on the left.

女：
慢在右台列祖宗，
慢在左台圣花婆。

F:
Farewell to forefathers on the right,
And grandmothers on the left.

50

男：
慢在高桌吃午餐，
慢在高台饮美酒。

M:
Farewell to high table where I have lunch,
And the high table for banquets.

女：
慢在高桌吃午餐，
慢在高台饮美酒。

F:
Farewell to high table where I have lunch,
And the high table for banquets.

51

男：
慢在平口煮菜锅，
慢在铁铸三脚卯。

M:
Farewell to the cooking pan,
As well as the metal tripod.

女：
慢在平口煮菜锅，
慢在铁铸三脚卯。

F:
Farewell to the cooking pan,
As well as the metal tripod.

52 男：
慢在四柱大碗柜，
慢在四角大楼房。

M:
Farewell to the four-pillar large cupboard,
And the four-angled grand house.

女：
慢在四柱大碗柜，
慢在四角大楼房。

F:
Farewell to the four-pillar large cupboard,
And the four-angled grand house.

53 男：
慢在花绿大瓷盆，
慢在画凤大瓷碗。

M:
Farewell to the colored porcelain basin,
And the phoenix-patterned porcelain bowl.

女：
慢在花绿大瓷盆，
慢在画凤大瓷碗。

F:
Farewell to the colored porcelain basin,
And the phoenix-patterned porcelain bowl.

54 男：
慢在门前李果树，
慢在窗前莎树木。

M:
Farewell to the plum tree in front of the door,
And the cedar tree in front of the window.

女：
慢在门前李果树，
慢在窗前莎树木。

F:
Farewell to the plum tree in front of the door,
And the cedar tree in front of the window.

55

男：
慢在楼角共晒台，
慢在亭榭共堂殿。

M:
Farewell to the terrace at the corner of the floor,
And the pavilion used as the hall.

女：
慢在楼角共晒台，
慢在亭榭共堂殿。

F:
Farewell to the terrace at the corner of the floor,
And the pavilion used as the hall.

56

男：
慢在水井共饮用，
慢在水槽共洗涤。

M:
Farewell to the well where we have water,
And the water slot where we do the wash.

女：
慢在泉井共饮用，
慢在水槽共洗涤。

F:
Farewell to the well where we have water,
And the water slot where we do the wash.

57

男：
慢在佑村土地庙，
慢在佑民神公堂。

M:
Farewell to community temple protecting the village,
And the God court blessing the villagers.

女：
慢在佑村土地庙，
慢在佑民神公堂。

F:
Farewell to community temple protecting the village,
And the God court blessing the villagers.

58

男：
骑马过坡路，
蛛网拦眼前。

M:
We're riding on the steep incline,
While entangled by the web of the spiders.

女：
骑马过坡路，
蛛网拦眼前。

F:
We're riding on the steep incline,
While entangled by the web of the spiders.

59

男：
到岔路穿鞋，
到沙滩穿袜。

M:
We leave traces at the crossroad,
We leave footprints on the sandy beach.

女：
到岔路穿鞋，
到沙滩穿袜。

F:
We leave traces at the crossroad,
We leave footprints on the sandy beach.

60

男：
歇息抽口烟，
歇好再上路。

M:
Taking a rest I wanna have a smoke,
After good rest we'll hit the road.

女：
歇息抽口烟，
歇好再上路。

F:
Taking a rest I wanna have a smoke,
After good rest we'll hit the road.

61

男：
抽烟妹抽烟，
抽罢又赶路。

女：
抽烟妹不会，
郎抽罢赶路。

M:
Why not have a smoke?
After smoking we can go.

F:
Smoking is not my want,
After your smoke we'll go.

62

男：
骑马扬起鞭，
留连同赶路。

女：
上马同挥鞭，
留连同赶路。

M:
Raising the whip I ride the horse,
On our journey without pause.

F:
Riding the horse I raise the whip,
On our journey without pause.

63

男：
骑马上红坡，
有何在前拦。

女：
骑马上红坡，
蜘蛛在前拦。

M:
Riding the horse up a red earth slope,
What hold us back on the road?

F:
Riding the horse up a red earth slope,
Spiders hold us back on the road.

64

男：
马不走催鞭，
流连几千里。

女：
马不走催鞭，
流连几千里。

M:
Whipping the horse I make it gallop,
For thousands of miles without a stop.

F:
Urging the horse forward we can find,
Thousands of miles soon behind.

65 男：
走到岔路我俩去，
瞧见好圩咱停行。

M:
We arrive at a cross road,
Seeing a fair and we go.

女：
走到岔路我俩去，
到好圩停步。

F:
We arrive at a cross road,
We see a fair we shall go.

66 男：
上街买花种，
赶圩寻花路。

M:
We go to the street for flower seeds,
We go to the fair for flower market.

女：
远方寻花路，
平川询好种。

F:
We look for flowers in this district,
Here we are to find rare seeds.

67 男：
几多宽都去，
几多远都寻。

M:
How broad the road I will go,
How far the way I will seek.

女：
道路多宽我俩去，
街道多远一起走。

F:
How broad the road together we go,
How far the street together we seek.

68 男：
来呀，妹来呀，
一起安排欲赶街。

M:
Come on, please come along!
Let’s go to the fair together.

女：
随哥一起来，
一起欲赶街。

F:
I’d go with you,
We will go to the fair together.

69

男：
渐渐走到大街头，
渐渐行到大闹市。

M:
We get to the main street,
We arrive at the bustling market.

女：
渐渐走到大街头，
不知好花有没有？

F:
We get to the main street,
Are nice flowers awaiting me?

70

男：
渐渐到了大街头，
既从远方赶来到。

M:
We get to the main street,
Far away from our district.

女：
既从异地下来到，
须寻得花种。

F:
We come here from another district,
We need to find our flower seeds.

71

男：
马栓在街头，
骡绑在巷尾。

M:
The horse is tied at the upper street,
And the mule at the lane.

女：
马栓在街头，
骡绑在巷尾。

F:
The horse is tied at the upper street,
while the mule at the lane.

72

男：
两丁把马来栓好，
两伊把骡来绑固。

M:
Two boys tie up the horses,
Two girls tie up the mules.

女：
两丁来把马栓好，
两伊来把骡绑固。

F:
Two boys tie up the horses,
Two girls tie up the mules.

73

男：
来呀，妹来呀，
寻找歇户来投宿。

M:
Come on, please come on!
We shall look for lodging for tonight.

女：
随哥找歇户，
找得合意共投宿。

F:
Let's find the lodging for tonight,
An ideal place to stay for the night.

74

男：
进家抽烟共歇息，
歇息同抽烟。

M:
Let's go into the lobby for a smoke,
We can have a rest while I smoke.

女：
歇息等哥抽口烟，
抽罢流连欲赶集。

F:
You have a smoke and I await for you,
After smoking we'll hit the road.

75

男：
赶集寻花种，
逛街觅花路。

M:
We go to the fair for flower seeds,
We go to the street for flower market.

女：
赶集寻花种，
逛街觅花路。

F:
We go to the fair for flower seeds,
We go to the street for flower market.

76

男：
走下第一街，
未曾有货出来卖，
未见花种出来摆。

M:
Walking along the first street,
We see nothing to be sold,
No flower seeds on the shelves.

女：
走下第一街，
未曾有货出来卖，
未见花种出来摆。

F:
Walking along the first street,
Chicks and ducks are to be sold,
No flower seeds can be seen.

77

男：
我俩绕出来，
寻找另条街。

M:
We move out of the street,
And look for another one.

女：
随哥绕回来，
又找另条街。

F:
I follow you from this street,
And we look for another street.

78

男：
未曾见有花种卖，
未曾看见有花摆。

M:
No flower seeds to be sold,
No flowers on the shelves.

女：
未曾见有花种卖，
同去另外新一街。

F:
No flower seeds to be sold,
To another street we will go.

79

男：
哪巷有种我俩找，
哪街有花我俩寻。

M:
We go through the lanes for flower seeds,
We search the streets for flowers.

女：
哪巷有种我俩找，
哪有好花我俩寻。

F:
We go through the lanes for flower seeds,
We search the place for flowers.

80 男：

走下第二街，
此街有豌豆出卖，
未见花种出来摆。

M:

Going along the second street,
Being sold on the shelves are some peas,
No flower seeds we can see.

女：

走下第二圩，
到处瞧仔细，
不见好花摆上市。

F:

Going along the second street,
We look carefully for flower seeds,
No rare flowers can be seen.

81 男：

此街未叫卖，
我俩又去另一街。

M:

No sales calls on this street,
We'd move to another street.

女：

此街未曾卖花种，
同赶新一街。

F:

No flower seeds on this street,
We'd turn to another street.

82 男：

走下第三街，
见有笋出卖。

M:

Going down the third street,
We see the bamboo shoots indeed.

女：

走下第三街，
见有笋出卖。

F:

Going down the third street,
Bamboo shoots we can see.

83

男：
未见花种出来卖，
未见花种出来摆。

M:
We look for flower seeds on the street,
But for sales are no flower seeds.

女：
未见花种出来卖，
一起欲赶新一街。

F:
No flower seeds in this street,
We'll go to another street.

84

男：
走下第四街，
处处客到齐，
好花种未摆。

M:
Walking down to the fourth street,
Wherever people can be seen,
No flower seeds we can see.

女：
走下第四街，
处处客来到，
未见花种出来摆。

F:
Walking down to the fourth street,
Wherever people can be seen,
No flower seeds can be seen.

85

男：
每街我俩去，
未有好花种摆卖。

M:
We go to every street together,
But see no seeds of flowers.

女：
这街我俩去，
未见有花种摆卖。

F:
We walk in this street together,
But see no seeds of flowers.

86 男：
花种未有卖，
花种未曾摆。

M:
No flower seeds we can see,
No flower seeds we can meet.

女：
花种未见卖，
同去别圩新一街。

F:
No flower seeds to be sold,
To another street we'll go.

87 男：
同转另一街，
欲去新一巷。

M:
We move out to another street,
And wanna find a new market.

女：
随哥转别街，
欲去新一巷。

F:
Going with you to another street,
We wanna find a new market.

88 男：
走下第五街，
他人也来贩牛马，
不见花种摆出来。

M:
Going down to the fifth street,
Cows and horses are on sale,
But no flower seeds to be sold.

女：
走下第五街，
有牛马交易，
未有花出卖。

F:
Going down to the fifth street,
Cows and horses are on sale,
But no flowers to be sold.

89

男：
见有卖欲买，
买来解开心头意。

M:
If there are seeds to be sold,
I'd buy them to achieve my goal.

女：
见有卖欲买，
讨得依人有名头。

F:
If there are seeds to be sold,
I'd buy them to fulfill this mission.

90

男：
他人成双多欢喜，
郎却叹气攀高坡。

M:
How delighted they are to be in couples,
Uttering a sigh I've to climb the upper slope.

女：
妹盼异地好花种，
拼命来会哥。

F:
I also hope to find a good partner,
So I join you to this area.

91

男：
盼见花种欲想要，
不知是否卖给吾？

M:
I hope to see flower seeds,
Whether or not they'd sell to me?

女：
盼见花种欲想要，
我俩有名才罢休。

F:
I expect to have flower seeds,
Till we get what we need.

92

男：
每街都空行，
未见有花种摆卖。

M:
We get nothing in the streets,
No flower seeds we can see.

女：
想去另一街，
欲赶新一巷。

F:
Let's go to another street,
Let's go to another alley.

93

男：
走下第六街，
此圩有绿纸出卖，
花种未曾摆。

M:
Walking down to the sixth street,
Green papers we can see,
But no flower seeds can be seen.

女：
走下第六街，
劳碌走几圩，
未见有摆卖。

F:
Walking down to the sixth street,
We have sought in several streets,
But no flower seeds to be seen.

94

男：
爱花几多街也去，
苦在好花种未露。

M:
I'll seek in many streets,
Until I find my flower seeds.

女：
爱花地多宽妹找，
爱花路多远妹行。

F:
No matter how long the way may be,
For desirable flower I'll seek.

95

男：
爱花真情去寻花，
既挂名声找花种。

M:
Seeking my dear flower with loyalty,
And the right flower seeds I am earnest.

女：
好种未有卖，
花乖未曾摆。

F:
No good seeds are sold,
No good flowers for sale.

96

男：
一起到别街，
一起找新市。

M:
We get nothing in the streets,
No flower seeds we can see.

女：
随哥走别街，
随郎找新市。

F:
Follow you to another street,
Follow you to another fair.

97

男：
走下第七街，
此街有辣椒出售，
未见花乖摆出来。

M:
Going down to the seventh street,
There are peppers in this street,
Still no flowers I can see.

女：
走下第七街，
渐临午饭时，
未见花乖摆出来。

F:
Going down to the seventh street,
Lunch time it's getting near,
No good flowers we can see.

98

男：
若妹重花就寻找，
我俩欲下新一街。

M:
If you don't give up,
Let's go to another street.

女：
为了重花才赶来，
随郎找新街。

F:
I come here for flowers,
And will always be your follower.

99

男：
边走又边找，
边行又边瞧。

M:
Where are flower seeds we can see?
Where are the flowers we can meet?

女：
边走妹边找，
边行娘边瞧。

F:
Where are flowers seeds I can see?
Where are the flowers I can meet?

100

男：
此圩有布匹出卖，
未见花乖摆出来。

M:
I see cloths on this street,
But no flowers I can meet.

女：
哪里有花种出卖？
银圆付几多也买。

F:
Where are the flower seeds?
For them any price I can give.

101

男：
我俩跨别路，
我俩找新街。

M:
We step across to the other road,
We are looking for another street.

女：
随哥转别街，
随郎逛新巷。

F:
I'll follow you to the street you go,
I'll follow you to the lane you roam.

102

男：
走下第八街，
这街有摘刀①出卖，
未有花种摆出来。

M:
Going down the eighth street,
Removable knives ① are on sale,
But no flower seeds available.

女：
走下第八街，
日照田头和地角，
未见花种摆出来。

F:
Going down the eighth street,
Sunshine lights up the field and land,
But no flower seeds are on the shelves.

103

男：
铁匠铸刀口出卖，
若妹有钱多就买。

M:
Blacksmith's knife blades are on sale,
You should buy one if you can.

女：
他人铸刀口出卖，
苦妹家里穷糯谷。

F:
Knife blades are on sale,
I'm too poor to afford one.

---

①摘刀，旧时用来剪糯谷穗的摘刀。

① Removable knife, a knife used in the old times to cut rice ears.

104

男：
买一把也行，
日后摘谷用容易。

M:
You'd better buy a sickle,
It'd be useful for harvest on land.

女：
为了爱花才得来，
不是找摘刀。

F:
For my beloved flowers I come,
Not for sickles on the sale.

105

男：
若妹说不买也罢，
欲同赶新街。

M:
If you don't wanna buy,
Let's go to another way.

女：
随哥转别巷，
随郎转新街。

F:
I'll follow you to another street,
I'll follow you to another lane.

106

男：
走下第九街，
这街有酒米出卖，
未见花乖摆出来。

M:
Walking down the ninth street,
Wine and rice you can buy,
No flowers are in my sight.

女：
走下第九街，
九街九去找，
未见花种摆出卖。

F:
Walking down the ninth street,
Nine streets we've found,
No flower seeds come in sight.

107

男：
请妹把酒买几斤，
日后坐月妹易喝。

M:
You'd better buy some wine,
For drinking in the confinement time.

女：
阿妹爱异路花种，
令不爱别处酒茶。

F:
I love flower seeds from far away,
But not wine or tea from other place.

108 男：
日后来买路也远，
自酿不如他人香。

M:
It's hard to buy in some later day,
And the wine here is of repute.

女：
他乡酒不要，
同去新街找花种。

F:
I won't buy the wine from elsewhere,
Let's go for flower seeds in another fair.

109 男：
若妹拒买又拒要，
欲同去新街。

M:
Now that you don't wanna buy,
Let's go to another street and try.

女：
随哥去别街，
随郎赶新集。

F:
I'll follow you to another street,
I'll follow you to another market.

110 男：
走下第十街，
这街有笔墨出卖，
这街有花布出摆。

M:
Walking down the tenth street,
Pens and ink are on sale,
Cotton cloth prevail.

女：
走下第十街，
笔墨也有卖，
花布也有摆。

F:
Walking down the tenth street,
Pens and ink to be sold,
Cotton patterned cloth prevail.

111 男：
请妹买笔墨红纸，
日后方便写情书。

M:
Pen and ink and red paper,
You need to buy them for love letter.

女：
笔墨属男孩，
女孩不会写不买。

F:
Pen and ink are boy's matter,
Illiterate girl won't consider.

112

男：
各样都有卖，
唯有花种未曾摆。

M:
All things are present,
But no flower seeds are on sale.

女：
不见有花种出卖，
欲同去赶新一街。

F:
No flower seeds we can see,
Let's try another street.

113

男：
不见名花种出卖，
不见花乖摆出来。

M:
No flower seeds are on sale,
Nor rare flowers on the shelves.

女：
不见何为好，
又去新一街。

F:
What a pity we can't find,
Let's go to another street for a try.

114

男：
我俩街街去，
未遇好花种。

M:
We seek on every street,
But see no flower seeds.

女：
这街也没有，
又赶新一街。

F:
No flower seeds on this street,
We'd go on for a new market.

115

男：
这就走别街，
欲同赶新集。

M:
Let's go to another street,
Together we join a new market.

女：
随哥另街走，
欲同赶新巷。

F:
I'll follow you to any street,
And go with you to a new market.

116 男：
走下十一街，
渐渐走得远，
何好来盘算。

M:
Walking down the eleventh street,
A long way from where we leave,
What if no flower seeds we can meet?

女：
走下十一街，
靛染布有卖，
未见花种摆出来。

F:
Walking down the eleventh street,
Indigo-dyed cloth is on sale,
But no flower seeds we can meet.

117 男：
靛染红黑布，
日后成亲妹好取。

M:
Indigo dyed cloth in black and red,
For your marriage you need to get.

女：
靛染土布妹有多，
只缺花种未曾得。

F:
Indigo-dyed cloth I already have,
Only flower seeds I need to get.

118 男：
边走又边找，
不见花种摆出来。

M:
We move forward for another try,
No flower seeds are in our sight.

女：
样样有齐全，
未见有花种摆卖。

F:
Other things are in our sight,
No flower seeds are in our eyes.

119 男：
又到上面街，
又往新一处。

M:
We move forward to the upper town,
A new place is to be found.

女：
随哥攀上街，
随郎往新处。

F:
I'll follow you to that street,
And a new place we are to arrive.

120

男：
新街也未见，
远客早来齐。

M:
No flower seeds on this street,
Though it's crowded with people indeed.

女：
新街客也多，
未见卖花种。

F:
Visitors are many on this street,
But no flower seeds we can see.

121

男：
我俩转别街，
我俩到新巷。

M:
We move on to another street,
We arrive at another market.

女：
随哥走别街，
随郎赶新巷。

F:
I'll follow you to another street,
I'll follow you to another market.

122

男：
走下十二巷，
意重妹去找，
我俩一起寻。

M:
Walking down the twelfth street,
You're so kind to follow me,
We're together for flowers seeds.

女：
走下十二街，
妹意重如山，
我俩一起寻。

F:
Walking down the twelfth street,
I'm so sincere indeed,
For the flower seeds we go to seek.

123

男：
几多找得花才来？
寻得花种才回返。

M:
When can we find what we need?
So as to return home with flower seeds.

女：
请哥仔细瞧，
好种不乱摆。

F:
Please look around carefully,
Those easily obtained are no good seeds.

124 男：
十街十去找，
来了十二街。

M:
We shall go to every street,
We've arrived at the twelfth street.

女：
十二街找遍，
好花在此街摆卖。

F:
Seeking through twelve streets,
We find good flower here indeed.

125 男：
十二花种都有卖，
十二名花街上摆。

M:
Twelve flowers seeds are on sale,
Twelve good flowers are on the shelves.

女：
样样名花都有卖，
十二花种街上摆。

F:
All the good flowers prevail,
Twelve flower seeds are on the shelves.

126 男：
请妹上前问，
请娘询价格。

M:
Please go forward to make inquiry,
About the price of the flower seeds.

女：
粤语妹不通，
请郎去问价。

F:
I can't speak Cantonese,
You are required to do this.

127 男：
价格它写有，
眼俐娘自瞧。

M:
Price is marked,
As you can see.

女：
价格也写有，
银圆不知花多少。

F:
It is marked indeed,
How many silvers do they need?

128

男：
价格它标好，
银元多少也得掏。

M:
The price is marked,
No matter how much I will pay.

女：
请哥看好花价格，
价钱多贵阿妹付。

F:
Please take note of the price,
No matter how expensive I'll pay.

129

男：
牡丹三两一，
玫瑰七两三，
海棠三两四。

M:
Peony needs three Liang and one,
Rose sells at seven Liang and three,
Crabapple is priced at three Liang and four.

女：
牡丹三两一，
玫瑰七两三，
海棠三两四。

F:
Peony needs three Liang and one,
Rose sells at seven Liang and three,
Crabapple is priced at three Liang and four.

130

男：
菁福[①]四两五，
兰花六两三，
红掌[②]二两四。

M:
Jingfu[①] is four Liang and five,
Orchid is six Liang and three,
Hongzhang[②] is two Liang and four.

女：
菁福四两五，
兰花六两三，
红掌二两四。

F:
Jingfu is four Liang and five,
Orchid is six Liang and three,
Hongzhang is two Liang and four.

---

①菁福，即幸福花。
②红掌，即红掌花。

① Jingfu, namely happy flowers.
② Hongzhang, namely anthodium.

131

男：	M:
水仙①二两三，	Shuixian needs① two Liang and three,
月桂四两三，	Laurel is four Liang and three,
金雀②七两八。	Jinque sells② at seven Liang and eight.
女：	F:
水仙二两三，	Shuixian needs two Liang and three,
月桂四两三，	Laurel is four Liang and three,
金雀七两八。	Jinque sells at seven Liang and eight.

132

男：	M:
芙蓉三两五，	Lotus sells at three Liang and five,
常春③五两三，	Changchun sells③ at five Liang and three,
凤梨④四两二。	Fengli is④ four Liang and two.
女：	F:
芙蓉三两五，	Lotus sells at three Liang and five,
常春五两三，	Long spring sells at five Liang and three,
凤梨四两二。	Bromeliads is four Liang and two.

133

男：	M:
十二名花买得齐，	Twelve good flowers we have bought,
十二好种买得全。	Twelve flower seeds we've got.
女：	F:
十二名花买得齐，	Twelve good flowers we have bought,
十二好种买得全。	And twelve flower seeds we've got.

①水仙，即水仙花。 ① Shuixian, namely narcissus.

②金雀，即金雀花。 ② Jinque, namely gold Spink.

③常春，即长春花。 ③ Changchun, namely roseus.

④凤梨，即凤梨花。 ④ Fengli, namely Bromeliads.

134

男： 银圆重如山， 再多哥也掏。	M: Silver means a lot to me, To pay full price I will do.
女： 银圆重如山， 我俩共来付。	F: Silver means a lot to us, But we can share payment for the flowers.

135

男： 银圆多厚重， 身上掏尽钱， 千两银哥付。	M: Thick and heavy are the silver coin, From my pocket they've gone, For thousand Liangs of silver I can afford.
女： 银圆多厚重， 身上掏尽钱， 千两银哥付。	F: Thick and heavy are the silver coin, From my pocket they've gone, For thousand Liangs of silver you can afford.

136

男： 欢欣获花种， 获花种高兴。	M: So delighted to get the flower seeds, They bring us joy indeed.
女： 欢欣获花种， 获花种高兴。	F: We're delighted to get the flower seeds, They bring us joy indeed.

137

男： 得花种回家， 得花种回屋。	M: With flower seeds we'll go back, With flower seeds we'll return.
女： 得花种回家， 得花种回屋。	F: With flower seeds we'll go back, With flower seeds we'll return.

138

男：
一起返上来，
歇息找住处。

M:
From the market we'd go away,
And look for a hotel to stay.

女：
得花种欲回，
歇息找住处。

F:
We'll be back with flower seeds,
But first we shall look for an inn.

139

男：
歇息共品茶，
歇脚同抽烟。

M:
We take a rest and have some tea,
After a smoke I feel at ease.

女：
歇息共品茶，
品罢嘱东家一言。

F:
We take a rest and have some tea,
We thank the inn keeper for good deed.

140

男：
抽罢一起嘱客栈，
吩咐歇户话一席。

M:
We thank the boss after the meal,
And bid him farewell for the night.

女：
安在客栈尊长老，
异地女儿欲返回。

F:
I bid farewell to the elders in the inn,
And start the journey to my town.

141

男：
嘱罢一起转，
我俩欲回家。

M:
We say goodbye to other lodgers,
And we return home together.

女：
嘱罢一起转，
我俩欲回家。

F:
We say goodbye to other lodgers,
And we return home together.

142

男：
挎帽在身上，
请娘前面走。

M:
We're packed up and ready to leave,
After you I'd follow your lead.

女：
挎帽在身上，
请郎在前行。

F:
We're packed up and ready to leave,
You go first and take the lead.

143

男：
两童来哥道，
两丁来哥讲，
两伊来哥说。

M:
You kids please come over,
I have errands for you both,
You can do them as I want.

女：
两童听哥道，
两丁听哥讲，
两伊听哥说。

F:
You kids thus come over,
He has errands for you both,
You can do them as he wants.

144

男：
两童把马牵出槽，
两伊马背配好鞍。

M:
The boys lead the horse out of the manger,
The girls match the horse with saddles.

女：
两童把马牵出槽，
两伊马背配好鞍。

F:
The boys lead the horse out of the manger,
The girls match the horse with saddles.

145

男：
骏马配花鞍，
哪匹乖妹骑。

M:
The steed is fitted with a red saddle,
And this horse suits you well.

女：
公马配紫鞍，
花鞍配母马，
哪匹乖哥骑。

F:
The stallion is fitted with a purple saddle,
The mare with a red saddle,
You can choose one matches you well.

146 男：
两童把马缰牵好，
欲同远程返回家。

M:
The boys lead the horses to us,
We'll ride home by the horses.

女：
两童牵马登路程，
买得花种返回家。

F:
Two boys lead the horses to us,
With flower seeds we'd return home.

147 男：
扬鞭跨上马，
流连几千里。

M:
We jump onto the horses with a whip,
The horses gallop thousands of miles.

女：
扬鞭跨上马，
流连几千里。

F:
We jump onto the horses with a whip,
For thousands of miles the horse gallop.

148 男：
十坡并作一坡驰，
十隘归作一隘闯，
流连回到嗅故地。

M:
Over ten hills the horses gallop,
And through ten passes it wouldn't stop,
After a long journey we return home.

女：
十坡并作一坡驰，
十隘归作一隘闯，
流连回到嗅故地。

F:
Over ten hills the horses gallop,
And through ten passes it wouldn't stop,
After a long journey we return home.

149 男：
回屋多欢欣，
到家开心同欢喜。

M:
How delighted we're returning home,
How joyful we're to be at home.

女：
到屋共育花，
到家共育种。

F:
Then we grow flowers together,
And breed the flower seeds together.

二、上天求雨
II Praying for Rain

150

男：
哪天下雨育花种，
哪天露绕栽名花。

M:
We'll breed flower seeds when it's rainy,
And plant flowers when it's dewy.

女：
栽花没有雨，
哪天等有露。

F:
We want to plant but there's no rain,
We'll wait for a dewy day.

151

男：
无露水难栽，
无雨更难育。

M:
It's hard to plant flowers without dew,
It's even harder without rain.

女：
几时等下雨得栽？
何时等降露得育？

F:
How long we need to wait for rain?
How long we need to wait for dew?

152

男：
下雨栽花齐欢欣，
降露育花皆欢喜。

M:
We're delighted to plant when it's rainy,
We're joyful to breed when it is dewy.

女：
哪天得栽齐欢喜，
何日育种皆欢欣。

F:
We'd be delighted the day we can grow,
We'd be joyful the day we can sow.

153 男：
若妹盼栽就求雨，
若娘想育去求露。

M:
Pray for rain if you want to plant,
Pray for dew if you want to breed.

女：
谁会上天去求雨？
谁能登天去求露？

F:
Who would go to Heaven for rain?
Who could ascent to Heaven for dew?

154 男：
哥来说妹一两句，
提示娘妹一两题。

M:
I wanna have words with you,
And some tips to prompt you.

女：
哥说妹哪句？
使妹惊骇魂魄乱。

F:
What do you wanna talk with me?
Don't you shock me or terrify me?

155 男：
托妹请道来求雨，
托娘请麽来求雾。

M:
Please invite the priest to pray for rain,
Please invite the master to pray for dew.

女：
妹去求道都愿来，
再求麽师也来帮。

F:
The priest I invited would come,
And the master I invited would help.

156 男：
道师来祈使雾降，
麽师来求给雨落。

M:
The priest prays for dew,
The master prays for rain.

女：
道师上天去求雨，
麽师登天去求露。

F:
The priest ascents to heaven for rain,
The master goes to heaven for dew.

157

男：	M:
道师为郎去求雾，	To heaven the priest pray for dew,
麽师上求给雨下。	To heaven the master pray for rain.
女：	F:
求露使露降，	Praying the heaven for dew,
求雨给雨落。	Praying the heaven for rain.

158

男：	M:
道师为郎护好命，	The priest protects my life,
麽师为哥佑好魂。	The master blesses my soul.
女：	F:
道师护命多完好，	The priest protects your life intact,
麽师佑魂稳又牢。	The master blesses your soul in peace.

159

男：	M:
命莫上天宫，	Allow not your life to heavenly palace,
魂莫归青云。	Allow not your soul return to the sky.
女：	F:
命莫上天宫，	Allow not your life to heavenly palace,
魂莫归青云。	Allow not your soul return to the sky.

160

男：	M:
道师画符往上托，	The priest draws magic figure and prays,
麽公画好先上报。	The master has finished and relates.
女：	F:
道师画法往上托，	The priest draws magic figure and prays,
麽师画好先上报。	The master sends the message to heavenly state.

161 男：
法上我俩升，
符升我俩上。

M:
The message ascends with our prayers,
The talisman rises with our promises.

女：
法上一起升，
符升一起上。

F:
The message ascends with our promises,
The talisman rises with our prayers.

162 男：
放符第一张，
渐渐到天上，
何日重见太阳出？

M:
Praying with the first magic figure,
It goes up to the sky,
When can we see the sun arise?

女：
放符第一张，
渐渐到天上，
太阳躲角落。

F:
Praying with the first magic figure,
It goes up to the sky,
But the sun is a little shy.

163 男：
太阳复出去求雨，
红日重升去求露。

M:
We pray for rain as the sun rises,
We pray for dew when the sun shines.

女：
明天日升去求雨，
明天见日去求露。

F:
Tomorrow we pray for rain when the sun shines,
Tomorrow we pray for dew as the sun rises.

164 男：
故地未有雨，
凡间未有露。

M:
No rain falls at my hometown,
Nor dew drops on earthly world.

女：
未有露求天，
未有雨求云。

F:
Praying the Heaven for dew,
Praying the cloud for rain.

165

男:
放符第二张，
哥来妹同来，
何日下雨来得到。

M:
Praying with the second magic figure,
Let' come along together,
Let's pray for some rain.

女:
放符第二张，
哥来妹同来，
何日雨来妹也到。

F:
Praying with the second magic figure,
I'll come and join you,
We're expecting for some rain.

166

男:
何日等得天开门？
何时天上降春雨？

M:
When will the Heaven open its gate?
When comes the spring rain to this state?

女:
何日天下雨，
何日天降露。

F:
We're longing for some rain,
We're looking forward to the dew.

167

男:
天公不下雨咋办？
我俩咋个好？

M:
What if no rain would fall?
How can we find a way?

女:
雨不落咱求，
为我俩降露。

F:
We'll pray for the rain,
We'll pray for the dew.

168

男:
让天开雨门，
让天揭露窗。

M:
The Heaven open its gate for rain,
The Heaven open its window for dew.

女:
盼天下大雨，
盼天降浓露。

F:
We're expecting heavy rain,
We're longing for some dew.

169 男：
符使天雨下，
法使天降露。

M:
The magic figure makes it rain,
The message is sent for some dew.

女：
符求天下雨，
法使天降露。

F:
The magic figure makes it rain,
The message is sent for some dew.

170 男：
放符第三张，
上到让雨落。

M:
Praying with the third magic figure,
It'll rise till the rain falls.

女：
放符第三张，
盼到有雨落。

F:
Praying with the third magic figure,
We're waiting for the rain.

171 男：
盼雨落未落，
盼露降未降，
凡间未有水。

M:
Praying for rain but no rain,
Praying for dew but no dew,
No water in the earthly world.

女：
求雨落未落，
求露降未降，
何日秧种栽名花？

F:
Praying for rain but no rain,
Praying for dew but no dew,
When can we plant the famed flowers?

172 男：
道师做法上去求，
麽师放符上去讲。

M:
The priest casts a spell to pray,
The master uses magic figure to pray.

女：
道师来祈求，
麽师施符来上报。

F:
The priest comes and prays,
The master joins in the rite.

173

男：	**M:**
放符第四张，	Praying with the fourth magic figure,
四处天漆黑，	Though it's late at night,
雨在远方未曾落。	We see no rain as we desire.
女：	**F:**
放符第四张，	Praying with the fourth magic figure,
四处天漆黑，	Though it is late at night,
雨在远方未曾落。	It has no rain as we desire.

174

男：	**M:**
天未开窗雨未落，	The heaven doesn't open the window to let down rain,
日未开门露未降。	Nor the sun opens its door to offer some dew.
女：	**F:**
天未开窗雨未落，	The heaven doesn't open the window for rain,
何日才得育花种？	How long shall we have to wait?

175

男：	**M:**
天上未开门，	The gate of heaven keeps closed,
天公未开窗。	And the window of haven remains shut.
女：	**F:**
天开雾门给郎君，	The gate to let out dew will be open,
天开雨门给阿哥。	And the gate to shed rain won't closed.

176

男：	**M:**
使它为露开天门，	Please open the gate to let out dew,
打开雨窗给阿哥。	Please open the window to shed rain.
女：	**F:**
天上开雾门，	May Heaven open the gate for dew,
揭窗让雨下。	May Heaven open the window for rain.

177 男：
开窗让咱去，
开门让咱登。

M:
Please open the window for us sake,
Please open the gate for us sake.

女：
开门上天去求雨，
揭窗上天去求雾。

F:
We shall pray for rain through the gate,
We shall pray for dew via the window.

178 男：
天门未曾开，
天窗未曾亮。

M:
The gate of heaven is not open,
And its window remains closed.

女：
天上未开门，
天公未开窗。

F:
The gate is not open,
The window is still closed.

179 男：
又放第五符，
天公未有雨，
天上未有雾。

M:
Praying with the fifth magic figure,
It still looks without rain,
It still shines without dew.

女：
放符第五张，
天公未有雨，
怎么育花种？

F:
Praying with the fifth magic figure,
It's still clear without rain,
How can we breed the flower seeds?

180 男：
天公未开窗下雨，
让咱怎么办？

M:
The window is not open for rain,
To whom we shall need to pray?

女：
天公未开窗下雨，
天上未开门降雾。

F:
The window is not open for rain,
The gate is not open for dew.

181	男： 放符第六张， 怕妹随绿符上天， 人情真难算。	**M:** Praying with the sixth magic figure, We should share weal and woe together, It's always hard to perceive each other.
	女： 放符第六张， 劳碌登几门， 雨符连露符。	**F:** Praying with the sixth magic figure, It calls at every door with sincerity, Praying for dew and rain with magic figures.
182	男： 求得露育种， 求得雨栽花。	**M:** Praying for dew for seed breeding, Praying for rain for flower planting.
	女： 求得露栽花， 求雨来育苗。	**F:** Praying for dew for flower planting, Praying for rain for seed breeding.
183	男： 若妹想栽花做人， 咱欲上天再次求。	**M:** If you wanna grow flowers, We'll appeal to heaven again.
	女： 情愿上天去求雨， 不愿育种下旱地。	**F:** I wanna pray for some rain, Rather than seedling in the dry land.
184	男： 求天开门给， 继续放黄符。	**M:** We pray to heaven for opening the gate, With yellow magic figures burned away.
	女： 求天开门给， 让哥再放新黄符。	**F:** We pray to the heaven for opening the gate, You should show your sincerity in this way.

185

男:	M:
放符第七张,	Praying with the seventh magic figure,
渐渐上到天,	Gradually it rises up to the heaven,
天上未开窗。	The window of sky is not yet open.
女:	F:
放符第七张,	Praying with the seventh magic figure,
渐渐上到天,	Gradually it rises up to the heaven,
未见有雨露。	The rain and the dew would not appear.

186

男:	M:
天未开窗给我俩,	The window of heaven keeps closed,
天未开门不许上。	The gate of heaven remains shut.
女:	F:
天未开窗为何好?	What if the window is not open?
怎么上去求浓露?	How to go up to pray for the dew?

187

男:	M:
边上咱边求,	We're praying for some rain,
开门咱求露。	We're praying for some dew.
女:	F:
边上咱边求,	We're praying for the rain,
求露咱栽花。	We pray for dew to plant flowers.

188

男:	M:
盼天开窗落场雨,	We expect rainfall from the sky window,
我俩育种栽名花。	Then good flowers we can grow.
女:	F:
盼天开窗落场雨,	We expect rainfall from the window,
我俩育种栽名花。	Then good flowers we can grow.

189

男：
雨落种花想娘妹，
露降栽花想妹人。

M:
In rainy day I grow flowers with loneliness,
It comes the dew and I miss my love.

女：
天公不应我俩意，
晓得栽花能不能。

F:
Heaven lord does not grant our wish,
Growing flowers is mysterious to us.

190

男：
放符第八张，
到处充满太阳光，
我俩何为好。

M:
Praying with the eighth magic figure,
The sun is shining all round,
But still no rain can be found.

女：
放符第八张，
到处充满太阳光，
何逢吉日降春雨？

F:
Praying with the eighth magic figure,
The sun is shining all over,
When can we have spring shower?

191

男：
道师画法未停手，
麽师画符未出来。

M:
The priest is performing magic art,
The master is drawing magic figure.

女：
请道画法往上送，
请麽画法往上说。

F:
The priest is sending away magic message,
The master prays with magic figure.

192

男：
画毕才上去，
画好才能上。

M:
The priest need to perform magic art,
The master has to drawn the magic figure.

女：
请道画法要画好，
咱才能上去求雾。

F:
After they've present their supplication,
We can pray for the rain and dew.

193 男：
道师画法来上祭，
边跪又边求，
给我俩求露。

M:
The priest is presenting his supplication,
He kneels down while praying,
Praying dew for you and me.

女：
道师画法来上祭，
边跪边上求，
让我俩求露。

F:
The priest is presenting his supplication,
He kneels down while praying,
Praying for you and me.

194 男：
天门还关紧，
天门还关密，
怎么上得去？

M:
The gate of heaven keeps closed,
The gate of heaven remains shut,
How can the pray go inside?

女：
天门还关紧，
天门还关密，
难晓上去求迷露。

F:
The gate of heaven keeps closed,
The gate of heaven remains shut,
It is hard for message to go inside.

195 男：
放符第九张，
天公还请酒和茶，
上天未去成。

M:
Praying with the ninth magic figure,
Wine and tea shall be provided,
Chance to go up to heaven is limited.

女：
放符第九张，
天公还请酒和茶，
他也未许来求雾。

F:
Praying with the ninth magic figure,
Wine and tea need to be provided,
Heaven lord may not grant our wish.

196

男：
哪时等得天门开，
我俩欲上天求露。

M:
When the gate of heaven is open,
We'll go to heaven for some dew.

女：
盼得天公来开门，
我俩欲上天求雾。

F:
We'd entreat the heaven lord,
Opening the gate we can pray for fog.

197

男：
边放法边求，
边放符边上。

M:
Performing magic art while praying,
The magic figure is burnt to smoke rising.

女：
边放法边求，
边放符边上。

F:
Performing magic art while praying,
The magic figure is in smoke rising.

198

男：
让咱上求雨，
让咱到天上求露。

M:
Please allow us go to heaven for rain,
Please allow us go to heaven for dew.

女：
让咱上求雨，
让咱到天上求露。

F:
Please allow us go to heaven for rain,
Please allow us go to heaven for dew.

199

男：
露降咱栽花，
雨下来育苗。

M:
We'll grow flowers when it's foggy,
We'll raise seedlings when it's rainy.

女：
露降咱栽花，
雨下来育苗。

F:
We'll grow flowers when it's foggy,
We'll raise seedling when it's rainy.

200 男：
何日栽花得成蔸？
何日育花得成簇？

M:
When can the flowers grow up?
When can the flowers flourish?

女：
何日栽花得成蔸？
何日育花得成簇？

F:
When can the flowers grow up?
When can the flowers flourish?

201 男：
放符第十张，
门门上去求，
路路都去请。

M:
Praying with the tenth magic figures,
It's expected to appeal at every door,
It's sure to make clear to whom to appeal.

女：
放符第十张，
门门上去求，
路路都去请。

F:
Praying with the tenth magic figures,
It will try at every door,
To make clear to whom we should appeal.

202 男：
天公欲开门，
天上欲开窗。

M:
The Heaven is to open its door,
The sky is to open its window.

女：
天公欲开门，
天上欲开窗。

F:
The Heaven is to open its door,
The sky is to open its window.

203 男：
开窗欲下雨，
开门欲降露。

M:
Opening the window to shed some rainfall,
Opening the door to let out dew water.

女：
天公开窗欲下雨，
天公开门欲降露。

F:
The Heaven opens the window for rain,
The Heaven opens the door for fog.

204

男：	M:
雨欲下吾方，	The rain will fall at this region,
露欲降田垌。	The dew will drop on our farmland.
女：	F:
雨欲下吾方，	The rain will fall at this region,
露欲降田垌。	The dew will drop on our farmland.

205

男：	M:
露降垌栽花，	People will grow flowers when it's foggy,
雨下来育苗。	And nurse seedlings when it's rainy.
女：	F:
露降咱栽花，	We'll grow flowers when it's foggy,
雨来咱育苗。	We'll nurse seedling when it's rainy.

206

男：	M:
放符十一张，	Praying with the eleventh magic figures,
上到十一殿，	And it goes up to the eleventh palace,
见露咱欢喜。	We're so glad to see the dew.
女：	F:
放符十一张，	Praying with the eleventh magic figures,
上到十一殿，	And it goes up to the eleventh palace,
见露咱欢喜。	We're so glad to see the dew.

207

男：	M:
见露齐欢欣，	So joyful we feel to see the dew,
见雨齐欢喜。	So delighted we're to see the rain.
女：	F:
见露妹欢欣，	I feel so joyful to see the dew,
见雨齐欢喜。	We're so delighted to see the rain.

208 男：
放符十二张，
窗窗都开毕，
门门都开尽。

M:
Praying with the twelfth magic figures,
Every window is now open,
Each door is now open.

女：
放符十二张，
窗窗都开毕，
门门都开尽。

F:
Praying with the twelfth magic figures,
Every window has been opened,
Each door has been opened.

209 男：
开窗让露降，
开门让雨落。

M:
The window is open for dew,
The door is open for rain.

女：
天公开窗露欲降，
天上开门雨欲落。

F:
The Heaven opens the window for the dew,
The sky opens the door for the rain.

210 男：
落雨泥巴紧，
天晴泥巴滑，
我俩何为好？

M:
It's muddy after it rains,
It's slippery on sunny days,
What can we do on the day?

女：
落雨泥巴紧，
天晴泥巴滑，
我俩何为好？

F:
It's so muddy with the rain,
It's so slippery on sunny days,
What we'll do you can say.

211 男：
落雨有云来遮阴，
降露有风来挡住。

M:
It's cloudy on rainy days,
It's windy on foggy days.

女：
落雨有云天变阴，
降露有风来挡住。

F:
It becomes cloudy on rainy days,
It becomes windy on foggy days.

212

男：
落雨随云要往下，
随雾随风要回屋。

M:
The rain will fall from the cloud,
With the wind and mist to the ground.

女：
雨落就回家，
雾来就回屋。

F:
We'll be back when the rain starts,
We'll return home when the fog comes.

213

男：
往上过天门，
回头下天窗。

M:
I wish to step across the gate of the heaven,
And come back through its skylight.

女：
升登过天门，
回家下天窗。

F:
Going up across the gate of the heaven,
And returning from its skylight.

214

男：
妹请道师来收魂，
魂命一起回到家。

M:
You invited the priest to collect the soul,
The soul and life are returning home.

女：
道师来收魂，
魔师收魂命。

F:
The Priest came and collected the soul,
The Master collected the life and soul.

215

男：
命莫留在青天上，
魂莫留在天宫里。

M:
Life shouldn't be left in the sky,
Nor the soul stayed in the heavenly palace.

女：
命也来得齐，
好魂来得尽。

F:
All Lives have come around,
Good souls have all arrived.

216	男： 道师握法保得准， 魂去哪里都招回。	M: The Priest has magic power, He can call back all the soul.
	女： 道师持法保得好， 魂去哪里都招回。	F: The Priest has super power, All the spirit will be back.
217	男： 道师握命下来齐， 麽师收魂下来整。	M: All lives are recalled by the Priest, All souls are collected by the Master.
	女： 命也来得齐， 好魂全部回。	F: All lives have come around, All souls have just returned.
218	男： 三十魂来尽， 九十命到齐， 好魂来如故。	M: All the thirty souls have come, All the ninety lives have returned, They have all returned to the earth.
	女： 三十魂来尽， 九十命到齐， 好魂来如故。	F: The thirty souls have come, And all the ninety lives have returned, They have been recalled back again.
219	男： 回来，妹回来， 回来到家栽名花。	M: Come on, please come home, Let's plant flowers together.
	女： 回来，哥回来， 回来到家栽名花。	F: Come on, please return home, We can plant flower of our own.

三、育花种
III Breeding Flower Seeds

220 男：
请妹去找育花地，
请娘去找育苗圃。

M:
Please find some land to grow flowers,
And a garden for breeding.

女：
妹也去找育花地，
找圃来育花。

F:
I would like to find the land,
And the garden for breeding.

221 男：
找得育花地，
找得育花圃。

M:
The land for flowers would be obtained,
The garden for breeding could be found.

女：
何地适育花？
哪圃宜育种？

F:
What kind of land is good for flowers?
What garden is suitable for breeding?

222 男：
晓妹寻得圃没有？
晓娘找得圃未曾？

M:
Have you found the land?
Could you found the garden?

女：
瘠地倒是有，
沃土难找着。

F:
I've got a piece of barren land,
Fertile land is hard to find.

223 男：
来哥想说妹两句，
来郎想盘娘两题。

M:
I have something to talk to you,
And some questions to ask you.

女：
哥知说出来，
娘傻想借听。

F:
Tell me what you want to say,
And the questions you want to ask.

224 男：
咱到坡地去育花，
咱到田坝去育种。

M:
Let's cultivate the flowers on the slope,
And do the breeding in farmland.

女：
随哥到坡地育花，
随郎到田坝育种。

F:
I'll follow you to the slope,
And accompany you to the farmland.

225 男：
育苗长成蔸才回，
栽花长成簇才归。

M:
We'll be back when the seedlings grown up,
And the flowers grown into clusters.

女：
育苗长成簇，
栽花长成簇。

F:
The seedlings will grow up,
And the flowers will grow into clusters.

226 男：
下雨泥巴软，
天晴泥巴松，
欲下地栽花。

M:
The soil is muddy in rainy day,
And become soft in sunny day,
I wanna grow the flowers in the land.

女：
下雨泥巴软，
天晴泥巴松，
欲下地栽花。

F:
It's muddy in rainy day,
And become soft in sunny day,
I wanna grow the flowers in the land.

227

男：
道师择凤日出门，
帮选吉日栽花。

M:
The Priest selects good day for beginning,
And an auspicious day for our plantation.

女：
道师择凤日栽花，
我俩选吉日去种。

F:
He selects a lucky day for planting,
The good day we will plant together.

228

男：
今日是阴天，
我俩种花下恒心。

M:
It is cloudy today,
We decide to plant flowers this day.

女：
阴天好种花，
我俩开眸播花种。

F:
It's right time to plant flowers,
We're to plant flowers together.

229

男：
哥栽妹培土，
郎种妹护花。

M:
I plant the flowers and you earth them up,
You'd be the gardener after I plant them out.

女：
同栽同培土，
同栽同护花。

F:
We plant and earth them up together,
We plant and take care of them together.

230

男：
花种嫩芽长得齐，
晓妹中意不中意？

M:
The flower sprouts are growing evenly,
Desirable or not you can tell me.

女：
花种吐芽长得齐，
美似仙女下凡间。

F:
The flower buds are growing evenly,
They're beautiful as the fairies.

231

男：
下雨要啥来掩护？
日照要啥来遮阴？

M:
How to protect them if it rains?
How to shade them if the sun shines?

女：
下雨要绿绸来挡，
日出用白缎来护。

F:
With green silk to protect in rainy days,
And white satin to shade them from sunray.

232

男：
芙蓉吐嫩芽欢欣，
牡丹吐嫩芽欢喜。

M:
Lotus are in full green buds,
Peonies are shooting out new green.

女：
芙蓉吐嫩芽欢欣，
牡丹吐嫩芽欢喜。

F:
Lotus are in full green buds,
Peonies are shooting out new green.

233

男：
花长平灶高，
每棵高平膝。

M:
Flower trees are as tall as the hearth,
Each grows up abreast the knee.

女：
花长似灶高，
每棵高似膝。

F:
Flower trees rise to the hearth's height,
And each grows up abreast the knee.

234

男：
苗长成移栽，
我俩用心把花种。

M:
It's time to make transplantation,
Let's work together with our passion.

女：
苗长欲移栽，
既逢阴天把花种。

F:
It's time to make transplantation,
On cloudy day we plant them together.

235

男：
俩童来哥道，
俩丁来哥讲，
俩伊来哥说。

M:
You kids please come over,
I have errands for you both,
You can do them as I want.

女：
俩童来哥道，
俩丁来哥讲，
俩伊来哥说。

F:
You kids please come over,
He has errands for you both,
You can do them as he wants.

236

男：
送哥到地里栽花，
送哥到田坝育苗。

M:
You go with me to the farmland,
And accompany me to the fields.

女：
随哥去地里栽花，
随郎去田坝育苗。

F:
We go to the land for planting,
And we go to the fields for seedling.

237

男：
哥种沙滩上，
水淹花不生。

M:
The flowers I plant above the beach,
Or they may get drowned by flood.

女：
哥种沙滩上，
哪蔸乖先长。

F:
You plant flowers above the beach,
The strong ones are growing well.

238

男：
外边山顶哥种花，
生怕乌鸦来叼拔。

M:
I plant flowers at the mountaintop,
Fear that the crow may carry them off.

女：
山顶哥种花，
凤凰来欣赏。

F:
You plant flowers at the mountaintop,
Phoenixes come to appreciate them all.

239

男：	M:
花哥种田里，	I plant flowers in the fields,
牛马来践踏。	Horses and cattle come to tread.
女：	F:
花哥种田里，	You plant flowers in the fields,
牛马来观看。	Horses and cattle may come to see.

240

男：	M:
生怕栽花挂空名，	What if I plant but harvest nothing?
日后愧对好恩情。	It may be unworthy of your kindness.
女：	F:
我俩种花真有名，	We plant flowers with sincerity,
将来不达情也爱。	No matter what the outcome will be.

241

男：	M:
若妹真是重恩情，	If you really care for me,
石壁莫给郎栽花。	Allow not me to plant on the cliff.
女：	F:
阿妹种花是真情，	I plant flowers with sincerity,
石壁拼命去种花。	So I risk to plant on the cliff.

242

男：	M:
心想出名种堂上，	I want to plant them in the hall,
生怕别人先结情。	Lest others may pick them first.
女：	F:
有意堂前种一丛，	Plant some in front of the hall,
给妹一道来护理。	Together we look after them all.

243

男：
盼妹育花勤浇水，
怕妹选路不同道。

M:
I hope you can water them everyday,
Fear that you choose another way.

女：
妹想来回同护花，
生怕有人赶上前。

F:
The flowers we can care for,
I am afraid others may have them all.

244

男：
种花盼富贵，
莫许费力白白空。

M:
I plant flowers with hope,
Allow not my efforts go in vain.

女：
妹盼栽花结出种，
莫许妹成卑贱人。

F:
I hope the flowers can have seeds,
Don't let my hope fail indeed.

245

男：
哥种花草不长叶，
唯郎栽花不生枝。

M:
The flowers I plant grow no leaves,
The flowers I plant grow no ticks.

女：
何花不长叶？
怕郎分轻重。

F:
What flowers you plant grow no leaves?
Have you plant them by heart indeed?

246 男：
请妹为郎种枝花，
请娘为哥栽花苗。

M:
Please plant one flower for me,
Please grow the seedling for me.

女：
妹栽哥培土，
娘种郎理苗。

F:
I plant flowers and you earth them up,
I do the planting you trim the yard.

247 男：
种花留功名，
才是女孩呈本事。

M:
If the flowers you plant are in blossom,
You'd be cherished by others.

女：
种花留功名，
结交恋情连到老。

F:
The flowers we plant will be in blossom,
We're holding hands until the end of time.

四、上坡砍树
Ⅳ Chopping Trees from the Hills

248

男：
哥种妹培土，
郎栽娘妹围。

M:
I plant flowers and you earth them up,
I grow flowers and you fence round.

女：
同栽同培土，
园里长花一起围。

F:
We plant the flowers and earth them up,
We fence them up as they grow up.

249

男：
种花还围园，
围园找木条。

M:
We plant flowers and fence them up,
Wood sticks are needed to build the fence.

女：
种花本围园，
围园用木条。

F:
Flowers need to be fenced up,
Woods can be used to build the fence.

250

男：
俩童来哥道，
俩丁来哥讲，
俩伊来哥说。

M:
You kids please come over,
I have errands for you both,
We can do them as I want.

女：
俩童来哥道，
俩丁来哥讲，
俩伊来哥说。

F:
You kids please come over,
He has errands for you both,
You can do them as he wants.

251 男:
一童架锅上火灶,
一伊取柴火来烧。

M:
A boy should put up the pot on fireplace,
A girl should fetch some wood for fire.

女:
一童提锅上火灶,
一伊要柴火来烧。

F:
The boy puts up the pot on fireplace,
The girl gets some wood for fire.

252 男:
米下一筒多,
水放一瓢半。

M:
Over one tube of rice to cook,
With one and a half bails of water.

女:
米煮一筒多,
水放一瓢半。

F:
Over one tube of rice to cook,
With one and a half bails of water.

253 男:
寅时同煮饭,
卯时煮午餐,
一起安排去找木。

M:
We cook the rice at four a.m.,
And cook some for lunch at five a.m.,
We need to go out for firewood.

女:
寅时同煮饭,
卯时煮午餐,
安排上坡找木条。

F:
We cook the rice at four a.m.,
And cook for lunch at five a.m.,
We'd go out together for firewood.

254 男:
布袋装午饭,
欲上山林砍木条。

M:
The lunch is packed in the cloth bag,
I'll go to the forest and cut the trees.

女:
布袋装午饭,
随郎林中砍木条。

F:
The lunch is packed in the cloth bag,
We'll go to the forest to cut the trees.

255

男：
一童把刀找出来，
一伊把斧准备好。

M:
The boy finds out the hacking knife,
The girl prepares the ax ready.

女：
一童把刀找出来，
一伊把斧准备好。

F:
The boy finds out the hacking knife,
The girl prepares the ax ready.

256

男：
妹出后门去磨刀，
哥到门前磨斧头，
流连上山砍木条。

M:
You sharpen the knife at back yard,
I sharpen the axe at front door,
We climb the mountain to cut the trees.

女：
妹出后门去磨刀，
哥到门前磨斧头，
流连上山砍木条。

F:
I sharpen the knife at back yard,
You sharpen the axe at front door,
We climb the mountain and cut down the trees.

257

男：
走上第一林，
木似牛排弯，
来围乖花锁不住。

M:
I go to the first forest on the way,
The trees are bending like the steak,
They are not suitable for the hedge.

女：
走上第一林，
木似牛排弯，
随郎去找新一坡。

F:
I go to the first forest on the way,
The trees are bending like the steak,
We shall go to the forest via another way.

258 男：
砍树砍老树，
选木选直木，
来做园柱才稳当。

M:
We'll cut down the old trees,
And select the straight ones,
They'd be firm to be hedge poles.

女：
砍树砍老树，
选木选直木，
来做园柱才稳当。

F:
We shall cut down the old trees,
And select the straight ones,
They'd be firm to be hedge poles.

259 男：
这林树木全是弯，
一起去到另一山。

M:
The trees here are not straight,
We've to move another way.

女：
这林树木全是弯，
一起去到另一山。

F:
The trees here are not straight,
We'll choose another way.

260 男：
走上第二林，
这林有椿树来拦，
未见一棵老甜竹。

M:
The second forest we have arrived,
Chun trees are on the right,
No old bamboos in my sight.

女：
走上第二林，
这林有椿树来拦，
未见一棵老甜竹。

F:
The second forest we have arrived,
Chun trees are on the right,
No old bamboos in our sight.

261 男：
既嘱父母出门来，
找得好木才归还。

M:
We've promised as we're out,
We won't return till fine wood are found.

女：
既然背刀出门来，
找得木才还。

F:
We come out with hacking knife,
We won't be back with nothing in hands.

262

男：	**M:**
边找咱边去，	We walk along and look around,
未见好木怎么办？	What if fine wood cannot be found?
女：	**F:**
边找咱边去，	We walk along and look around,
哪里有好材就砍。	We'd cut the trees that are good enough.

263

男：	**M:**
咱上别山林，	We go to another forest,
又走新一坡。	After climbing over another hill.
女：	**F:**
随哥上别山，	I follow you climbing the hill,
随郎走新林。	And we soon get to another forest.

264

男：	**M:**
走上第三林，	The third forest we've arrived,
这林金竹还嫩小。	Golden bamboos are tender and young.
女：	**F:**
走上第三林，	The third forest we've arrived,
这林金竹还嫩小。	Golden bamboos here are still too young.

265

男：	**M:**
未见老树笔直木，	No old and straight trees we can see,
再到另山新一林。	We'd go to another hill to seek.
女：	**F:**
未见老树笔直木，	No old and straight trees we can see,
再到另山新一林。	We'd go to another hill for the forest.

266	男： 走上第四林， 到处都找遍， 不见好材怎么办？	M: The fourth forest I've arrived, What I want aren't in my sight, What if fine wood I can't find?
	女： 走上第四林， 到处都找遍， 不见好材怎么办？	F: The fourth forest we've arrived, What we want aren't in our sight, What if fine wood we can't find?
267	男： 找了几片林， 下了几条溪。	M: I seek over one forest after another, And go thru several streams as well.
	女： 找了几片林， 下了几条溪。	F: We seek over one forest after another, And go thru several streams as well.
268	男： 边走又边去， 见好木就砍。	M: We go along and search around, We cut the woods that we want.
	女： 边走又边去， 见好木就砍。	F: We go along and search around, We cut the woods that we want.
269	男： 每蔸从根看到梢， 每蔸弯似牛排样。	M: The trees are long from bottom to top, They're bending like the steak.
	女： 每蔸从根看到梢， 弯似牛排难去砍。	F: The trees are long from bottom to top, The bending woods are hard to log.

270

男：	**M:**
这林弯木也有多， 又去别山新一林。	No straight woods in this forest, For another forest we've to leave.
女：	**F:**
这林木似牛排弯， 随郎去别山新林。	The woods are bending like the steak, For other forest we'd change our way.

271

男：	**M:**
走上第五林， 这林幼木也有多， 眼灵娘自瞧。	The fifth forest we've arrived, Small trees are growing up, You have sharp eyes for the fine.
女：	**F:**
走上第五林， 幼木也有多， 想砍树皮未够老。	The fifth forest we've arrived, Young trees are in my sight, I want to cut but they are too young.

272

男：	**M:**
幼木不宜来做橹， 没得几天就损坏。	Saplings can't be used as poles, They are easily broken off.
女：	**F:**
幼木不宜做木桩， 雨淋几天就损坏。	Saplings can't be used as poles, They'd soon get rotted by the rain.

273

男：	**M:**
幼木咱不砍， 又到新一坡。	The young wood we won't cut, So we're going to another slope.
女：	**F:**
幼木咱不砍， 砍来围园也不稳。	The young wood we won't cut, They aren't solid for fencing up.

274	男： 边走又边找， 边行又边寻。	M: We are advancing on the way, Looking for ideal wood we can't wait.
	女： 边走又边找， 眼灵郎自瞧。	F: We keep on seeking on the way, You have sharp eyes for proper ones.
275	男： 找了几片林， 下了几个坳。	M: We try forest after forest, And search from one col to another.
	女： 找了几片林， 去找哪蔸都是嫩。	F: We seek over the forests, The woods are too young when we meet.
276	男： 这林找遍了， 未见好木合适砍。	M: We've sought over this forest, But find no one to meet our need.
	女： 这林找遍了， 未见好木怎么办？	F: We've sought over this forest, But why good wood we can't meet?
277	男： 这林树不好， 又到新的一片林。	M: The trees here are not what we want, And we climb over to another forest.
	女： 这林树不好， 随郎去片新树林。	F: The trees here are not good, We go to another forest with new hope.

278

男：
走上第六林，
这林有恩桃拦路，
给郎空找好几粱。

M:
The sixth forest we've arrived,
Entao trees come into sight,
We've finally found them alright.

女：
走上第六林，
这林有恩桃拦路，
给郎空找好几粱。

F:
The sixth forest we've arrived,
Entao trees come into sight,
We finally find them alright.

279

男：
不得难知返回家，
难把花园围。

M:
We won't be back empty-handed,
With none to have garden fenced.

女：
不得难知返回家，
难把花园围。

F:
We won't be back empty-handed,
We've to take some as the hedge.

280

男：
找见老树欲砍要，
找见直木欲砍回。

M:
I'll cut down the old trees,
And choose the straight wood I meet.

女：
哪林有老树才要，
哪林有直木才砍。

F:
We'd get only the old trees,
We'd cut only the straight we need.

281

男：
碰蔸老树想要砍，
来做园柱多容易。

M:
I wanna cut down the old tree,
A nice pole of the fence it may be.

女：
未见一蔸直树木，
老木立柱才稳固。

F:
No straight wood is in this forest,
Only old tree can meet our need.

282 男:	M:
未见这林有老木,	No tree's old enough in this forest,
又去选别处,	To find the good trees I've to leave,
又去新一林。	Over the hill is another forest.
女:	F:
未见这林有老木,	No tree's old enough in this forest,
随哥选别处,	To find the good ones we shall leave,
又去找新林。	Over the hill there is another forest.
283 男:	M:
走上第七林,	The seventh forest we've arrived,
这有五杯子[①]拦下,	Wubeizi [①] trees catch our eyes,
别人砍去起晒台。	They're good for building terrace.
女:	F:
走上第七林,	The seventh forest we've arrived,
渐渐走得远,	A long journey we've gone,
未见好材我们砍。	We see no trees that we want.
284 男:	M:
嫩木不宜编篱笆,	Young trees can't make up the fence,
五杯子树不能编。	Wubeizi trees can't be used as hedge.
女:	F:
嫩木不宜编篱笆,	Young trees can't make up the fence,
五杯子树不能编。	Wubeizi trees can't form a hedge.

①五杯子,树名,其碳捣碎成末与硝合拌为制造火药原料。

① Wubeizi, a tree whose carbon mashed with nitrate to make powder.

285

男： 老树人先砍， 只有幼林等我们， 嫩木不宜做柱子。	**M:** Old trees have been cut by others, Leaving only young trees to us, They're unsuitable for the fence.
女： 老树人先砍， 只有幼林等我们， 让咱怎么办？	**F:** Old trees have been cut by others, Leaving here only the young growth, It's not fair for us.

286

男： 既咱持刀进林子， 欲转新一坡。	**M:** We've carried hacking knife with us, Why not look for another forest?
女： 既咱持刀进林子， 欲转新一坡。	**F:** We've carried hacking knife with us, We'll try to find another forest.

287

男： 走上第八坡， 红日照山林， 欲进山林歇歇脚。	**M:** The eighth mountain we've arrived, Sprinkling into the forest is the sunlight, Let's go into the forest and have a rest.
女： 走上第八坡， 日照山林间， 我俩欲稍息。	**F:** The eighth forest we've arrived, Sprinkling into the forest is the sunlight, We're too tired and need a rest.

288

男： 稍息咱抽烟， 抽烟歇歇气。	**M:** Having a smoke I take a rest, I need a smoke to catch my breath.
女： 间歇候哥抽口烟， 待郎抽烟筒。	**F:** While you smoke I'd take a rest, You need to smoke for a rest.

289

男： 抽烟妹抽烟， 抽好烟再找。	**M:** Why not join me and have a smoke, After smoking we can go.
女： 妹不懂抽烟， 抽烟娘不会。	**F:** I can't joint you to have a smoke, I'm a girl I won't smoke.

290

男： 抽罢就去找， 又去新地方。	**M:** After a smoke we'll go, Another forest is over the hill.
女： 歇罢就去找， 随郎上新林。	**F:** After a rest and we need to go, To another forest for our hope.

291

男： 边去边看树， 边巡坡边走。	**M:** We're looking for trees on the way, Over the mountains we survey.
女： 边走又边去， 眼灵郎自瞧。	**F:** We're looking for trees along the way, Let's keep eyes open on our way.

292

男： 未见一丛笔直树， 想砍木还嫩。	**M:** Straight trees we can't find, And the ones we meet are too young.
女： 未见一蔸笔直树， 我俩上新林。	**F:** We can't meet a straight tree, We've to find another forest.

293

男：
又走另一坡，
再找新一林。

M:
We've climbed over another hill,
The forest is on top of the hill.

女：
随哥找另山，
随哥找别林。

F:
I'll follow you to another hill,
The new forest is in our view.

294

男：
走上第九坡，
这坡枫树也有多，
睁乖娘自瞧。

M:
The ninth mountain we've arrived,
The maple trees here have thrived,
Please don't miss the ones we want.

女：
走上第九坡，
枫树有很多，
睁乖郎帮瞧。

F:
The ninth mountain we've arrived,
The maple trees here have thrived,
We'll keep sharp eyes for what we want.

295

男：
哪蔸老才要，
哪根直才砍。

M:
We wanna get only the old trees,
And the straight ones that we need.

女：
哪蔸老咱要，
哪根直咱砍。

F:
We wanna get only the old trees,
And cut the straight ones for our need.

296

男：
就地砍两棵，
同处根两根。

M:
Here we cut down two trees,
Their roots are twisting in the deep.

女：
就地砍两棵，
同处根两根。

F:
Here we cut down two trees,
Their roots are twisting in the deep.

297

男：	**M:**
老树别人已砍多，	We find no many old trees,
幸好不断餐空回。	Though we return without our hands empty.
女：	**F:**
老树别人已砍多，	The old trees we seldom meet,
哪蔸好要完。	We'll cut the ones meet our need.

298

男：	**M:**
攀上几重坡，	We climb over one slope after another,
走下几个坳。	And we search thru one col to another.
女：	**F:**
随哥攀几坡，	I'll follow you up to the hills,
随郎翻几坳。	I'll follow you down thru the cols.

299

男：	**M:**
同上另一坡，	After climbing another hill,
又到新一林。	We come across another forest.
女：	**F:**
随哥去别山，	I follow you to another hill,
随郎找新林。	Together we get to another forest.

300

男：	**M:**
走上第十坡，	The tenth hill we've arrived,
十蔸十成柱，	Ten trees useful we've found,
砍来做木桩。	We'd cut them down to make the fence.
女：	**F:**
走上第十坡，	The tenth hill we've arrived,
十蔸十成柱，	Ten trees useful we finally find,
砍来做木桩。	We'd cut them down to be fence poles.

301

男：
围木未找着，
篱木还未寻。

M:
We still need woods for building fence,
And need sticks to make the hedge.

女：
围木咱未找，
篱木咱未寻。

F:
Let's look for trees for the fence,
Let's look for sticks to make hedge.

302

男：
既上树林来，
还找围园木。

M:
Since we're here in the forest,
Let's look for the right thing for the fence.

女：
既上树林来，
我俩找围木。

F:
Since we're here in the forest,
We'd look for sticks to make the hedge.

303

男：
走上十一坡，
渐渐走得远，
好木也找见。

M:
The eleventh hill we've arrived,
A long journey we've traveled,
Here we may find the right materials.

女：
走上十一坡，
渐渐走得远，
好木也找见。

F:
The eleventh hill we've arrived,
A long journey we've traveled,
Here we may find the right materials.

304

男：
遇上篱笆木，
遇着木桩树。

M:
Trees for fence here we see,
Sticks for hedge here we meet.

女：
咱要篱笆木，
咱砍木桩树。

F:
Trees for fence here we see,
We'd cut them down for our need.

305 男：
这坡已砍遍，
我俩又到别山林。

M:
We are in need of something more,
Another forest we'll leave for.

女：
随哥上别山，
随郎去新处。

F:
I'll follow you to another hill,
For a new forest we'll leave.

306 男：
走上十二林，
根根成柱子，
砍哪蔸都得。

M:
The twelfth forest we've arrived,
The trees are good for the poles,
We can choose the one we like.

女：
走上十二林，
根根成柱子，
砍哪蔸都得。

F:
The twelfth forest we've arrived,
The trees here are fence poles,
We can choose any one we like.

307 男：
篱木真有多，
既咱有缘来遇着。

M:
Sticks for hedges are many,
To meet them here we're lucky.

女：
篱木真有多，
既咱有缘来遇着。

F:
Sticks for hedges are many,
To meet them here we're lucky.

308 男：
砍木已足够，
生怕路遥难盘算。

M:
The wood for fence we've obtained,
But the way back home is far away.

女：
砍木已足够，
苦死路遥途又远。

F:
The wood for fence we've obtained,
But the way back home is too far away.

309

男：	**M:**
搬来推在地头边，	The wood are piled up in the field,
日后邀众来帮扛。	We'll have them carried away.
女：	**F:**
搬来推在地头边，	We pile them up in the field,
日后邀众来帮扛。	We'll ask people to carry them away.

310

男：	**M:**
搬到地头沙滩上，	We've moved them in the field,
我俩欲想把家回。	And now we wanna go back home.
女：	**F:**
木头堆满沙滩上，	The wood are piled up in the field,
我俩欲想把家回。	We are ready we've to leave.

311

男：	**M:**
娘妹先到家，	You arrive at home happily,
娘妹先回屋。	I'd accompany you home before I leave.
女：	**F:**
随哥回到家，	You accompany me to my home,
随郎来到屋。	Together we both come back home.

312

男：	**M:**
回屋求众齐来帮，	We ask the villagers to come over,
到家求亲来帮忙。	They're gathering and give counsel.
女：	**F:**
回屋求众齐来帮，	We ask the villagers to come over,
到家求亲来帮忙。	They're gathering and give counsel.

313 男：
俩童来哥道，
俩丁来哥讲，
俩伊来哥说。

M:
You kids please come over,
I have errands for you both,
You can do them as I want.

女：
俩童来哥道，
俩丁来哥讲，
俩伊来哥说。

F:
You kids please come over,
He has errands for you both,
You can do them as he wants.

314 男：
一童下寨去请人，
一伊上村去找酒。

M:
A boy should go to the village to invite some people,
A girl should go to the village for some wine.

女：
一童下寨去找人，
一伊上村去找酒。

F:
The boy goes to the village for people,
The girl goes to the village for some wine.

315 男：
请老人进餐，
请众来喝酒。

M:
The elderly are invited to the seat,
All the villagers are invited to drink.

女：
俩童叫老人进餐，
俩伊邀众来喝酒。

F:
The boys lead the elderly to seat,
The girls invite the folks to drink.

316 男：
老人也来帮，
众人也来齐。

M:
Even the elderly come to help,
All the villagers give their hands.

女：
老人来帮工，
众人来帮忙。

F:
Even the senior come to help,
They come together for our need.

五、要木围花园
V Enclosing Garden with Hedge

317

男：
木料搬到家，
我们围园把花种。

M:
The woods were carried home,
We grow flowers with hedge round.

女：
木料搬到家，
明天围园把花种。

F:
The woods were carried home,
Tomorrow we'll grow flowers fenced by the wood.

318

男：
立好木桩围花园，
栏木捆三轮。

M:
The woods were erected as the poles,
The poles were tied up with tightropes.

女：
每根木桩插得深，
栏木捆三轮。

F:
Each pole was struck into the soil,
They were tied up with tightropes.

319

男：
围园网三道，
先把牡丹栽。

M:
The garden was fenced by three layers,
We grow peony first in the garden.

女：
篱笆三道网，
首先栽棵牡丹花。

F:
The fences contained three layers,
We grow peony first in the garden.

320 男：
二来围花园，
众友一起到，
齐手种上玫瑰花。

M:
Then we start making the fence,
All the friends come to help,
The roses we grow with join hands.

女：
二来围花园，
众友一起到，
齐手种上玫瑰花。

F:
Then we start working on the fence,
All the friends come to help,
The roses we grow with join hands.

321 男：
三来围花园，
齐种海棠花。

M:
We're working on the fence,
And we plant Begonia in the garden.

女：
三来围花园，
齐种海棠花。

F:
We're working on the fence,
We plant Begonia in the garden.

322 男：
四来围花园，
众友帮栽幸福花，
长在门前真好看。

M:
We're working on the fence,
Happy flowers would be grown by join hands,
They'll be blooming just behind garden gate.

女：
四来围花园，
众友帮栽幸福花，
长在门前别人管。

F:
We're working on the fence,
Happy flowers were grown by join hands,
They should be taken care by our hands.

323 男：
五来围起兰花园，
长在晒楼别人摘。

M:
Then we enclose the orchid garden with fence,
They can be picked up at the terrace.

女：
五来围起兰花园，
长在晒楼哥护理。

F:
Then we enclose the orchid garden with fence,
Near the terrace they need your hands.

324

男：
花栽别处才好看，
苦郎在远难得理。

M:
The flowers are blooming on other land,
I'm too far away to care for them.

女：
栽花只盼花朵靓，
好花等郎来护理。

F:
We plant flowers for their fame,
Good flowers are waiting for your hands.

325

男：
六来围起红掌花，
贵花否到我们手？

M:
We're enclosing the anthurium with hedge,
Will precious flowers belong to us?

女：
六来围起红掌花，
栽花盼贵如人家。

F:
We're enclosing the anthurium with hedge,
I wish my love as noble as the flower.

326

男：
七来围起水仙花，
郎在遥远也难盼。

M:
It's time to hedge the daffodil,
It's hard to come to you from over the hill.

女：
七来围起水仙花，
别人在远也期盼。

F:
It's time to hedge the daffodil,
You can easily come if you have the will.

327

男：
得围不得瞧，
得种不得摘。

M:
I hedge them but can't appreciate them,
I plant them but can't enjoy them.

女：
得围咱得瞧，
得种也得摘。

F:
We hedge them and we can appreciate them,
We plant and we can enjoy them.

328 男：
八来围起月桂花，
月桂远在别人乡，
花好咱命苦不受。

M:
It's time to hedge the laurel flowers,
They're growing in land of others,
I'm too poor to get their favors.

女：
八来围起月桂花，
月桂在异地不远，
我俩命好一起围。

F:
It's time to hedge the laurel flowers,
Though they originally grow in land of others,
We're fortunate to obtain their favors.

329 男：
九来围起金雀花，
有朝成人如别个。

M:
It's time to hedge the broom,
One day they'll be in full bloom.

女：
九来围起金雀花，
使妹成人如别个。

F:
It's time to hedge the broom,
I expect to be as charming as the broom.

330 男：
围花盼得变富有，
生怕成鬼死在前。

M:
I hedge the flower with good wish,
I'm afraid I can't wait their growth.

女：
哪蔸都是园中花，
围花得共家才罢。

F:
Each one in the garden can grow,
They'll be in full bloom as we hope.

331 男：
十来围起芙蓉园，
盼它常开多么好，
郎在远方讨欣赏。

M:
It's time to hedge the hibiscus,
I expect them to open forever,
I live too far away to enjoy them closer.

女：
十来围起芙蓉园，
花亮得很远，
见美哥才来。

F:
Let's hedge the hibiscus together,
They're charming and proud,
Attracting the appreciator come around.

332

男：
花它蓝朵伴紫朵，
粉红配火红。

M:
Blue flowers match well with violet ones,
The flowers in pink match those in crimson.

女：
花它蓝朵伴紫朵，
粉红配火红。

F:
The blue flower matches well with violet one,
The flowers in pink match those in crimson.

333

男：
蓝朵是英台，
红朵是山伯。

M:
The blue one reminds Yingtai of a love canon,
The red one may be Shanbo of the legend.

女：
蓝朵是英台，
红朵是山伯。

F:
The blue one reminds Yingtai of a love canon,
The red one may be Shanbo of the legend.

334

男：
人说山伯与英台，
赏花当作早晚饭。

M:
For the two lovers of the story,
Enjoying flowers as their meals.

女：
人说山伯与英台，
理花当饭不觉饥。

F:
The lovers of the story,
Enjoying flowers they forget hunger.

335

男：
论人说到己，
是否有点小名头？

M:
Let's talk about things of our own,
Do you have good wish and the hope?

女：
论人说到己，
是否有点小名头。

F:
We'll talk about things of our own,
We have good wishes and we have hope.

336 男：
想来白费围花园，
既不依人得爱财。

M:
I'm afraid my efforts go in vain,
Nothing is gained from what I've sowed.

女：
别人围园发爱财，
怕郎围空园难办。

F:
People gain by what they've sowed,
You gain nothing from what you've sowed.

337 男：
讲多话也多，
咱欲去围新花园。

M:
It's no use talking too much,
Let's go to the garden to fence them up.

女：
讲多话也多，
随郎去围新花园。

F:
It's no use talking too much,
We'll go to the garden and fence them up.

338 男：
十一来围常春花，
心想依人享情缘。

M:
Let's enclose for the periwinkle,
I expect my true love to be encountered.

女：
十一来围常春花，
我俩结情才罢休。

F:
We'd enclose the periwinkle together,
Mutual affection establishes between lovers.

339 男：
围花只盼结种子，
有朝结情像别个。

M:
I hope to get seeds by growing flowers,
I envy those lovers could be together.

女：
妹盼围花结种子，
怕郎见不好难办。

F:
I hope to get seeds by growing flowers,
What kind of lover would you prefer?

340

男：	**M:**
从前有莵常春花，	There was once a periwinkle,
英台昼夜来相会。	It attracted Zhu Yingtai and her lover.
女：	**F:**
从前有莵常春花，	There was a periwinkle,
有朝结情像别个。	I hope to be one of the legendary lovers.

341

男：	**M:**
古时围园发情财，	Hedging the garden and love gained,
天下唯英台做到。	It's only Yingtai who could obtain.
女：	**F:**
古时围园发情财，	During the hedging love gained,
山伯英台才做到。	Shanbo and Yingtai could obtain.

342

男：	**M:**
十二围莵凤梨花，	Let's enclose the pineapple flowers,
凤梨逢时它才开。	It only blooms in the right hour.
女：	**F:**
十二围莵凤梨花，	We'll enclose the pineapple flowers,
凤梨逢时它才开。	It only blooms in the right time.

343

男：	**M:**
四季也是此时见，	It's blooming right this time,
在哪等得新一春。	I can't wait till the new spring comes.
女：	**F:**
四季也是此时开，	It's blooming right this time,
新年立春也快来。	After new year the spring will come.

344

男： 凤凰也是此时飞， 情侣也是那时会。	**M:** The phoenixes fly at this time, The lovers date at the same time.
女： 凤凰结对才起飞， 连情同家才罢休。	**F:** The phoenixes fly in pairs, Perusing love till a happy end.

345

男： 凤梨还有酸和甜， 不如古时蝴蝶兰。	**M:** Pineapples are sour and sweet, Not as enjoyable as moth orchid.
女： 酸果嫁接变甜果， 恰似古代蝴蝶兰。	**F:** By grafting the sour become sweet, They're just like the moth orchid.

346

男： 哪莞酸妹撩， 哪莞甜妹理。	**M:** You can care for sour fruit, You can attend to the sweet ones.
女： 哪莞酸同撩， 哪莞甜同理。	**F:** Let's care for the sour ones, Let's attend to the sweet ones.

347

男： 妹来嫁接酸变甜， 种在晒台妹来理。	**M:** You may graft the sour to become sweet, They grow by the veranda for your care.
女： 妹撩哥嫁接， 哪莞甜共理。	**F:** Let's graft the sour fruit tree with sweet sticks, We'd attend to the sweet ones together.

348 男：
他人嫁接还结果，
我俩育种不生芽。

M:
The trees grafted by others bear fruits,
But our breeding grows no shoots.

女：
他人石上还种果，
它还早熟先得吃。

F:
Someone plants their fruit trees on the rock,
But they harvest fruit earlier to eat.

349 男：
随哥转别句，
欲道新一题。

M:
I'm going to lead the song to another way,
We'd start a new topic as I say.

女：
随哥转别句，
随哥道新题。

F:
I'll follow you to another way,
To start a new song as you say.

350 男：
十二名花都围齐，
园里每蔸长得好。

M:
We've enclosed for all the twelve flowers,
Each one in the garden grows well.

女：
十二名花都围齐，
园里每蔸长得好。

F:
We've enclosed for all the twelve flowers,
They're in the garden and all grow well.

351 男：
名花园中长，
每蔸根部成培土。

M:
Famed flowers grow in the garden,
Each one need to be earthed up.

女：
名花园中长，
每蔸都成来培土。

F:
Famed flowers grow in the garden,
They all need to be earthed up.

六、栽花快长
Ⅵ Growing Flowers

352 男：
来咱种花给它大，
来咱种花给它长。

M:
Let's plant flowers for them to grow,
Let's plant flowers to make them flourish.

女：
随哥种花使它大，
来咱种花使它长。

F:
Let's plant flowers for them to grow,
Let's plant flowers to make them flourish.

353 男：
使它长欲看，
使它大想瞧。

M:
Make them grow for appreciation,
Make them flourish for admiration.

女：
它长一起看，
它大一起瞧。

F:
Let's care for them together,
Let's enjoy them together.

354 男：
牡丹远方才有卖，
名花京城才有摆。

M:
Peonies are only sold far away,
Rare flowers are on stalls in urban place.

女：
远方牡丹真有多，
京城名花摆满市。

F:
Peonies are plentiful far away,
Rare flowers are on shelves in urban place.

355

男：
来呀，妹来呀，
一起来论古话题。

M:
Come on, dear girl, please come on,
Let's start a topic together.

女：
随哥一起来，
一起来论古话题。

F:
I'll certainly follow you,
And start a topic together.

356

男：
这方有名花出卖，
我国有名花出售。

M:
Rare flowers are for sale in this region,
Rare flowers are for sale in our land.

女：
这方有名花出卖，
随郎有钱多就买。

F:
Rare flowers are for sale in our region,
Buy more if you can afford them.

357

男：
在家身子腻，
在村衣服脏，
想去远方栽花朵。

M:
I'm feeling lazy at home,
Wandering the village in dirty clothes,
I want to grow flowers far from home.

女：
在家身子腻，
在村衣服脏，
远去不懂路。

F:
You're lazy at home,
Roaming the village in dirty clothes,
I don't know where the way is.

358

男：
同来栽培花一枝，
大家论起从前事。

M:
Let's grow flowers in joint effort,
And talk about the past together.

女：
随哥栽培花一枝，
大家论起从前事。

F:
We'd grow flowers in joint effort,
And talk about the past together.

359 男：
一来先栽牡丹花，
花开辉映神台前。

M:
First we grow the peonies,
Their flowers would be shining at the altar.

女：
一来先栽牡丹花，
亮在别人晒台上。

F:
So we grow the peonies first,
Blossoms are decorating others' veranda.

360 男：
哪天妹闲见了它，
培土又浇水。

M:
If you are available,
Please earth up and water them.

女：
得空妹去瞧一次，
远处有好人淋水。

F:
I'll see them when available,
But some nice person may water them.

361 男：
浇水渗透花根须，
使它长成蔸。

M:
Water will infiltrate the root,
Flowers will finally bloom.

女：
浇水渗透花根须，
生怕遭人来嫉妒。

F:
Water will infiltrate the root,
Envy may be caused by the people in tow.

362 男：
使它长成丛，
使它长成蔸。

M:
May them grow into clusters,
May them grow to maturity.

女：
望它枝繁又叶茂，
日后长大别人管。

F:
May them spread out branches,
Then being taken care of by others.

363

男：	**M:**
哪枝倒妹扶，	You're to support the one that falls down,
枯死妹补种。	And reseed the one that dies off.
女：	**F:**
倒的妹用木来撑，	The slant I'll support with woods,
枯死妹补种。	The dead I'll replace with new seeds.

364

男：	**M:**
种花别去婆家久，	Don't grow flowers back in your mother-in-law's home,
栽花别去夫家在。	Don't grow flowers back at your husband's house.
女：	**F:**
妹婆远在花根旁，	My mother-in-law doesn't live far,
哥眸伶俐自知明。	You're smart enough to figure out her home.

365

男：	**M:**
栽花莫贪住几天，	Please stay not too long there,
日后不晓花结种。	Or you'll miss the blooming period.
女：	**F:**
妹穷讨饭去几天，	I need to return home for a few days,
望郎闭眼莫要怪。	It's kind of you not to blame me.

366

男：	**M:**
花靠妹去护理好，	Flowers need your good care,
让哥远郎讨得瞧。	So that I'd have the chance to admire.
女：	**F:**
妹想把花护理好，	How I want to nurse the flowers well,
怕郎嫌远不来种。	But wonder if you fear the distance between us.

367 男：
牡丹长在大平川，
哪有生在陡壁上，
哪到阿哥手头摘？

M:
Peonies are growing in the plain,
But not on the sheer cliffs,
How can I have the chance to pick them?

女：
牡丹长在大平川，
若在井边长才好，
给妹挑水来回看。

F:
Peonies are growing in the plain,
I wish them grow near the well,
So that I can see while fetching water.

368 男：
皇帝府中常观花，
仙在天上常欣赏。

M:
The Emperor enjoys flowers in his palace,
Gods admire flowers in the heaven.

女：
皇帝府中常观花，
妹在远方望莫及。

F:
The Emperor enjoys flowers in his palace,
But I can't enjoy the flowers from long distance.

369 男：
花平膝盖哥培土，
何日共园一起在？

M:
Earth them up as to my knee's height,
When can we be together in the garden?

女：
培土浇水哥有意，
终能共园一起在。

F:
If you're sincere enough to water the flowers,
Someday we'll be in the same garden.

370 男：
浇水花才开，
我俩欲去瞧。

M:
They'll bloom if being watered,
So we have the chance to admire together.

女：
盼它早开花，
靠郎勤浇水。

F:
If we long for the blossoms,
You should water them more.

371

男：
盼它含蕾快开花，
是否能到咱手头。

女：
妹也期望它开花，
盼郎似仙来相会。

M:
Hope the flowers in bud soon,
I doubt if we can get them in hand.

F:
Hope the flowers in bud soon,
Long for meeting you as in fairy tales.

372

男：
莫让羞颜哥落空，
莫让丢脸郎白劳。

女：
只要哥愿来，
怕郎嫌差就难办。

M:
Don't let me down,
Don't have my efforts go in vain.

F:
If you're willing to come to me,
Your dream won't fail.

373

男：
时刻忧心惦花朵，
有朝讨瞧得罪人。

女：
哥想栽花就快到，
若想捕鱼就别来。

M:
I always miss the flowers,
But for fear of offending others.

F:
Come if you want to grow flowers,
Or just go somewhere else if not sincere.

374

男：
心想拼命把花栽，
生怕阿哥命不受。

女：
想花不种莫要来，
切莫怪命不受投。

M:
I'm in the mind for growing flowers,
But fear that I'm not destined for the fortune.

F:
Don't come if you are unwilling,
Don't make excuse in your destiny.

375 男： 莫要空栽园中花， 长在异地也惦念。	**M:** I wish the flowers can bloom, I miss them however far from their home.
女： 妹盼同园来栽花， 日后共家一起瞧。	**F:** I wish to grow flowers together, Expect the day for us to enjoy together.
376 男： 想栽名花得一茬， 怕人蜚语传远方。	**M:** I want to grow rare flowers, Afraid of the spread-out rumors.
女： 有意种花出了名， 不成夫妻情还在。	**F:** If you're sincere to grow rare flowers, Blossom or not is the destiny of ours.
377 男： 怕不中意怎么好， 日后流泪永不干。	**M:** I'm afraid you dislike them, With tears from the eyes later.
女： 妹也入眼见中意， 怕郎嫌差更难办。	**F:** I like them with my affection, I'm afraid you dislike them even.
378 男： 开口眼泪流， 远花难得理。	**M:** Words are uttered as my eyes welled with tear, Flowers in distance are hard to care.
女： 有意天涯若比邻， 无意在近也不找， 我俩结对见中意。	**F:** If you're sincere distance can't keep us apart, Indifferent heart can make us afar, We'd become a couple if we follow our heart.

379

男：
牡丹绿朵配红朵，
我俩能否享富贵。

M:
Red peony goes well with green ones,
If we can be together to enjoy the wealth.

女：
牡丹绿朵配红朵，
它才富贵结成双。

F:
Red peony goes well with green ones,
Pairing off to enjoy the wealth.

380

男：
二来栽种玫瑰花，
园中玫瑰开得亮。

M:
Let's grow some roses,
Blossoms are shining in the garden.

女：
随哥来种玫瑰花，
有心共到园里种。

F:
Along with you is my heart,
Grow them together in the yard.

381

男：
花开灿烂映园外，
映到皇宫金梯前。

M:
The flourishing roses radiate from the garden,
Shinning onto the palace's golden stairs.

女：
红花照到哥脸上，
怕郎另奔不会合。

F:
Red roses are shining on your face,
I'm afraid you fall into someone else's embrace.

382

男：
玫瑰映入妹门口，
早晚喂猪容易看。

M:
Roses are shining on your doorway,
You can enjoy them when feeding pigs.

女：
玫瑰映入哥村寨，
郎耕田地自己瞧。

F:
Roses are shining on your village,
You can admire them while plowing the land.

383 男：
辉映至远方，
好花能否到手头。

M:
They're shining far away,
If I can get a good one in my way.

女：
映入哥村来，
怕郎不找也难办。

F:
They're reaching onto your village,
Fearing that you aren't eager for them.

384 男：
得理盼得赏，
得育盼得栽。

M:
Being taken care they wish to be admired,
Being cultivated they wish to grow well.

女：
花盼共园一起长，
怎么让哥独自栽。

F:
In the same garden they wish to grow,
I won't leave you to plant alone.

385 男：
不种苗快老，
哪天依人发爱财。

M:
Seeds need to be sewed in good timing,
Someday you'll gain the fruits of love.

女：
不栽花仍未衰老，
怕郎男汉不重情。

F:
It's never too late to grow flower,
Fear you don't value the love ever.

386 男：
见花成丛真高兴，
开心如榕遮天下。

M:
I'm glad to see the flowers thrive,
As the banyan shading all of us.

女：
花长成丛看得喜，
怕郎无心去栽它。

F:
I'm glad to see the flowers thrive,
But fear you won't bear it in mind.

387

男： 给哥来回得护花， 哪天讨得有脸面。	**M:** I'd always take care of them, Hoping someday to have claim on them.
女： 盼哥来回常护花， 名花让给我俩种。	**F:** Wish you always take care of them, Together rare flowers we'd plant.

388

男： 人说玫瑰美天下， 拼命去护理。	**M:** It's said that roses are the fairest, So I treat them with carefulness.
女： 妹处有蔸玫瑰花， 未有谁敢下去栽。	**F:** Here I have the roses, Who dares to grow them?

389

男： 心想护好园中花， 别人登门在前头。	**M:** I want to care the flowers well, But someone else may get ahead.
女： 它自长在园里头， 还未有人上门瞧。	**F:** They're growing inside the garden, Yet no one come to make claim.

390

男： 在哪得看哥得摘， 千金在手也白望。	**M:** Where I can see and pick the flowers, Much money in hand may go in vain.
女： 不嫌去看又去摘， 有心一抓就到手。	**F:** To see and pick them if you care, You can take hole of them as a claim.

391

男：
一蔸有花十二朵，
怕有多路来会合。

M:
There are twelve flowers in a tree,
I'm afraid others may get ahead.

女：
一蔸有花十二朵，
它等我俩同路栽。

F:
There are twelve flowers in a tree,
Waiting us to plant together.

392

男：
别人从根包到梢，
让郎拼死也白劳。

M:
They're nursed from root to top,
My greatest efforts seem to be lost.

女：
独妹从根理到梢，
未有后生前来瞧。

F:
Only I nurse them from root to top,
No one has yet come to enjoy.

393

男：
有意把花护理好，
远方阿哥赶来栽。

M:
I intend to take good care of them,
And I come from afar to grow them.

女：
阿妹自理花欲开，
等郎进园来种花。

F:
Flowers will bloom with my care,
Waiting for you to come and admire.

394

男：
栽花使花结花种，
有朝成人表爱慕。

M:
Let's grow flowers to produce seeds,
Someone will show affections in deed.

女：
名花等哥栽结籽，
郎择吉日哪时得。

F:
Rare flowers are waiting to be planted,
Whenever the lucky day you choose will do.

395

男：
三来栽莵海棠花，
长在平川别人育，
远方郎哥也空盼。

M:
Let's grow begonias,
In plain they're cultivated by others,
I have no chance to make a claim.

女：
随哥种莵海棠花，
长在平川没有名，
等郎结交成伴侣。

F:
With you I grow begonias,
In plain they remain nameless,
Waiting for you to become mates.

396

男：
园中海棠多灿烂，
千里远客还来瞧。

M:
How splendid the flowers are,
Even guests come to see from afar.

女：
海棠辉映千里遥，
郎择吉日前去栽。

F:
The splendor radiates a thousand mile away,
You choose a lucky day to grow anyway.

397

男：
别人靠近又靠边，
他欲决沿毁界线。

M:
People approach close to the flowers,
They want to destroy the boundary.

女：
没人靠近想靠边，
没人决沿毁界线。

F:
No one intends to approach,
No one wants to destroy the boundary.

398

男：
见妹把花护起来，
它欲攀亲常来往。

M:
I'm afraid others may shelter you,
And want to claim kinship with you.

女：
有纱盼织布，
有儿盼结姻，
有铜盼合铁。

F:
With voile I want to weave,
If I have a son we'll be relatives,
As I hope to integrate copper with iron.

399

男： 名花栽培才壮大， 好花栽培才快长。	**M:** Cultivation makes rare flowers grow stronger, Cultivation makes good flowers grow faster.
女： 名花茁壮靠哥栽， 好花快长靠哥育。	**F:** It's you that grow the flowers stronger, It's you that grow the flowers faster.

400

男： 哥栽妹培土， 郎观娘围园。	**M:** I grow them and you earth them up, You watch them and I make a fence.
女： 我俩一同来栽培， 好花长在一园中。	**F:** Let's cultivate them together, Make them grow well in the same garden.

401

男： 有心护花长起来， 莫许分孽长寄生。	**M:** Flowers will grow up with care, No parasitic branch is allowed to generate.
女： 妹也护花长起来， 怕郎分岔不合拢。	**F:** Flowers grow up with my care, Fear that you'll go your own way.

402

男： 花美胜嫦娥， 花乖天天瞧不怨。	**M:** Flowers are fairer than Change①, Admiring flowers isn't boring everyday.
女： 花差不称心， 人看嫌郁闷。	**F:** If flowers are unsatisfactory, People would be too depressed to enjoy them.

① A Goddess in Chinese legend.

403

男：
别让花期白白误，
莫许青苗废栽期。

女：
我俩似花一起长，
似金樱同开，
郎嫌路远难得算。

M:
Don't miss the flowering period,
Don't waste the seeding season.

F:
We grow up together like the flowers,
And bloom like the cherokee rose,
Fear you aren't coming due to distance.

404

男：
生怕栽花没有名，
种姜变金樱。

女：
妹盼栽花出美名，
莫许姜种变金樱。

M:
Fear that the flowers have no fame,
The homebred ginger becomes cherokee rose.

F:
Wish the flowers become famous,
Stop the ginger from becoming cherokee rose.

405

男：
心想种花得来往，
怕开成朵被人摘。

女：
有意栽花得来往，
盼花盛开一起瞧。

M:
Growing flowers facilitates mutual exchange,
Fear that flowers will be picked by others.

F:
Growing flowers facilitates mutual exchange,
Wish to enjoy them together when they bloom.

406

男：
栽花命不受也难，
言语多甜也是假。

女：
哥命相已出，
花还等郎君，
莫给竹象①叮嫩笋。

M:
If I'm not destined to grow flowers,
The honeyed words will go futile.

F:
You're destined to grow flowers,
They're waiting for you to admire,
Don't allow insects to bite bamboo shoots.

---

①竹象，甲虫类，专啃嫩竹笋，形状似象状的昆虫。

407 男：
四来栽培幸福花，
长在门口被人摘。

女：
随哥栽培幸福花，
有朝一起养猪鸡。

M:
Happy flowers are grown at doorway,
Someone else may pick them away.

F:
I want to grow happy flowers with you,
Someday we'd raise chicks and pigs together.

408 男：
请妹护花等郎哥，
有朝变身共坟墓。

女：
山伯英台哪敢比，
死后同墓共灵牌。

M:
Please protect the flowers and wait for me,
Someday we can be buried together.

F:
We shan't compare with Shanbo and Yingtai,
To be buried together when we die.

409 男：
护花如山伯英台，
死后仍结双成对。

女：
盼如山伯与英台，
怕郎安排不到家。

M:
Protecting flowers are like Shanbo and Yingtai,
Who are still a pair even after they die.

F:
Wish we can be Shanbo and Yingtai,
Though fear that my dream may finally die.

410 男：
阿妹自身去盘算，
怕移大园被人管。

女：
花儿阿妹自栽培，
盼郎下园里去栽。

M:
You grow the flowers by yourself,
Or they'd be ruled after being removed.

F:
I'll grow flowers by myself,
Wish you'll go and pick the flowers.

411	男： 盼得来回共育花， 我俩如人得相伴。	M: Hope to grow flowers together, As we have so long companies each other.
	女： 妹盼哥来护理花， 让它长大共栽培。	F: Hope you come and nurse the flowers, They grow up and we nurse them together.
412	男： 育花多劳碌， 栽花得成人， 使它结种才罢休。	M: Nursing flowers needs hard work, Growing flowers achieve maturity, We won't stop until they bear seeds.
	女： 育花多辛苦， 哥来关顾花才开， 决心育它出良种。	F: Nursing flowers needs hard work, You're the very one to make them bloom, We're determined to nurse good flower species.
413	男： 我俩栽花共一园， 犹如同在共一家。	M: We grow flowers in the same garden, As if we were members of the same family.
	女： 我俩栽花共一园， 盼望同在共一家。	F: We grow flowers in the same garden, Hope we can be members of the same family.
414	男： 咱似有金不觉穷， 怕如破镜照影子， 不知落入谁手头。	M: It seems as if we had gold and were not poor, But fear that's shadow from a broken mirror, Who can catch a mirror shadow?
	女： 咱似真金永不变， 别人瞧不见， 好比获金银做宝。	F: True golds withstand testifying, No one but we can see our true feeling, As we get gold and silver as treasure.

415 男：
咱似花儿共一枝，
本是同根生。

M:
We're like the flowers in one branch,
And we're born from the same root.

女：
咱如花儿共一园，
好似同屋在一起。

F:
We're like the flowers in the same garden,
As if living in the same shelter.

416 男：
有意来回勤理花，
切莫忘咱种花情。

M:
Nurse them often if you're sincere,
Don't forget our friendship forever.

女：
妹勤来回护理花，
怕郎安家在前头。

F:
I'll nurse the flowers more often,
Afraid that you'd marry another woman.

417 男：
我俩栽花一起赏，
莫给嫩鸭去觅食。

M:
We grow flowers and enjoy them together,
Don't let ducks forage and ruin the flowers.

女：
花有人种才得赏，
怕郎多心难得算。

F:
Flowers should be planted first,
But I'm afraid you're only fiddling.

418 男：
鸭刮花根坏，
那时给咱难会合。

M:
Ducks digging the roots damage the flowers,
Making it difficult for us to meet each other.

女：
鸡鸭根旁去观花，
凤凰飞来把花恋。

F:
Chicks and ducks are onlookers,
Only phoenixes can fly among the flowers.

419

男：	**M:**
花落人讥笑，	People laugh at the fallen flowers,
想来埋头往前行。	I lower my head and walk forward.
女：	**F:**
但凡阿哥重情意，	If you think highly of our friendship,
切莫不许花脱落。	Don't let the flowers fall off.

420

男：	**M:**
五来栽棵蝴蝶兰，	Let's grow moth orchid,
啥花美不及。	Which is the fairest flower.
女：	**F:**
随哥栽棵蝴蝶兰，	I'd grow moth orchid with you,
蜜蒙再香难攀比。	The most fragrant has to admit inferior.

421

男：	**M:**
从前花幼不相逢，	No chance to meet when they're young,
现花长高被人管。	When they're grown up they've been claimed.
女：	**F:**
从前花幼就寻找，	They dream to be together when they're young,
现花长高才祈盼。	They keep the dream when grown up.

422

男：	**M:**
别人从根管到梢，	They're nursed from root to top,
我俩白白围花园。	The fence we make seem futile job.
女：	**F:**
别人岂敢靠花根，	Nobody dare to cling to the flowers,
妹用荆棘围起来。	As I use thistles and thorns to make fence.

423	男： 好坏也是属咱俩， 栽花务必有功名。	**M:** No matter good or bad they belong to us, Growing flowers would achieve something good.
	女： 我俩似花初绽放， 它盼我俩共栽培。	**F:** We're like flowers newly blooming, The flower would expect us to plant together.
424	男： 栽花莫要贪家务， 日后园中花欲落。	**M:** Do less housework if you grow flowers, Someday the flowers will fall down.
	女： 理花如管家， 日复月自长。	**F:** Nursing flowers is like housekeeping, Day after day they grow up with care.
425	男： 切莫忘记园中花， 日浇月培土。	**M:** Don't forget the flowers in the garden, Water them and earth them up often.
	女： 妹不忘却园中花， 苦妹无家真难办。	**F:** I won't forget the flowers in the garden, Without a home I can't do anything even.
426	男： 怕妹婆家去几天， 日后不晓花结籽。	**M:** If you go to mother-in-law's home for days, You wouldn't know when they produce seeds.
	女： 妹婆与猴在悬崖， 与哥无缘情还在。	**F:** My mother-in-law and monkey are in the cliff, Friendship remains if we're destined to part.

427

男：
怕妹偷偷去婆家，
日后花叶青变黄。

M:
If you go to mother-in-law's homesecretly,
Later the green leaves would turn yellow.

女：
妹婆在哥家，
怕郎橙叶找辛苦。

F:
My mother-in-law is at your home,
Making it hard to find orange leaves.

428

男：
即使妹要去婆家，
莫忘我俩种的花。

M:
If you go to mother-in-law's home,
Don't forget the flowers we grow.

女：
给去婆家妹依从，
吉日怕哥找不到。

F:
I'd comply if you permit,
The lucky day how you find it.

429

男：
种花莫给哥白栽，
栽花莫给哥空回。

M:
Don't waste my good intentions,
Don't have me go back with nothing.

女：
情深意重栽次花，
哪朵最靓让哥摘。

F:
Grow flowers with deep affection,
You could pick the fairest without hesitation.

430

男：
空栽手脚软，
咱情丢下河。

M:
My hands and legs go limp if in vain,
Throw our love into the river away.

女：
名花绽放时时艳，
怕郎无心去栽培。

F:
Rare flowers bloom and always shine,
Fear that you treat them without sincerity.

431 男:
阿哥爱花刻心中,
不许来空看。

M:
Flowers are engraved in my heart,
You can't come and see them only.

女:
栽花莫生多心眼,
稍下有场狂风乱。

F:
Don't be in two minds while growing flowers,
Later there will be strong wind.

432 男:
十五进庙妹上香,
上千仙家下赏花。

M:
You burn incense in temple on full moon day,
Thousands of fairies come down to admire flowers.

女:
妹还进庙化成仙,
怕哥上香丢了杆。

F:
In the temple I change into a fairy,
Fear that you lose the incense sticks easily.

433 男:
凤凰从根站满梢,
它愿我俩发爱财。

M:
Phoenixes are standing from root to top,
Hope that we could reap the fruit of love.

女:
凤凰挤满花丛中,
生怕别人先发财。

F:
Phoenixes hustle and bustle among flowers,
Fear that others may get the fruit first.

434 男:
凤凰进庙先求雨,
许愿我俩配成双。

M:
Phoenixes pray for rain first in the temple,
Wishing that we can become a couple.

女:
凤凰进庙去求雨,
花种将结又落空。

F:
Phoenixes pray for rain in the temple,
Wishes may finally come to naught.

435

男：	**M:**
六来栽棵红掌花，	Let's grow anthurium,
不知得享富贵福。	Wondering if I could enjoy wealth and honor.
女：	**F:**
六来栽培红掌花，	Let's grow anthurium,
靠哥能否享富贵？	Can I depend on you to enjoy wealth and honor?

436

男：	**M:**
怕妹忘却红掌花，	I'm afraid you'll forget the anthurium,
怕妹专讲小孩话。	I'm afraid you just have empty talk.
女：	**F:**
阿妹不忘红掌花，	I won't forget the anthurium,
靠郎一生享富贵。	I'd rely on you for fortune.

437

男：	**M:**
凤凰兴奋飞上天，	Phoenixes are excited to fly to the sky,
乌鸡欲配难高翔。	Crows aren't qualified to fly high.
女：	**F:**
凤凰上天任它飞，	Phoenixes fly free in the sky,
真心不改变。	I'll never change my original mind.

438

男：	**M:**
哪愿下田伴乌鸦？	How can phoenixes land to accompany crows?
哪愿安家贫穷地？	How will you settle down in my poor house?
女：	**F:**
凤凰随风落田坝，	Phoenixes will land with the wind,
想与乌鸡结成双。	Wishing to make pairs with the crows.

439 男：
轮不到哥来护花，
岂能到哥得栽培。

M:
I don't have the chance to nurse flowers,
Nor to cultivate the flowers.

女：
盼哥来种花才开，
先祖让咱来栽培。

F:
You grow flowers to make them bloom,
We're designated by our ancestors.

440 男：
得种不得收，
免得有损好名头。

M:
Grow them without harvest,
My reputation will be damaged.

女：
得种盼收成，
得种非得收不可。

F:
Hope to get harvest as you grow them,
It's necessary you have claim on them.

441 男：
哥是异地远方人，
花好命不受。

M:
I'm an outlander faraway,
My fate is blocking my way.

女：
命合不怕远，
命好才相逢。

F:
Distance doesn't matter if we follow our fate,
Our fate would lead us to meet each other.

442 男：
白白替人来种花，
他人先择好吉日。

M:
I grow flowers for others,
Others choose a lucky day first.

女：
栽花别替人说媒，
给妹吸空螺。

F:
Don't act as a matchmaker,
Or my hope fails to attain whatever.

443

男：
不种始祖早已定，
种来却成他人妻。

M:
We aren't destined to grow flowers together,
You'd finally become someone else's wife.

女：
古有始祖定下来，
栽花不成妻也妾。

F:
Even if I can't be your wife,
To be concubine is acceptable.

444

男：
若妹还念红掌花，
莫忘哥嘱心里话。

M:
If you still think about the anthurium,
Don't forget what I've confined to you.

女：
阿妹重视红掌花，
听郎贵言心头安。

F:
I'm so concerned about the anthurium,
I feel at ease to listen to you.

445

男：
哥说妹记牢，
郎话娘听好。

M:
Listen to my words carefully,
Commit what I've said to your memory.

女：
哥说妹牢记，
怕郎重如碎米粒。

F:
I'll remember them heartedly,
Your words weight heavily.

446

男：
我俩栽花已成名，
即使无缘情还在。

M:
We've become famous by growing flowers,
Without predestination our affection remains.

女：
巴望栽花得出名，
怕哥多情不投合。

F:
Wish to become famous by growing flowers,
Fear that you're too amorous to be in love.

447 男：

有朝造地共一沿，
有朝共盒晌午饭。

M:

Someday we reclaim the same wasteland,
Someday we share the same box of lunch.

女：

巴望耕地共一沿，
希望共盒晌午饭。

F:

I wish to reclaim the same wasteland,
And share the same box of lunch.

448 男：

哥想搬家来靠近，
晓妹给起上或下，
早晚借盐容易点。

M:

I want to remove my house closer to you,
It can be above or below your house,
Make it easy to borrow salt regularly.

女：

有心搬来一起住，
共一锅更好，
怕郎讲假真难办。

F:

Remove to live with me if you're sincere,
To use the same pot will even be better,
I'm afraid you don't mean what you say.

449 男：

七来种蔸水仙花，
天上仙女下来会。

M:

Let's grow daffodils,
Fairies from heaven come down to admire.

女：

七来种蔸水仙花，
我俩似仙配成双。

F:

Let's grow daffodils,
We'd be a couple as immortals.

450

男：	**M:**
水仙映在脸庞上， 怕妹说假就难安， 日后熟菜又发芽。	Daffodil is shining on the face, I'm worried that you won't take me serious, The ripe vegetables may spout out again.
女：	**F:**
水仙灿烂映红天， 怕有乌云下来拦， 使妹怎么办？	The splendid daffodils flame the sky, I fear they'd be covered by the dark clouds, What should I do in that case?

451

男：	**M:**
怕妹护花不周到， 怕娘后抛不顾情。	Fear you aren't considerate enough, And abandon it regardless of our love.
女：	**F:**
阿妹护花很周到， 莫怕后抛不顾情。	I'm so considerate of the flower, I'll never abandon the flower.

452

男：	**M:**
护花还勤把水浇， 日后好移栽。	Water the flower diligently, In case someday we remove it easily.
女：	**F:**
靠哥护花才壮大， 使它绽朵一起瞧。	It's you who make flowers stronger, When they bloom we can see together.

453

男：	**M:**
有意护花尽到头， 莫怕别人笑一生。	Nurse the flowers till the end of life, Don't fear the laughter from others.
女：	**F:**
阿妹护花尽到头， 怕郎途中就丢弃。	I'll do it till the final day, But fear you'd give up halfway.

454

男：
种花使它长成丛，
让它映在脸庞上。

M:
Grow the flowers into clusters,
So that they'd reflect on the faces.

女：
盼哥种花长成丛，
让它讨得好脸面。

F:
Wish you grow flowers into clusters,
Let them gain some honors.

455

男：
从前种花有来历，
仙家种花成双对。

M:
Growing flowers has a history,
Growing flowers pair off the fairies.

女：
从前种花结姻缘，
我俩要给结成双。

F:
Growing flowers enables gardeners to get marry,
We'd match into a pair as fairies.

456

男：
仙家栽花出种子，
交情结缘才罢休。

M:
Fairies' flowers will sprout the seeds,
They never give up until they get fancy.

女：
栽花盼出种，
人生这时才珍贵。

F:
Wish to grow flowers that can sprout,
Life is just precious by now.

457

男：
生怕栽花不出名，
生怕女孩说谎话。

M:
Fear that growing flowers get no honor,
And you girls are kidding the other.

女：
栽花要有名，
妹是女孩就讲过。

F:
Growing flowers should win honor,
As a girl I'm not a liar.

458 男：
让妹继续护好花，
咱种千年不觉闷。

女：
妹也继续护好花，
让郎择日来栽培。

M:
If you take good care of the flowers,
It isn't boring here a thousand years.

F:
I'll continue to take care of them,
You can cultivate them at your leisure.

459 男：
心不忘种花，
命不出也难，
犹如高山把海隔。

女：
心莫忘种花，
家族让哥来，
护花成丛莫能丢。

M:
I never forget to grow flowers,
But I don't have the luck to grow them well,
Just as a mountain separating the sea.

F:
Never forget to grow flowers,
Waiting for you to take care,
Never give up the flowers in clusters.

460 男：
八来种蔸月桂花，
月桂长在遥远处，
咱命多好才相投。

女：
随哥种蔸月桂花，
长在异地另一园，
未得同家在一起。

M:
Let's grow laurel flowers,
Which is planted faraway,
How lucky we're to acquire them!

F:
I'd grow laurel flowers with you,
But they're in another garden,
Failing to be in the same one.

461 男：
得接月桂真高兴，
见它长高真爱栽。

女：
月桂成丛欲开花，
怕郎不敢下来种。

M:
I'm so glad to receive the laurel flowers,
I'd like to grow it when it grows taller.

F:
Laurel flowers in clusters are blooming,
Will you dare come down to grow them?

462

男：	M:
种它成蔸哥勤来， 花开成朵哥勤到。	I'll come more often if they flourish, I'll come more often if they bloom.
女：	F:
种花开了想去见， 洁白如银不变色。	I want to see the blooming flowers, They keep to the end their silver color.

463

男：	M:
来插路口敬神仙， 来插路旁敬凤凰。	Flowers are inserted by roadside To worship Gods and phoenixes.
女：	F:
插在岔路敬行人， 插在路上敬情侣。	Flowers are inserted by roadside To worship pedestrians and lovers.

464

男：	M:
山伯沿途来观花， 英台追踪来欣赏。	Shanbo enjoys the flowers along the way, Yingtai is following him all the way.
女：	F:
山伯沿途来观花， 英台追踪来欣赏。	Shanbo enjoys the flowers along the way, Yingtai is following him all the way.

465

男：	M:
人说山伯与英台， 观花当餐不觉饿。	Shanbo and Yingtai the legendary lovers, They don't feel hungry when admiring flowers.
女：	F:
人说山伯与英台， 观花当餐也做得。	Shanbo and Yingtai the legendary lovers, They enjoy flowers as meals and dinner.

466

男：
边种咱边看，
请守金身等待哥。

M:
I'm growing flowers while watching,
Please keep your integrity for my returning.

女：
哥种妹讨看，
妹守金身等郎哥。

F:
You grow flowers I'd enjoy,
I'll keep my integrity for you.

467

男：
早晚妹去把水浇，
日后花种容易结。

M:
You water them evening and morning,
They'll sprout easily sooner or later.

女：
妹自护花长起来，
怕郎另奔不合拢。

F:
I'll grow them with care,
Fear that you choose someone else.

468

男：
要来敬天化成月，
花变英台配成双。

M:
Turn into moon if you wish to worship heaven,
Turn into Yingtai if you want to fall in love.

女：
要来敬天化成月，
我俩结对如英台。

F:
To worship heaven we can turn into the moon,
We should pay homage to Yingtai if we'd be in love.

469

男：
山伯英台哪能比，
他们有鞋来作证。

M:
Shall we compare with Shanbo and Yingtai?
They have shoes as love token.

女：
盼如山伯配英台，
我俩有众来作证。

F:
Wish to be Shanbo and Yingtai,
We have many people as witness.

470	男： 月桂成丛亮得好， 苦郎在远难得栽。	**M:** Laurel flowers in clusters look bright, It's too far and hard for me to grow.
	女： 月桂成丛在园中， 让哥来同住一家。	**F:** Laurel flowers in clusters are in the garden, You may come to live under the same roof.
471	男： 在近早理晚也理， 在远哪天也空盼。	**M:** I can nurse them everyday if near, Too faraway it'd be beyond my power.
	女： 妹自晚理早也理， 盼郎哪天也是空。	**F:** I'll nurse in the morning and evening, Looking forward to your coming.
472	男： 从前种花得交情， 今朝恋爱都空谈。	**M:** Friendship used to form while growing flowers, I fear that no friendship is real today.
	女： 从前种花有财发， 今天像观天上月。	**F:** People used to grow flowers for fortune, Now it's like desiring the moon in vain.
473	男： 阿哥种花白费工， 哪得发财像别人。	**M:** It's in vain for me to grow flowers, I can't make fortune as others.
	女： 别人种花共一园， 怕郎去多家不回。	**F:** Other people grow flowers in one garden, I'm afraid you grow in several gardens.

474

男：
九来种棵金雀花，
怕长路上别人摘。

M:
Let's grow brooms,
Others may pick them if we grow by the road.

女：
随哥种棵金雀花，
命好才得今日逢。

F:
I grow brooms with you,
Our fate leads us to meet today.

475

男：
它在花园欲培土，
它在大园欲栽种。

M:
I want to earth it up in the garden,
I want to plant it in the big yard.

女：
园中长棵金雀花，
眼见结种还未栽。

F:
There is a broom in the garden,
Its seeds are waiting to be planted.

476

男：
种它使其长得好，
来敬龛前众祖先。

M:
I want to plant it and cultivate it well,
Then put it before the niche to worship ancestors.

女：
分给阿妹种一枝，
日后讨看更容易。

F:
Give me one and I'll plant it,
So I may have claim to look at it.

477

男：
祖师下来找，
他也喜欢咱种花。

M:
The priest is looking for the flowers,
He likes us to grow flowers.

女：
祖师很想来观花，
他给我俩一起种。

F:
The priest longs for enjoying the flowers,
He asks us to grow flowers together.

478 男：
插在龛前映红光，
早晚容易讨富贵。

M:
The broom is flaming before the niche,
And people would find it easy to get rich.

女：
插在岔路有多亮，
山伯英台争来瞧。

F:
The broom is illuminating at the crossroad,
Shanbo and Yingtai strive to admire them.

479 男：
我俩培根又护梢，
生怕别人先发财。

M:
We nurse the tree and trim the branches,
Fear that others may overtake us to get rich.

女：
我俩培根又护梢，
有朝发财先谢哥。

F:
We nurse the tree and trim the branches,
I'd be grateful if I get rich someday.

480 男：
有朝同屋一起观，
有朝同家一起瞧。

M:
We'd admire flowers in the same house someday,
We'd enjoy flowers in the same home someday.

女：
有朝得共屋和家，
有朝共园一起种。

F:
We'd be in the same house someday,
We'd grow flowers in the same garden anyway.

481 男：
怕妹听人说巧话，
日后金雀变异花。

M:
You shouldn't listen to others' artful words,
Or the broom will become alien.

女：
妹不听人说巧话，
花未结种等待哥。

F:
I won't listen to their artful words,
Waiting for you until the flowers produce seeds.

482

男：	**M:**
有意把花来护理，	If the flowers are well nursed,
再说不见好也罢。	Whatever they'll be good enough.
女：	**F:**
护花难见花一面，	It's hard to see flowers bloom,
见金难得金到手。	And equally hard to have golds in hand.

483

男：	**M:**
再说不得种也见，	I'd grow them however hard it may be,
天不公平也为难。	I feel sorry that God is unfair.
女：	**F:**
得种盼得见，	I grow flowers with the hope for them to bloom,
古人分给咱成双。	Ancestors designated us to be a couple.

484

男：	**M:**
莫忘我俩种的花，	Don't forget the flowers we grow,
再说不共家也罢。	Even if we can't reach our goal.
女：	**F:**
盼哥一起来栽培，	I wish you to come and grow the flower,
栽花想必共一家。	It's hopeful that we'd be a couple.

485

男：	**M:**
栽花不服见到花，	I'm not convinced to let others benefit,
花不结种被人论。	Gossips appear if they sprout no seeds.
女：	**F:**
栽花绽朵让人见，	The blossoms are for people to admire,
载花非要结花种。	The flowers would certainly produce seeds.

486 男：
指望有情来护花，
我俩栽花长新叶。

M:
Hope you nurse the flowers with sincerity,
The flowers we plant sprout new leaves.

女：
妹早有情护理花，
怕郎嫌差也为难。

F:
I'm nursing the flowers with sincere passion,
Fear that I'm not equal to your expectation.

487 男：
十来种棵芙蓉花，
芙蓉花开千百朵，
天仙飞来赏。

M:
Let's grow hibiscus,
Thousands of flowers bloom in clusters,
Fairies from heaven fly to admire the flowers.

女：
一起种棵芙蓉花，
芙蓉花开上千朵，
照到皇宫大地方。

F:
We'd grow hibiscus together,
Thousands of flowers bloom in clusters,
Shining directly into the imperial palace.

488 男：
芙蓉绿朵配红朵，
青蓝朵朵嫩。

M:
The green hibiscus matches the red ones,
All are very tender in whatever color.

女：
绿朵喻英台，
红朵是山伯。

F:
The green one is like Zhu Yingtai,
The red one is like Liang Shanbo.

489 男：
日里蝴蝶满天飞，
它是山伯与英台。

M:
Butterflies are flying everywhere,
They're incarnation of Yingtai and Shanbo.

女：
日里化蝶去恋花，
它是山伯与英台。

F:
Butterflies are hovering among flowers,
They're Yingtai and Shanbo.

490

男：
化作蝴蝶双双飞，
昼夜一路把花赏。

M:
They become butterflies flying by pair,
Admiring the flowers day and night.

女：
蝴蝶结对比翼飞，
常在路上把花赏。

F:
They pair off to fly side by side,
Admiring the flowers all the way.

491

男：
人说山伯与英台，
死后还是结成双。

M:
The lovers Shanbo and Yingtai
Are still a pair after they die.

女：
人说山伯与英台，
死后同墓共灵牌。

F:
The lovers Shanbo and Yingtai
Share the tomb and tablet when they die.

492

男：
山伯观花当午饭，
英台拼命在一块。

M:
Shanbo and Yin Tai are enjoying flowers,
Disregarding adversaries whatever.

女：
山伯惜花胜过饭，
英台拼命在一块。

F:
Shanbo and Yingtai cherish the flowers,
Which outweighs the meal hour.

493

男：
说人话我俩，
是否有点小名气。

M:
As concerning ourselves,
I wonder if we're a little famous.

女：
说人话我俩，
照镜不见哥身影。

F:
As concerning ourselves,
I can't see you in the mirror.

494 男：
思来栽花也白种，
犹如弯月落山快。

M:
Growing flowers is in vain,
Just as the crescent moon that sets soon.

女：
我俩似花不同坡，
见面散快如弯月。

F:
We're two flowers in different hillsides,
As the crescent moon dispersing soon.

495 男：
不栽古已定下来，
想栽我俩情未深。

M:
We aren't meant to grow flowers,
We aren't close enough to be lovers.

女：
山伯为种花同死，
英台为栽花同墓。

F:
Shanbo and Yingtai died together,
Until death they grew flowers together.

496 男：
芙蓉美丽长成蔸，
生怕手摘它又变。

M:
Hibiscus grow beautifully in stalks,
To pick them may be an insult to the flowers.

女：
芙蓉花蕾将绽放，
怕郎不敢下去栽。

F:
Hibiscus are about to bloom,
You have to touch them with tenderness.

497 男：
我俩犹如树梢果，
好似天上挂明月。

M:
We're the fruits hanging on the tree,
Fair and bright as the moon in the sky.

女：
我俩犹如树梢果，
亮如十五月。

F:
We're the fruits hanging on the tree,
Shining as the full moon in the sky.

498 男：
要是妹想去婆家，
先栽好花再出走。

M:
If you want to go back home,
Do it after you grow flowers.

女：
妹婆就在阿哥家，
同园栽花住一块。

F:
Your home is my very home,
We'd grow flowers and live together.

499 男：
有空妹来耘花根，
使它亮如十五月。

M:
Earth them up when you're free,
Make them shine as full moon brilliantly.

女：
人说山伯常来游，
却不见影来观花。

F:
People say Shanbo comes here frequently,
I never see him enjoy flowers actually.

500 男：
亮如圆月看见影，
得种不得收也恋。

M:
They're as bright as full moon,
Without harvest we still love to grow them.

女：
靠哥同护见身影，
得种盼得收同住。

F:
I count on you to nurse them with me,
I wish to reap in harvest with you.

501 男：
别人攀梢嫁接果，
我俩白栽莫丢情。

M:
Others may graft the fruit trees,
We can't lose our friendship even go in vain.

女：
别人嫁接还结果，
开花无籽被人说。

F:
Others may graft fruit trees,
Flowers without seeds will cause comments.

502 男：
人说名花难逾期，
郎才拼命去种它。

M:
People say rare flowers can't stay long,
So I grow them with all my efforts.

女：
名花难逾期，
代代栽花永不老。

F:
Rare flowers can't stay long,
So we grow them year after year for ever-blooming.

503 男：
十一来种长春花，
一年四季亮光华。

M:
Let's grow periwinkles,
Shining bright all seasons.

女：
十一来种长春花，
见郎数载不觉闷。

F:
Let's grow periwinkles,
I won't be bored for several years.

504 男：
鲜花映入妹脸庞，
妹将当家不觉闷。

M:
Flowers are shinning on your face,
I won't be bored if you'd keep my house.

女：
鲜花映入咱脸庞，
有朝娶嫁得欢快。

F:
Flowers are shinning on our face,
Someday we'll be cheerful to get married.

505 男：
从前有棵长春花，
栽它非得享富有。

M:
There used to be a stalk of periwinkles,
Planting it makes people wealthy.

女：
从前有棵长春花，
等郎来年未曾栽。

F:
There used to be a stalk of periwinkles,
Waiting to be planted by you.

506

男：	M:
别人种花早发财，	Others gain love after planting,
我俩种来白白空。	While we only have emptiness.
女：	F:
古时栽花至终年，	People plant flowers all year round,
让咱一起活到老。	May we together live a long life.

507

男：	M:
别人先游进花根，	I'm afraid others may get ahead first,
靓花不到哥守候。	I'm not destined to protect the flowers.
女：	F:
妹得护花得培土，	I look after them and earth them up,
未有人下园里摘。	They haven't been picked by anyone else.

508

男：	M:
别人围上金樱刺，	The garden is enclosed by cherokee rose thorns,
郎在园外空空瞧。	I can only look at them from outside.
女：	F:
别人开园几道门，	Others' garden is with several entrances,
哪有荆棘拦花根。	No thistles or thorns used as fence.

509

男：	M:
种花也替别人栽，	Flowers are also planted for other people,
烧火还得炭。	Making fire needs coals.
女：	F:
种花完全为我俩，	Flowers are completely for us two,
花瓣落入哥怀中。	Petals will fall into your arms.

510 男：
我俩怎么办？
栽花成丛被人摘。

M:
What should we do?
Our flowers are picked by others.

女：
种花别说为什么，
路途多远走到头。

F:
Don't plant flowers with preset intention,
We'd keep walking till the end however far.

511 男：
阿哥自想在心头，
不得栽培心不安，
语言多甜河里丢。

M:
In mind I do always bear,
Worrying that I can't plant the flower,
Sweet words are cast into a river.

女：
莫要思三又想四，
有意哥种勤护花，
才是意重情又深。

F:
You shouldn't blame hot or cold,
Take care of them as you behold,
Your deep love would be good as gold.

512 男：
若念远方那棵花，
我俩继续种好它。

M:
If you'd miss the flower from afar,
We should keep planting it by heart.

女：
妹念远方那棵花，
命好我俩继续种。

F:
I'd miss the flower from afar,
Destiny leads us to keep on by heart.

513 男：
种花开成朵，
让它并缔连。

M:
Flowers are blooming in clusters,
The fairest are twin flowers in one stalk.

女：
种花让花开成朵，
让它并缔连。

F:
Let them bloom in clusters,
Let there be twin flowers.

514

男：	**M:**
似蝶结对比翼飞，	As butterflies flying wing to wing,
有朝合葬共一墓。	Someday we may share the same tomb.
女：	**F:**
似蝶结对比翼飞，	As butterflies flying wing to wing,
情人路上共坟墓。	Lovers share the same tomb on the road.

515

男：	**M:**
十二种棵凤梨花，	Let's grow pineapple flowers,
凤梨仅是此时亮。	The flowers just bloom at this moment.
女：	**F:**
种棵凤梨花，	Let's grow pineapple flowers,
一年提前它先亮。	Making them bloom a year in advance.

516

男：	**M:**
凤凰仅是此时飞，	Phoenix would fly only at this moment,
情人仅是此时会。	Lovers meet just at this moment.
女：	**F:**
凤欲结对比翼飞，	Phoenixes fly wing to wing,
情人仅此才相会。	Lovers meet just at this moment.

517

男：	**M:**
凤梨有甜也有酸，	Pineapple tastes sweet or sour,
不比古时蝴蝶兰。	Not as good as moth orchid of yore.
女：	**F:**
酸果嫁接成甜柑，	By grafting sour fruit become sweet one,
凤梨亮在晒台前。	Pineapple can be placed at the veranda.

518 男：
哪棵酸妹撩，
哪蔸甜妹育。

M:
Cut the one that is sour,
Cultivate the one that is sweet.

女：
哪棵酸妹撩，
靠哥嫁接酸变甜。

F:
Cut the one that is sour,
You can make the sour sweeter.

519 男：
别人嫁接还结果，
我俩育种不长芽。

M:
Others graft trees to bear fruits,
The seeds we sewed would not sprout.

女：
别人石板还种果，
它却提前先得吃。

F:
Others plant trees on the flagstone,
In advance bearing fruits on their own.

520 男：
我俩似棵凤梨花，
过时就难连。

M:
We're like the pineapple flowers,
It'd be hard to meet again once we part.

女：
我俩似棵凤梨花，
跨年就难连。

F:
We're like the pineapple flowers,
It'd be hard to meet again over the year.

521 男：
酸果变甜妹嫁接，
有朝长在妹晒台。

M:
You graft the sour fruit tree to become sweet,
Someday they'll grow by your veranda.

女：
酸果变甜同嫁接，
不怕人刮根。

F:
We graft the sour fruit tree to become sweet,
Not worry about the roots being scraped.

522

男：
凤梨让妹栽，
有朝口苦妹易尝。

M:
You grow the pineapple,
Someday it's easy for you to taste.

女：
我俩种果晒台前，
非使吃甜才罢可。

F:
We grow the fruits before the veranda,
Tasting the sweet ones is our desire.

523

男：
何日护花得富有，
何日种梨结硕果。

M:
When to become wealthy by caring flowers,
When to harvest fruits by planting pineapples.

女：
有心护花得富裕，
有意种梨结硕果。

F:
If you set your mind you'll be rich,
And with the will you'll get fruits.

524

男：
果熟咱共享，
结果留种放来年。

M:
We share the ripe fruits,
Leaving the seeds to grow next year.

女：
花开并蒂咱得见，
结果留种放明年。

F:
We can see the flowers in twins,
Leaving the seeds to plant next year.

525

男：
名花十二蔸，
每蔸已种完。

M:
Twelve kinds of rare flowers altogether,
Every kind of flower has been planted.

女：
名花十二蔸，
每蔸咱种完。

F:
Twelve kinds of rare flowers altogether,
Every kind of flower has been planted.

526 男：
每蔸都种齐，
娘妹心好去护理。

M:
Every kind of flower has been planted,
How nice of you to take care of them.

女：
每蔸都种齐，
将择吉日结成双。

F:
Every kind of flower has been planted,
Choosing a lucky day to make pairs.

527 男：
有意育花花结籽，
育它结果才罢休。

M:
It'll produce seeds if you're sincere,
Only fruits can meet your desire.

女：
有意同育花结籽，
让它结果才罢休。

F:
It'll produce seeds if we're both sincere,
Only fruits can meet our desire.

528 男：
名花自古种出来，
我俩吉日去栽培。

M:
Rare flowers need planting,
We plant them on a lucky day.

女：
名花自古种出来，
今找我俩去栽培。

F:
Rare flowers need planting,
We're lucky to plant them.

529 男：
吉日种名花少有，
才栽凤梨赏名花。

M:
They're rare to be planted on lucky day,
We also plant pineapple in this way.

女：
今栽名花品种多，
它也结对似英台。

F:
Now there are a variety of rare flowers,
They make pairs as legendary lovers.

530

男：	**M:**
别人想栽没花苗，	Without seeds others fail to plant rare ones,
特在村口种凤梨。	So they plant pineapple at the village entrance.
女：	**F:**
别人想栽没花苗，	Without seeds others fail to plant rare ones,
凤梨柠檬当不得。	Pineapple and lemon make no sense.

531

男：	**M:**
栽花是否还恋花，	I wonder if you long for the flowers,
种花是否还恋情。	Or the romance by growing them.
女：	**F:**
妹总惦念凤梨花，	I keep missing the pineapple flowers,
栽花依人享富有。	For they enable people to enjoy prosperity.

532

男：	**M:**
恋也白白恋，	My affection may all go in vain,
不如从前祝英台。	Not as the legendary love can maintain.
女：	**F:**
恋花就要护到底，	You should keep your affection anyway,
记好中途莫丢弃。	Remember not to give up halfway.

533

男：	**M:**
山伯他种花到死，	Shanbo planted flowers till he died,
英台她栽花共坟。	With Yingtai he'd stay dead or alive.
女：	**F:**
我俩栽花共一园，	We plant flowers in the same garden,
种花给成家共屋。	Till we share the same house together.

534 男：
论人话自身，
得种难为不得收。

M:
As is concerning ourselves,
What if I get no harvest by planting flowers?

女：
论人话自身，
栽花能共一家室。

F:
As is concerning ourselves,
We can be together by growing flowers.

535 男：
想来白误好花期，
好花属别个。

M:
If we miss the flower period,
The good ones would belong to others.

女：
莫许白误好花期，
种来不发也怪命。

F:
Don't miss the flower period,
It's fate if they aren't ours.

536 男：
我俩去平川种花，
命不投空回，
别人先把爱财发。

M:
We can plant flowers in plain,
It's fate if they aren't ours,
While others get ahead of me.

女：
我俩去远方种花，
咱命合才去，
择吉日才走。

F:
We can plant flowers in a distant place,
If our fates support each other,
We can choose a lucky day to go.

537 男：
栽花不见花结籽，
交情不见情结义。

M:
If the flowers produce no seeds,
Our affection would produce no love.

女：
栽花使花结成籽，
种花给结果才罢。

F:
Flowers are apt to produce seeds,
Why not maintain your affection to the end?

538

男：	**M:**
想来心头欲裂开，	I'm not optimistic as you,
本不比山伯英台，	We aren't Shanbo and Yingtai,
太阳难与月结对。	The sun and the moon will never be a couple.
女：	**F:**
我俩初逢还是客，	We're strangers when we first met,
面如山伯英台，	Gradually we learn from Shanbo and Yingtai,
离生不离死共坟。	They live apart but die together.

539

男：	**M:**
见妹说重情来往，	You value so much our affection,
咱还再次培花根。	We'll plant flowers together again.
女：	**F:**
种了还培土，	Earth up after planting the flowers,
花在园中才成长。	They'd grow up better and better.

七、培花给长
Ⅶ Cultivating Flowers

540 男：
莵莵成培土，
园园成培根。

M:
We earth up every flower,
And maintain each flower bed.

女：
莵莵成培土，
园园成培根。

F:
We earth up every flower,
And loosen the soil in the garden.

541 男：
一来培莵牡丹花，
晓妹是否还甜蜜。

M:
Let's cultivate peonies,
I wonder if you're still sweet.

女：
一来培莵牡丹花，
我俩甜比糖不变。

F:
Let's cultivate peonies,
We are as sweet as sugar.

542 男：
有意把花培好土，
死去变身还共坟。

M:
I'm sincere to cultivate peonies,
And desire our dust be mixed together.

女：
妹想把花培好土，
怕郎嫌遥远难办。

F:
I'm also sincere to cultivate peonies,
But fear you'd be hauled by the long distance.

543

男：
去婆家别久，
花长晒楼边欲坏。

M:
Don't stay long in your mother-in-law's home,
Exposed long to the sun the flowers will wither.

女：
妹来边栽边培土，
不怕我俩园花坏。

F:
I'd be cultivating the flowers,
They won't wither with my care.

544

男：
二来培蔸玫瑰花，
能盼上下得往来。

M:
Let's cultivate the roses,
It'd give us a chance to meet each other.

女：
二来培蔸玫瑰花，
使它快点开。

F:
Let's cultivate the roses,
Wishing them bloom as soon as possible.

545

男：
心想培蔸园中花，
怕娘提前去当家。

M:
I want to cultivate flowers in the garden,
But fear that you get marry first.

女：
重花培蔸花园中，
我俩同家才抵值。

F:
It's worth cultivating flowers,
If we can be in the same family.

546

男：
惹妹对花情意重，
我俩找锄来培土。

M:
You have deep feelings for the flowers,
So we find a hoe and earth them up together.

女：
重花培蔸园中花，
重花下花园培花。

F:
We'd cultivate flowers in the garden,
With all our focus attention.

547 男：
三来培莵海棠花，
海棠地阔长得亮，
有次得出名依人。

M:
Let's cultivate begonias,
The blossoms grow brilliant in extensive space,
It depends whether they'll gain a name.

女：
三来培莵海棠花，
海棠地阔也长名，
培花无缘情还在。

F:
Let's cultivate begonias,
The blossom should also gain a name,
Even without results our love will remain.

548 男：
请妹把花培好土，
日后郎想下园瞧。

M:
Please earth up the flowers well,
I'd come to enjoy them someday.

女：
妹早把花培好土，
请郎择日下来瞧。

F:
I've earthed up the flowers well,
You may come to see them on a lucky day.

549 男：
莫许让人摘头苗，
日后花园咱就败。

M:
Don't have others picked the first flower,
Or our garden will come to naught.

女：
别人不敢摘头苗，
还有我俩做它主。

F:
Others daren't pick the first flower,
For we're the master of our garden.

550 男：
四来培莵幸福花，
幸福长门口它嫩。

M:
Let's cultivate happy flowers,
Growing in the doorway they're tender.

女：
四来培莵幸福花，
盼它依人有名头。

F:
Let's cultivate happy flowers,
I hope they're known as our own.

551

男：	M:
笨人照问命出口，	The fool would rely on fate for fortune,
乖人名花造出来，	The wise would grow rare flowers,
我俩培花得共家。	We're to live together by growing flowers.
女：	F:
古时培花成情侣，	Cultivating flowers resulted in lovers,
想来女孩太低贱。	I wonder if girl's life is cheaper.

552

男：	M:
自古种名花结情，	Cultivating flowers resulted in lovers,
才有男女配成双。	Then we mortals can get into pairs.
女：	F:
自古种名花结情，	Cultivating flowers resulted in lovers,
培花有名得结对。	Growing rare flowers can leave people in pairs.

553

男：	M:
培花祈盼花结籽，	I expect the flowers to produce seeds,
有朝成人得欢喜。	I'd be glad to have my affection accepted.
女：	F:
培花祈盼得结籽，	I expect the flowers to produce seeds,
日后成人得结对。	Someday we'll become a couple indeed.

554

男：	M:
心想培花得成人，	I wish them to become full-grown,
怕未结种被人摘。	Afraid they're picked before producing seeds.
女：	F:
拼命培花得成人，	I work hard to make them grow up,
盼它结种才罢休。	Until they'd produce seeds.

555 男：
五来培蔸蝴蝶兰，
花在人家晒台长。

M:
Let's cultivate butterfly flowers,
Growing on the veranda of ours.

女：
五来培蔸蝴蝶兰，
花长晒台同护理。

F:
Let's cultivate butterfly flowers,
Take care of them on the veranda of ours.

556 男：
心想培蔸花成朵，
苦它长大被人管。

M:
I want to cultivate a stalk of flowers,
Fear they'd be taken over by others.

女：
培花给成朵，
让它大想瞧。

F:
I cultivate them till they bloom,
To admire them when they grow up.

557 男：
它长同寨想培土，
苦它长在别园头。

M:
I want them to grow in one garden,
But they're planted in another one.

女：
命好得守远乡花，
命好对接大花园。

F:
A good fate maintains the rare flowers faraway,
And being planted in a big garden anyway.

558 男：
六来培蔸红掌花，
懂得能否享富贵。

M:
Let's cultivate anthurium flowers,
I hope we can enjoy wealth and honor.

女：
六来培蔸红掌花，
靠哥是否得享福。

F:
Let's cultivate anthurium flowers,
I hope relying on you to enjoy wealth and honor.

559

男：
生怕落空来培花，
替人发情财不值。

M:
For fear that we'd finally have nothing,
The love I develop would only be for others.

女：
为了我俩结成双，
培花为我俩结对。

F:
You're cultivating flowers for us two,
Enabling us to finally become a couple.

560

男：
哥以为花期难逾，
才来死伴这蔸花。

M:
I think the flower period last short,
So I run all risk to accompany them.

女：
名花本难逾，
奇花本难老。

F:
Rare flowers can last long,
Rare flowers can keep young.

561

男：
先辈培花得交情，
有朝依人得好高。

M:
Ancestors attain love by growing flowers,
How deep they loved depending on their own.

女：
古代培花得嫁娶，
今莫许挂空名头。

F:
Cultivating flowers meant marriage in old time,
Don't have our affections exist only in name.

562

男：
心想培蔸花一茬，
怕遭他人遇冷眼。

M:
I want to cultivate a stalk of flowers,
Afraid that I'll get cold response.

女：
有意多点把花培，
有心人生培到底。

F:
Care them more if you're sincere,
Keeping on cultivating them forever.

563	男： 七来培莞水仙花， 水仙千年培不闷。	M: Let's cultivate daffodil, It won't be boring forever.
	女： 七来培莞水仙花， 此花千年培不闷。	F: Let's cultivate daffodils, It won't be boring forever.
564	男： 它在花园长提亮， 佛仙在千远来瞧。	M: Flowers are good to grow up in the garden, The fairy comes to see them from heaven.
	女： 名花本亮好， 仍有远客来观看。	F: Rare flowers are born to be good, There are still people coming from afar.
565	男： 它长成簇花欲开， 苦郎在远难相会。	M: Flowers are blooming in clusters, But it's hard to meet you cause' I'm faraway.
	女： 花等哥来才绽开， 有心不怕远忍来。	F: Flowers only bloom for your coming, If you like them distance would be nothing.
566	男： 相会也是一片刻， 却不得依人富有。	M: Our meeting is but temporally, We can't long keep company.
	女： 相会盼发财， 得交如昔似英台。	F: We expect to be long once in love, To be close as lovers in legendary story.

567

男：
莫忘我俩种的花，
重心只是在心头。

M:
Don't forget the flowers we plant,
Keep them in your mind when we apart.

女：
重哥在心间，
培花心念哥。

F:
I'd keep you in mind your affection,
Missing you while cultivating flowers.

568

男：
培花想到咱，
培花念咱当初情。

M:
I cherish you while cultivating flowers,
Sweet is our friendship from the beginning.

女：
培花如山伯英台，
培花使男女结对。

F:
We cultivate flowers as Shanbo and Yingtai,
Flowers make them wife and husband.

569

男：
请妹去卦卜给通，
让郎常往去培花。

M:
Please go for a divination,
Allowing me to cultivate flowers.

女：
妹身去卦卜早通，
让郎常往去培花。

F:
I'll go for a divination,
To let you cultivate flowers.

570

男：
八来培莵月桂花，
怕妹主意打不通，
日后难得常往来。

M:
Let's cultivate laurel flowers,
Afraid you haven't set your mind,
Making it hard for our appointment.

女：
八来培莵月桂花，
妹身主意早打通，
盼郎常来又交往。

F:
Let's cultivate laurel flowers,
I've already set my mind,
Expecting you to come for appointment.

571

男：
携哥培根待花开，
怕娘提前去安家。

M:
We earth up flowers and wait for blooming,
Fear that you get married without my knowing.

女：
携妹培花得种子，
有朝像人得成家。

F:
We cultivate flowers till they produce seeds,
Someday we'll get married as a natural course.

572

男：
莫许荒废丢花园，
眼见爱情落了空。

M:
Don't abandon the flower garden,
Or our love will meet failure.

女：
别人培花先有情，
切莫丢闲白荒废。

F:
Love comes from cultivating flowers,
Don't set it aside whatsoever.

573

男：
有意不断把花培，
才是我俩重恩情。

M:
Keep in mind our mutual flowers,
It shows we value our affections.

女：
妹独几天来培花，
却不见郎丢来看。

F:
I've planted flowers alone for some days,
You haven't come and see them anyway.

574

男：
培花如山伯英台，
死后安排得结对。

M:
Cultivating flowers like Shanbo and Yingtai,
Who were destined to be a couple after death.

女：
培花如英台，
谁当情乖配山伯。

F:
We grow flowers like Shanbo and Yingtai,
But they couldn't get married alive.

575

男：
九来培莵金雀花，
培花不连怪命哭。

M:
Let's cultivate brooms,
It's our fate to achieve no affections.

女：
九来培莵金雀花，
培花不见情灰心。

F:
Let's cultivate brooms,
Depressed I feel to achieve no affections.

576

男：
培花不见花也难，
犹如山拦把海隔。

M:
I'm depressed to find no blossoms,
Just as the mountain obstructing the sea.

女：
培花盼见花结种，
有朝连情得结对。

F:
I expect the flowers to produce seeds,
Hopefully we can become lovers someday.

577

男：
越培越灰心，
或说霉命才如此，
哪天象人和成功。

M:
My depression deepens with cultivation,
Maybe it's my unfortunate destiny,
I wonder when we can become a pair.

女：
成啥也成定，
拼命培育园中花，
再说不共家也罢。

F:
Whatever the result may be,
We just try our best,
Even if we can't be together at last.

578

男：
别人培花有名分，
我俩连情却扑空。

M:
Others get settled by flower cultivation,
But we get nothing from our affection.

女：
别人培花出名分，
我俩来连情到老。

F:
Others get settled by flower cultivation,
Forever I hope we can keep our affection.

579 男：
十来培莬芙蓉花，
芙蓉开心长成丛，
怕娘变卦心不好。

M:
Let's cultivate hibiscus,
Happy to see a crowd of flowers,
Fear that you'll change your mind.

女：
十来培莬芙蓉花，
芙蓉长成丛好看，
怕郎多心也为难。

F:
Let's cultivate hibiscus,
A crowd of flowers are so beautiful,
Fear that you're in two minds.

580 男：
园中芙蓉长嫩叶，
怕妹丢哥去当家。

M:
The hibiscus produce tender leaves,
I fear that you leave me to marry others.

女：
芙蓉长叶嫩又青，
人未流传咱成对。

F:
The leaves are tender and green,
I won't marry others but you.

581 男：
古时培花就得娶，
当今只是做名头。

M:
Marriage came after flower cultivation,
Now it's alright to have just a title.

女：
古时培花在园中，
今朝得共家才罢。

F:
People of the past planted flowers in the garden,
We at present aim at being wife and husband.

582 男：
心想培花至末端，
弃身予妹来关顾。

M:
I want to cultivate flowers till the end,
And commit myself to you to take care.

女：
有意培花至末端，
我俩似笋一起长。

F:
I want to cultivate flowers till the end,
We'd grow up together like bamboo shoots.

583 男：
名花长成丛难分，
有朝同墓共座坟。

M:
Rare flowers in a cluster are hard to separate,
We long to be buried in the same grave.

女：
分花如分园，
分花如分家难过。

F:
Separating flowers is like separating the gardens,
It's as sad as dividing a family into two.

584 男：
妹是培花有名分，
给哥得个空名头。

M:
By growing flowers a name you do obtain,
I get a name without real gain.

女：
妹嘴本说真，
培花给结种才罢。

F:
I've been telling the truth from the outset,
I won't stop until they produce seeds.

585 男：
芙蓉开花想结对，
懂得是否到咱手。

M:
The hibiscus would like to bloom in pair,
I'm not sure if they'd come to our hands.

女：
芙蓉开花得结对，
它还等哥来才得。

F:
The hibiscus will bloom in pair,
They're waiting for you to admire.

586 男：
十一培莵长春花，
晓娘是否重一时。

M:
Let's cultivate periwinkles,
I wonder you just have short attention.

女：
十一培莵长春花，
等郎得整年不来。

F:
Let's cultivate periwinkles,
You haven't come for a whole year.

587

男：
爱花似爱情，
出名也靠妹。

M:
Loving flowers is like loving you,
I depend on you for a good reputation.

女：
爱花如爱情，
拼命得共家才罢。

F:
Loving flowers is like loving you,
Let's strive to become a couple.

588

男：
有意培莞长春花，
见郎得一年也是。

M:
I'm sincere to cultivate periwinkles,
Even we can meet once in a year.

女：
妹很爱培长春花，
靠郎能否得有情。

F:
I love to cultivate periwinkles,
I wonder if you're reliable.

589

男：
名花园中开成对，
一年四季瞧不闷。

M:
The rare flowers bloom in pair,
They feast our eyes in four seasons.

女：
花开成对正合意，
怕郎嫌差更难办。

F:
The rare flowers bloom in pair,
I'm afraid you dislike them either.

590

男：
别人千里还来看，
怕娘变卦有多心。

M:
People come to see the flowers from afar,
Fear that you'll change your heart.

女：
别人先培开了花，
仅剩我俩情未深。

F:
Other people's flowers bloom first,
Only we two have no deep affection.

591

男：
十二培莵凤梨花，
有朝得连情依人。

M:
Let's cultivate pineapple flowers,
Someday they'd make people become pairs.

女：
十二培莵凤梨花，
靠郎是否有情意？

F:
Let's cultivate pineapple flowers,
Can you show your feeling to us?

592

男：
梨花处处有，
一年才是此时亮。

M:
Pineapple flowers are everywhere,
They're brilliant this moment every year.

女：
凤梨不难把花开，
哪如古时蝴蝶兰。

F:
It isn't hard for them to bloom,
They can't compare with butterfly flowers.

593

男：
丛中酸枝被人撩，
晒台甜枝被人管。

M:
The sour twigs are picked in the garden,
The sweet ones are basked in the veranda.

女：
酸枝嫁接变甜枝，
晒台甜枝让哥理。

F:
The sour are grafted with the sweet,
Basked in the veranda and cared by you.

594

男：
我俩似梨花，
过时难得盼。

M:
We're like pineapple flowers,
It's hard to meet if overdue.

女：
梨花别人多珍惜，
苦它却是提前开。

F:
Others still cherish the pineapple flowers,
But they bloom before the flower period.

595 男：
哪天培花有恋情，
哪天培凤梨开花。

M:
Romance comes after cultivating,
Pineapple flowers bloom after nurturing.

女：
别人石上种果树，
它仍早熟先得吃。

F:
Other people plant trees on the flagstone,
In advance bearing fruits on its own.

596 男：
培遍十二蔸名花，
我俩想去远方看。

M:
We've cultivated twelve kinds of flowers,
We're about to appreciate them afar.

女：
培遍十二蔸名花，
随郎去远乡欣赏。

F:
We've cultivated twelve kinds of flowers,
I'd follow you if you depart.

八、赏名花
Ⅷ Enjoying Rare Flowers

597

男：	M:
一来赏莵牡丹花，	Let's enjoy the peonies,
花它香嫩开得久。	The tender blossoms would last long.
女：	F:
随哥赏莵牡丹花，	I'd enjoy the peonies with you,
我俩爱如当初情。	We love them as we did before.

598

男：	M:
哪天得闲妹去赏，	You go to appreciate them when free,
切莫依人做多心。	Don't be oversensitive as others.
女：	F:
得闲去赏我俩花，	Let's enjoy the flowers together,
莫赏别人花一朵。	Never desire the flowers of others.

599

男：	M:
赏花莫忘我俩情，	We can't forget the flowers of ours,
仍念从前我俩恩。	And our affections from the outset.
女：	F:
不忘我俩那莵花，	I'd never forget the flowers we plant,
不忘我俩当初情。	And the love we have from the outset.

600 男：
从前有蔸牡丹花，
交情甜蜜爱到老。

M:
There was once a stalk of peonies,
Which loved each other forever.

女：
从前造蔸牡丹花，
几番交情次丢弃。

F:
There was once a tree of peonies,
Which abandoned their love more than once.

601 男：
赏花第一蔸，
妹爱就交情，
晓妹称心不称心。

M:
Let's enjoy the first flowers,
If you love them please say yes,
I wonder what your answer may be.

女：
赏花第一蔸，
爱哥重如山，
怕郎嫌羞就难办。

F:
Let's enjoy the first flowers,
My love for you is irremovable as a mountain,
Afraid that you aren't brave enough.

602 男：
若妹爱花是真情，
我俩未来想流名。

M:
If you truly love the flowers,
We'd strive to leave our names forever.

女：
妹早爱花表真情，
未来非得留美名。

F:
I've shown my true love for flowers,
We must leave our names forever.

603 男：
赏花第二蔸，
请妹主意打给通，
我俩常往想交情。

M:
Let's enjoy the second flowers,
Hope you go steady with me,
We'd like to go dating at our will.

女：
赏花第二蔸，
四处天明亮，
哪天得交情。

F:
Let's enjoy the second flowers,
The day is bright everywhere,
Hope to go dating steadily.

604

男：
心想把花赏到尾，
竹未长笋被人撩。

M:
I want to enjoy the flowers till the end,
But afraid they'd be picked before they bloom.

女：
赏不到牢世人笑，
赏不到头世人议。

F:
People laugh at us if we give up halfway,
They'd talk ill of us if we break up halfway.

605

男：
赏花第三蔸，
弃身给妹来关顾。

M:
Let's enjoy the third flowers,
I'd commit myself to you to take care.

女：
赏花第三蔸，
郎哥早有人关顾。

F:
Let's enjoy the third flowers,
You've had someone else to take care.

606

男：
心想到根去观赏，
怕坏名头一场空。

M:
I'd like to enjoy the whole flower,
Afraid I should damage its fame.

女：
有意摘枝来观赏，
不怕白费一场空。

F:
Pick one if you're sincere,
Don't make your efforts in vain.

607

男：
赏花第四蔸，
妹情不深也难做，
话有多甜也是假。

M:
Let's enjoy the fourth flowers,
You don't seem to be deeply affected,
Your sweet words don't seem reliable.

女：
赏花第四蔸，
怕哥还有多处赏，
似有一阵旋风刮。

F:
Let's enjoy the fourth flowers,
I suppose you have several places to go,
Like a whirlwind you come and go.

608 男：
只妹爱花就来交，
交到白头才罢休。

M:
We can date if you love flowers,
Till the end of the world forever.

女：
爱哥来回把花赏，
若不成妻也恩爱。

F:
I love both you and the flowers,
Even we can't be a couple ever.

609 男：
赏花第五蔸，
天下唯我俩，
交情密切胜他人。

M:
Let's enjoy the fifth flowers,
There are only two of us,
Our affection is beyond others'.

女：
赏花第五蔸，
妹已等几年，
靠郎是否得缘分。

F:
Let's enjoy the first flowers,
I've been waiting for years,
To see if you can give me a marriage.

610 男：
谁人把花赏到尾，
日后变身结良缘。

M:
Who will enjoy the flowers till the end,
Someday they'll form ties as they want.

女：
结缘比山伯英台，
有朝易发爱情财。

F:
Just as Shanbo and Yingtai of old day,
It's easy to develop relationship someday.

611 男：
生怕护花守不住，
日后很难应出口。

M:
I fear I can't protect the flowers,
Making it hard to make promise.

女：
妹也守花那么久，
怕郎听人话甜言。

F:
I've protected the flowers for so long,
Fear you listen to others' sweet words.

612

男： 赏花第六蔸， 劳碌赏花也是空， 令不依人发情财。	M: Let's enjoy the sixth flowers, Our efforts would come to nothing, We can't develop affection as others.
女： 赏花第六蔸， 劳碌给出名， 不达情也恋。	F: Let's enjoy the sixth flowers, Our efforts would win a name, Even if our love can't achieve the aim.

613

男： 带哥赏花花结种， 做事莫听人。	M: The flowers will produce seeds, Don't listen to others' gossips.
女： 带妹培花花出种， 莫听旁人来教唆。	F: The flowers will produce seeds, Don't listen to others' gossips.

614

男： 古时故此种名花， 别人连情交成妻。	M: Once people dated by planting flowers, Finally becoming a couple via affection.
女： 古时培花共一园， 赏花得住同一家。	F: Once people cultivated flowers in the same garden, Finally living in the same roof in addition.

615

男： 赏花第七蔸， 似鸭失散难回窝， 似针失线难得在。	M: Let's enjoy the seventh flowers, Just as the lost duck can't go back, A needle without thread can do nothing.
女： 赏花第七蔸， 妹似鸡鸭无笼住， 叫花当皇想不能。	F: Let's enjoy the seventh flowers, I'm like a chick or duck without hencoop, I'm too humble to achieve anything great.

616 男：
讲话离心也难办，
情有多甜也是丢。

M:
If we fail to communicate with each other,
Throw away the love however sweet.

女：
名花不乱赏，
话给对心才要得。

F:
Don't enjoy the flowers recklessly,
We should impart our true feelings.

617 男：
宁可以前不得栽，
栽不得赏白白丢。

M:
I'd rather not plant the flowers at the outset,
If I can't enjoy them after all.

女：
成啥已成定，
也是命成才如此，
赏花非让花结种。

F:
The outcome is definitely settled,
This is also our fate,
Hold on until seeds are produced.

618 男：
赏花第八蔸，
阳光照在田地上，
好花是否到手头？

M:
Let's enjoy the eighth flowers,
The sun shines upon the farmlands,
Shall we have claim on good flowers?

女：
赏花第八蔸，
赏花好似白赏哥，
赏郎似赏天上月。

F:
Let's enjoy the eighth flowers,
Enjoying flowers is like appreciating you,
You're the moon shining on us.

619 男：
别人到根早去赏，
生怕遭人吐苦言。

M:
Others go at the first time to admire flowers,
I'll be complained if I'm still there.

女：
别人未到根一次，
怕郎无心也难办。

F:
Others have never seen the real flower,
I fear the flower can't come into your favor.

620

男：
在近想进一次根，
在远难得算。

M:
I want to see them if they're near,
Wouldn't bother to go if they locate too far.

女：
有意不怕远，
好花仍等哥。

F:
It isn't far if you have intention,
Good flowers are still waiting for you.

621

男：
赏花第九蔸，
哪天请酒妹讲郎，
切莫先把橙子挂。

M:
Let's enjoy the nineth flowers,
Please tell me if you hold a wedding feast,
Don't hang up the orange leaves first.

女：
赏花第九蔸，
哥得十九就当家，
妹仍流浪找住处。

F:
Let's enjoy the nineth flowers,
You get married when still young,
I still roam about to find my Mr. Right.

622

男：
别人舂扁米①香甜，
郎在晒台空着看。

M:
Others grind the sweet bianmi①,
I can only watch beside the veranda.

女：
别人种糯成扁米，
给妹来帮摘，
讨看谷穗也是行。

F:
Others make bianmi from sticky rice,
And ask me to help pick them,
It's fine to just look on the earhead.

---

①扁米，姑娘后生们摘下即将成熟的糯谷，经蒸煮晒晾后舂出来的新米叫扁米，甜香可口，象征初恋。

① In September, Zhuang people in Napo and Jingxi usually pick some glutinous rice which is ready to be ripe to make "bianmi". Bianmi is very hard to make because it can only be done after certain procedures, namely steaming, cooking, drying and pounding. Bianmi is so delicious that people would never forget about it if they have a chance to have it. Good taste and unforgettable, local people use it to symbolize first love.

623

男:	**M:**
别人整天摘糯谷,	You harvest the rice all day,
明年留点谷种给。	Leaving some seeds for the next year.
女:	**F:**
妹种沙田倒分孽,	I have a good harvest in dry land,
哥种水田却欠收,	But you fail to harvest in paddy field,
要妹留种快些说。	Tell me if you want some seeds from me.

624

男:	**M:**
有意给吊把做种,	Give me some seeds if you want,
银子花多少就说。	And tell me how much they cost.
女:	**F:**
旱田不乱留谷种,	Dry land is not a place to leave seeds,
若种不成莫要怪。	Don't blame me if you get no harvest.

625

男:	**M:**
哥也空听口头讲,	I just say it by the way,
谷种切莫往外卖。	Don't sell the seeds to other people.
女:	**F:**
如果哥想要,	If you want to have some seeds,
日后收再说。	We'll talk later when they're ripen.

626

男:	**M:**
赏花第十蔸,	Let's enjoy the tenth flowers,
十盼又九盼,	I'm looking forward anxiously,
等娘哪街也是空。	Waiting for you to appear.
女:	**F:**
赏花第十蔸,	Let's enjoy the tenth flowers,
十盼又九盼,	I'm looking forward anxiously,
不见有信写字条。	Not receiving your note and reply actually.

627 男：
凤凰会结对赏花，
我俩分路各自在。

M:
Phoenixes will enjoy flowers in pair,
But we're apart from each other.

女：
给妹独在像乌鸦，
独来像老鹰。

F:
I'm like a crow to roam alone,
As an eagle I'd come and go.

628 男：
孤像潭上树一棵，
无依又无靠。

M:
You're like a tree by a pool,
Having nothing to depend on.

女：
给妹不知去靠谁，
早看晚不见。

F:
Who I can depend on?
Sooner or later they'd be gone.

629 男：
赏花十一莵，
渐渐结对又扑空，
渐渐连情又破灭。

M:
Let's enjoy the eleventh flowers,
Pairs fail to get what they want,
Affections gradually fade away.

女：
赏花十一莵，
正月到七月扑空，
不见有情来看望。

F:
Let's enjoy the eleventh flowers,
I fail to meet you from January to July,
You call on me at no time.

630 男：
哥把赏花当家住，
一年四季在外头。

M:
I regard enjoying flowers as living at home,
I'm outside all the year round.

女：
哥说赏花当家住，
整月不见郎来瞧。

F:
You said it's like your home,
But you didn't come to see me for months.

631	男： 花根当屋哥常往， 花丛当家哥常往。	**M:** I regard the flower stalk as the house, I regard the clusters as my home.
	女： 妹在花根看不见， 月三十天不相逢。	**F:** I'm always here but can't see you, I never meet you for an entire month.
632	男： 在哪赏花人变仙， 蛤蟆难得变麒麟。	**M:** I won't become a fairy anywhere, It's rare for a frog to turn into kylin.
	女： 别人土花还去赏， 郎嫌名花在远方。	**F:** Others enjoy even the ordinary flowers, How could you dislike the rare flowers faraway?
633	男： 赏花十二蔸， 到处有凤来游玩， 给咱侬人有名头。	**M:** Let's enjoy the twelfth flowers, Phoenixes are playing everywhere, Bringing us fame and social status.
	女： 赏花十二蔸， 让哥到根来观花， 我俩欢喜得交情。	**F:** Let's enjoy the twelfth flowers, I let you come in and enjoy closely, We're happy to establish affections.
634	男： 古时赏花有情缘， 今赏梨花被人讲。	**M:** Enjoying flowers aroused feelings ever, We're talked about for enjoying pineapple flowers.
	女： 爱花观赏园中花， 再不成家也恩爱。	**F:** Love and enjoy the flowers in the garden, Despite we can't be together even.

635 男：
十二名花已赏毕，
晓妹是否见中意。

M:
We've enjoyed twelve kinds of rare flowers,
Whether you like them or not I wonder.

女：
十二名花已赏毕，
见好要不得。

F:
We've enjoyed twelve kinds of rare flowers,
We can't get them though they are good.

636 男：
赏了咱同去，
咱去修花到远方。

M:
After enjoying the flowers We'd go away,
For trimming flowers somewhere faraway.

女：
名花赏完毕，
随郎修花去远方。

F:
I'll go with you after enjoying the flowers,
For trimming flowers somewhere faraway.

九、修花枝成簇

Ⅸ Trimming Flowers

637 男：
修花第一蔸，
出来六七位皇上，
他准许我俩去修。

M:
Let's trim the first flowers,
The emperor shows up,
He allows us to do the job.

女：
修花第一蔸，
天上有玉皇下来，
他准我俩去修花。

F:
Let's trim the first flowers,
The Jade Emperor shows up,
He allows us to do the job.

638 男：
一枝朝府金闪闪，
一枝朝京亮堂堂。

M:
One branch faces to the government office,
One to the capital court for promotion.

女：
一枝修朝吃饭桌，
一枝修朝饮酒台。

F:
One faces to the table praying for foods,
One to the bar counter for drinks.

639 男：
一枝修朝窗望月，
朝着晒楼盼情侣。

M:
One faces to the window to watch the moon,
One to the veranda to expect loving couples.

女：
一枝朝着岔路口，
一枝朝着大路上。

F:
One faces to the byroad for journey in peace,
One to the main road for safe travel.

640

男：	M:
修枝给妹去夫家，	Cut a bunch for you to take to your husband,
修枝给娘去家婆。	And one for you to present to your mother-in-law.
女：	F:
修枝朝进我俩面，	Trim the flowers towards us two,
给咱侬人成夫妻。	Making us a couple as we wish.

641

男：	M:
修花第二蔸，	Let's trim the second flowers,
修朝去远方，	Facing towards a far distance,
我俩何为好。	Whether it's good for us two.
女：	F:
修花第二蔸，	Let's trim the second flowers,
主意妹打好，	I've set up my mind,
修枝朝着好情人。	To trim them facing true lovers.

642

男：	M:
修枝朝村去看人，	A branch facing village to greet the dwellers,
修枝朝路去看客。	Another to the main road to welcome the guests.
女：	F:
修枝朝河看游鱼，	One faces the river to look at the fish,
日后妹当家容易。	It'll facilitate me to be a housewife.

643

男：	M:
修枝朝河看游鱼，	One faces the river to look at the fish,
修枝朝田看谷穗。	One faces the farm to oversee the corns.
女：	F:
修朝牧牛大草坪，	One faces the pasture to herd the cattle,
修朝练马大沙滩。	Another to the beach to exercise the horse.

644 男：
修朝地里去看花，
修朝田坝看金谷。

M:
One faces the fields to view the flowers,
Another faces the land to watch the grains.

女：
修朝阿哥大村头，
修朝阿哥大寨上。

F:
One faces your village,
Praying for marriage.

645 男：
修枝朝井共饮用，
修枝朝池共洗涤。

M:
One faces the well praying for water,
Another towards the pool for washing together.

女：
修朝管村土地庙，
修朝管寨土地宫。

F:
One faces the Earth Temple to govern the village,
Another towards Earth Palace to manage the stockade.

646 男：
吃水不忘井，
顾哥给成人，
日后正想常往来。

M:
Don't forget the well-diggers,
I'm for you to take care,
We can develop our affections gradually.

女：
吃水不忘井，
盼哥顾成人，
情缘给到老。

F:
Don't forget the well-diggers,
I wish I can be taken care,
So we can love each other forever.

647 男：
修花第三蔸，
苦郎半身还光棍。

M:
Let's trim the third flowers,
Half of my life past but I'm still a bachelor.

女：
修花第三蔸，
靠郎能否得情缘？

F:
Let's trim the third flowers,
Can I depend on you to be my lover?

648 男：
单身修花盼成双，
难办天公分不平。

M:
Trimming flowers I hope to get true love,
I'm afraid God is unequal.

女：
单身才修花多路，
不怕遭人瞟冷眼。

F:
Create more chances as I'm single,
I'm not afraid of being baffled.

649 男：
不修却是古始造，
修来咱情却未浓。

M:
We're destined not to trim flowers,
Our love isn't deep enough however.

女：
古时造修花安家，
今朝给我俩会合。

F:
People used to get married after trimming flowers,
Now we have chance to meet each other.

650 男：
情深如山伯英台，
修花如古男配女。

M:
Love is as deep as Shanbo and Yingtai,
We trim the flowers as people did in the past.

女：
情深如山伯英台，
修花得相爱才罢。

F:
Love is as deep as Shanbo and Yingtai,
We trim the flowers until we fall in love.

651 男：
山伯为修花致命，
英台为修花共坟。

M:
Shanbo died for trimming flowers,
Yingtai was buried together.

女：
人流传山伯英台，
死后仍安排结对。

F:
There's a tale of Shanbo and Yingtai
Who are still a pair after they die.

652

男： 修花第四蔸， 让妹主意打给通， 有朝依人常来往。	**M:** Let's trim the fourth flowers, You'd better set up your mind, Someday we'll date as lovers.
女： 修花第四蔸， 主意在哥是当头， 切莫贪心与人家。	**F:** Let's trim the fourth flowers, Your decision is the most important, Don't change your mind to love other people.

653

男： 带哥修花修到尾， 带郎交情到白头。	**M:** You trim the flowers to the top, Please stick to the love we develop.
女： 带妹修花早绽放， 带娘上下早往来。	**F:** If you took me to trim together, We could keep in touch earlier.

654

男： 修花莫忘我俩花， 切莫忘咱以往情。	**M:** Don't forget us when we trim flowers, Don't forget our affections in the past.
女： 妹不忘记咱俩花， 娘不忘记咱俩情。	**F:** I'll neither forget our flowers, Nor our affections in the past.

655

男： 修花第五蔸， 修枝朝下河看鱼， 修枝朝下田看谷。	**M:** Let's trim the fifth flowers, Make it face the river to see the fish, Another face the farm to oversee corns.
女： 修花第五蔸， 人家修花枝看鱼， 人家下田早看谷。	**F:** Let's trim the fifth flowers, Others trim them to see the fish, Others have already overseen the corns.

656

男：	M:
修朝树下去纳凉，	Trim them facing the trees to get some shade,
晓妹是否有恒心。	I wonder if you can insist on your true feelings.
女：	F:
修枝朝府看皇上，	Trim one facing the mansion to respect the Emperor,
修枝朝衙看官吏。	To government office to look up to the officials.

657

男：	M:
修枝朝进妹村来，	Flowers are trimmed towards your village,
日后下田妹常看。	You can see them often working in the fields.
女：	F:
修枝朝着哥路口，	Flowers are trimmed towards your crossroad,
修枝朝哥晒台前。	Flowers are trimmed towards your veranda.

658

男：	M:
在闷到路口看花，	View the flowers at crossroad when bored,
莫忘修花咱情缘。	Don't forget our love of trimming flowers.
女：	F:
在闷照影看水盆，	View the shadow in basin when bored,
眼见用手抓不到。	I can just see it but can't catch it.

659

男：	M:
修花第六蔸，	Let's trim the sixth flowers,
辛苦劳碌都无名，	I work so hard but earn nothing,
想来苦情独自在。	Full of bitterness and loneliness.
女：	F:
修花第六蔸，	Let's trim the sixth flowers,
妹心乱如油，	I'm confused and disconcerted,
哪天风流像人家。	Don't be dissolute as others.

660 男：	**M:**
修花渐渐去得远，	Trimming flowers make us drift apart,
得修难得来重合。	It's difficult for us to reunite.
女：	**F:**
人家修花共一岸，	Others trim the flowers on one side,
我俩修花共一家，	We trim flowers in the same family,
任哥修哪园都得。	Which garden you choose is up to you.
661 男：	**M:**
天下造写信排忧，	Letters are written to release anxiety,
修花到手才罢休。	We must achieve something from trimming flowers.
女：	**F:**
修花得看花解心，	Trimming flowers unlocks the heart,
见郎如吹风纳凉。	Meeting you is like enjoying the cool wind.
662 男：	**M:**
修花第七蔸，	Let's trim the seventh flowers,
初一妹进庙上香，	I pray in the temple on the first day①,
日后变仙易会合。	It's easy to meet if we become fairies.
女：	**F:**
修花第七蔸，	Let's trim the seventh flowers,
初一人宰鸡祭拜，	Kill the roster to perform the worship,
我俩空讲白费嘴。	Don't just have an empty talk.

① "The first day" here refers to the first day of lunar month in China. The followings are the same.

663 男：
修枝朝岔路往来，
一枝朝咱情会合。

M:
Trim the flowers towards the byroad,
Enabling us to meet each other.

女：
我俩似花共一园，
如共家同住。

F:
We're like the flowers in one garden,
Living together like members of the same family.

664 男：
名花长别处开花，
怕娘安家去别处。

M:
Rare flowers bloom in other places,
I'm afraid you settle down there first.

女：
名花等哥来才开，
等郎远方人来修。

F:
Rare flowers bloom until you come,
Waiting to be trimmed by you from afar.

665 男：
修花第八蔸，
花长膝高被人摘，
美花在远方难修。

M:
Let's trim the eighth flowers,
Flowers are picked when they're knee's height,
It's hard to trim the fair flowers so faraway.

女：
修花第八蔸，
日照根花开，
盼郎在远方来修。

F:
Let's trim the eighth flowers,
Flowers blossom when the sun shines,
I look forward to your coming from afar.

666 男：
美花早被人看重，
再有多少银也假。

M:
Fair flowers have been valued high,
With however much money I can't buy.

女：
花还幼时咱得培，
大来盼哥来修枝。

F:
We should cultivate them when they're young,
Waiting to be trimmed when they grow up.

667 男：
当初花还小咱培，
今长大园别人修。

M:
We cultivated the flowers when they were young,
Today they grow up to be trimmed by others.

女：
我俩似花共一园，
就苦未得同家住。

F:
We're like the flowers in one garden,
But still not yet member of a family.

668 男：
修花第九蔸，
花长平膝别人要，
不到咱手得修枝。

M:
Let's trim the ninth flowers,
Others would take them over by knee's height,
We won't have chance to acquire them.

女：
修花第九蔸，
以前得来哥共培，
等郎下园来修枝。

F:
Let's trim the ninth flowers,
You cultivated them with me before,
Still I'm waiting for you to work with me.

669 男：
得修不得要，
名头来落空。

M:
I trim them but can't get them,
I'd have claim to nothing.

女：
盼哥来园里修花，
修花得共家才罢。

F:
I expect you to trim the flowers,
Until we become family members.

670 男：
老人怕名花咱剩，
他把上园卖给人。

M:
The old worries the flowers be left over,
He sells the last garden to others.

女：
名花是妹自己栽，
未卖哪园给人家。

F:
I cultivate the rare flowers by myself,
None is sold to others.

671

男：
当初咱求露求雨，
今求情人落了空。

M:
We prayed for dew and rain before,
Now we fail to pray for a lover.

女：
当初咱上天求雨，
修花如人连成双。

F:
We prayed for the rain before,
Trimming flowers to make us a couple.

672

男：
修花第十蔸，
萤虫下根来，
映入眼和面。

M:
Let's trim the tenth flowers,
Fireflies fly down to the roots,
Glowing on our eyes and faces.

女：
修花第十蔸，
萤虫下花根观赏，
它催我俩来修花。

F:
Let's trim the tenth flowers,
Fireflies fly down to the roots,
They urge us to trim the flowers.

673

男：
我俩修枝花朵开，
晓得是否到手头。

M:
We trim the flowers till they bloom,
But in doubt if we could have claim to them.

女：
我俩修花拼成丛，
不许哪枝独立在。

F:
We trim the flowers into clusters,
No flower to be left in single.

674

男：
人家说就说，
花未大别卖，
切莫去贪他人财。

M:
You can ignore what others may suggest,
Don't sell the flowers while they're young,
Don't be greedy for others' fortune.

女：
咱似金叶难摘掉，
切莫不理丢路上，
人家追踪别要给。

F:
We're like golden leaves hard to be picked,
Don't throw them on the road away,
Don't give to those pursuing you.

675

男：	**M:**
修花十一蔸， 渐渐蔓成丛， 怕人来做主。	Let's trim the eleventh flowers, They gradually grow in clusters, I'm afraid others will claim for them.
女：	**F:**
修花十一蔸， 渐渐情缘深， 莫给妹拼死落空。	Let's trim the eleventh flowers, We gradually develop deep feelings, Never make me lose everything.

676

男：	**M:**
心想修花有姻缘， 生怕命不长先死。	I think trimming flowers brings marriage, Fear that life is short and I'll die early.
女：	**F:**
切莫抛弃咱名花， 先辈历来准许修。	Don't abandon our rare flowers, The ancestors allow us to trim them.

677

男：	**M:**
名花经常开开断， 我俩得合命还长。	The rare flowers always bloom, And we're a good match.
女：	**F:**
汇合修花共一园， 让它依人得共家。	We join together to trim flowers, Hoping to be in the same family.

678

男：	**M:**
心想修花有姻缘， 怕妹说过时难办。	I think trimming flowers brings marriage, Fear the appointed time has passed.
女：	**F:**
妹想修花添密切， 怕郎不合走另道。	I think trimming flowers promote intimacy, Fear you choose your partner with others.

679

男：	**M:**
修花十二蔸，	Let's trim the twelfth flowers,
朋友催我俩，	Friends are urging us,
修花给结缘成对。	To match as a couple by trimming flowers.
女：	**F:**
修花十二蔸，	Let's trim the twelfth flowers,
十处十赶到，	People come from near and far,
十路十来瞧。	Appreciating the flowers they admire.

680

男：	**M:**
古造修花得交情，	Trimming flowers brings affections,
不怕有人来乱管。	Not fearing that someone will take over.
女：	**F:**
自古修花有情缘，	Trimming flowers brings marriage,
今得睁眼结成对。	Now we can pair up as we wish.

681

男：	**M:**
我俩想结鸳鸯缘，	We want to form ties as the lovebirds,
修花必须朵朵红。	If we trim this red flower.
女：	**F:**
给它结成种，	We grow them to produce seeds,
给它配成双。	We grow them into pairs.

682

男：	**M:**
十二名花修完毕，	We've trimmed twelve kinds of flowers,
怕娘不称心难办。	For fear that you're still not content.
女：	**F:**
每蔸都修齐，	Every flower has been trimmed properly,
每园都修罢。	Every garden has been trimmed completely.

683 男：
修花给结籽，
明年还有人再种。

M:
Flowers will produce seeds after trimming,
With which we can plant next year.

女：
修花盼结籽，
下代还有人再种。

F:
We look forward to producing seeds,
With which next generation can cultivate.

684 男：
修罢咱收籽，
日后咱再种。

M:
We'd collect flower seeds after trimming,
Leaving them for planting later on.

女：
修罢咱收籽，
收籽放新年。

F:
We'd collect the seeds after trimming,
Reserving them to embrace the new year.

十、收名花种
X Collecting Seeds of Rare Flowers

685 男：
一来收花种，
牡丹收得七斤三，
哪个来问都别给。

M:
Let's trim the first flowers,
We get 7.3 jin[1] of peony seeds,
Never give anyone who asks for them.

女：
一来收花种，
牡丹收得七斤多，
哪个白要更别给。

F:
Let's collect the first seeds,
We get over 7 jin of peony seeds,
Never give anyone who wants them for free.

686 男：
理多辛苦才成花，
天旱求雨才结种。

M:
Only great efforts bring us blossoms,
Seeds from praying for rain in dry season.

女：
每天理花在园中，
哪座当作是妹家？

F:
You cultivate flowers in the garden everyday,
Which garden do you regard as my home?

687 男：
二来收花种，
玫瑰四斤四，
日后咱播更容易。

M:
Let's collect the second seeds,
We get 4.4 jin of rose seeds,
Later it'd be easy for us to sow.

女：
二来收花种，
玫瑰四斤四，
我俩开心得欢喜。

F:
Let's collect the second seeds,
We get 4.4 jin of rose seeds,
With the seeds we are delighted.

① Jin is a unit of weight. 1 jin is equal to 0.5 kilogram.

688 男：
名花收得种，
我俩再次得交情。

M:
Rare flowers harvest seeds,
We can form ties again.

女：
名花收得种，
我俩交情结成对。

F:
Rare flowers harvest seeds,
We can well be a couple.

689 男：
三来收花种，
海棠三斤四。

M:
Let's collect the third seeds,
We get 3.4 jin of begonia seeds.

女：
三来收花种，
海棠三斤四。

F:
Let's collect the third seeds,
We get 3.4 jin of begonia seeds.

690 男：
切莫卖出外一两，
郎仍围园再种花。

M:
Don't sell them out even a bit,
I'd enclose the garden and plant again.

女：
妹不卖出外一两，
我俩未富像人家。

F:
I won't sell them out even a bit,
We aren't as wealthy as others.

691 男：
名花种难求，
本地有才易。

M:
It's hard to ask for seeds of rare flowers,
It's easy only when there are local ones.

女：
名花种难要，
求人几多次才给。

F:
It's hard to ask for seeds of rare flowers,
You won't have any until appealing times.

692 男：
四来收花种，
到处都来收，
咱有切莫给。

M:
Let's collect the fourth seeds,
Everywhere people are doing the same,
Don't give them seeds in our possession.

女：
四来收花种，
到处都来找，
箐福四两五。

F:
Let's collect the fourth seeds,
People come from everywhere,
Seeds of happy flowers we have some.

693 男：
名花卖异地亏大，
日后去做别人皇。

M:
A great loss to sell rare flowers afar,
They'd breed flower to be the queen of others.

女：
名花卖近常见哥，
去远无依又无靠。

F:
It's easy to see the rare flowers sold nearby,
Without anyone to depend on if too faraway.

694 男：
五来收花种，
人家围园等种花，
它倒给咱白白爱。

M:
Let's collect the fifth seeds,
Others couldn't wait to plant them,
So my love for them would go in vain.

女：
五来收花种，
人家围园等有多，
妹死活不卖。

F:
Let's collect the fifth seeds,
Others are waiting for the seeds,
But I won't definitely sell them out.

695 男：
人家等就等，
我俩理花结出种，
还未成家像别人。

M:
I don't care if others are waiting,
The flowers we cultivate produce seeds,
But we can't be a family as others.

女：
人家不来也不成，
花种做主是我俩。

F:
Other people won't act recklessly,
We are the master of the seeds.

696 男：
六来收花种，
不知劳碌多少年，
我俩未富有别丢。

M:
Let's collect the sixth seeds,
I've worked hard for years,
Don't abandon our love even we're still poor.

女：
六来收花种，
劳碌盼美名，
有种不如人有情。

F:
Let's collect the sixth seeds,
I look forward to getting a name,
Seeds aren't equal to love.

697 男：
请妹找块种花地，
既咱有种再栽培。

M:
Find a place to grow flowers please,
Since we have the seeds.

女：
哪处成种让哥找，
哪里成种请哥说。

F:
You tell me where we can find the seeds,
You tell me where seeds are produced.

698 男：
七来收花种，
初一晒在阳台上，
公婆妹夫齐欣赏。

M:
Let's collect the seventh seeds,
Basking in the veranda on the first day,
Your parents-in-law and husband come to see together.

女：
七来收花种，
初一怕落雨，
谁见花种子？

F:
Let's collect the seventh seeds,
I'm afraid it'll rain the first day,
Who could see the seeds?

699 男：
有福公婆赐姻缘，
日后栽花容易长。

M:
You're blessed with marriage by parents-in-law,
It's easy for the flower to grow in the future.

女：
有福公婆赐姻缘，
却怕有虫蛀花根。

F:
If I were blessed with marriage by parents-in-law,
I fear that insects would bite the roots.

700

男：
公婆找地把园围，
给妹在家中观花。

M:
Your parents-in-law enclose a place to be garden,
For you to enjoy the flowers at home.

女：
公婆另有栽花处，
咱情未有园种花。

F:
The old generation have their own gardens,
But I don't have one to grow flowers.

701

男：
八来收花种，
日也光照田地间，
我俩欲种也白劳。

M:
Let's collect the eighth seeds,
The sun shines upon the farmlands,
Our desire to plant flowers may go in vain.

女：
八来收花种，
日头照山顶，
却照不到种花人。

F:
Let's collect the eighth seeds,
The sun shines upon the peak of the mountain,
But not on those who plant flowers.

702

男：
哥想下园去种花，
怕妹提前去当家。

M:
I want to plant flowers in the garden,
Fear that you get married to another one.

女：
妹想种花成配偶，
怕人撒种在前头。

F:
I want to accompany you plant flowers,
Fear someone has already sown the seeds.

703

男：
哥想种花在阳台，
怕娘不在去夫家。

M:
I want to plant flowers on the veranda,
Fear you'd not be home when I come.

女：
花园在哥家，
恩夫在哥屋。

F:
The garden is in your home,
My husband is in your house.

704 男：
九来收花种，
人家准备请喜酒，
给郎荒废把园围。

M:
We'd continue to collect the ninth seeds,
A wedding feast would be held for you,
Why waste my efforts to rail the garden?

女：
九来收花种，
酒米是哥才认领，
别的妹不接。

F:
We continue to collect the ninth seeds,
I'd accept wine and rice from you only,
I won't accept them from anybody else.

705 男：
娘妹快有喜酒喝，
郎却花园没找着。

M:
Your wedding feast will be held soon,
But I still can't find the one I love.

女：
请酒等哥来，
花园等哥种。

F:
I'm waiting for you to the feast,
The garden is waiting for you to plant.

706 男：
妹说种花流美名，
为何丢情在半路？

M:
You say planting flowers brings good fame,
Why abandon our love halfway?

女：
妹说种花本流名，
郎来不成夫也爱。

F:
I meant planting flowers for good fame,
Even if you can't be my husband anyway.

707 男：
十来收花种，
我俩生离白望空，
在哪结对如英台。

M:
We'd go on to collect the tenth seeds,
We are going to drift apart,
We aren't legendary lovers after all.

女：
十来收花种，
咱似十端月初升，
交郎不休成恩夫。

F:
We'd go on to collect the tenth seeds,
We're like the rising moon,
I'd go on until you become my husband.

708

男：	M:
收种不拆园， 我俩还没同一家。	We'd collect seeds but not break boundary, Cause' we haven't been in the same family.
女：	F:
花种属妹下功夫， 与哥未依他人亲。	The seeds are the results of your efforts, We aren't as close as others.

709

男：	M:
花园莫让人来栽， 莫留哥白看。	People aren't allowed to plant in this garden, Don't make my efforts come to nothing.
女：	F:
花园本是属我俩， 谁来也不让。	The garden belongs to both of us, It wouldn't be available to anyone else.

710

男：	M:
妹说去婆家就去， 先种好花才能走。	If you go to mother-in-law's home, Please plant the flowers in advance.
女：	F:
妹婆在郎家， 夫在哥屋里。	My mother-in-law is in your home, My husband is in your house.

711

男：	M:
十一收花种， 渐渐远离去， 何日又见好花逢？	We continue to collect the eleventh seeds, Gradually it's time to depart, When can we see the good flowers again?
女：	F:
十一收花种， 靛浆妹备好， 望哥快点找吉日。	We go on to collect the eleventh seeds, I've prepared the indigo pulp for clothing, Expect you to find a lucky day for wedding.

712	男： 妹说种花成恋人， 今收得种却抛弃。	M: You said planting flowers made us become lovers, But now I'm abandoned even we have seeds.
	女： 妹说种花成恋人， 天不公平也难办。	F: I said planting flowers made us become lovers, It's to no avail because God is unjust.
713	男： 拼命栽花结成种， 今不成人为何事？	M: I plant flowers desperately for the seeds, Why now my efforts prove futile?
	女： 妹说种花共一园， 收种同进共一家。	F: We share the same garden to plant flowers, We harvest seeds and become family members.
714	男： 当初想结流芳名， 今却丢情真是难。	M: Originally we want a good fame by pairing up, Now it's embarrassing to abandon our love.
	女： 拼命种花得出名， 交郎不成夫也爱。	F: Working hard to plant flowers wins a name, Even you can't be my husband love remains.
715	男： 十二收花种， 主意妹也多， 口说心头歪难办。	M: Let's collect the last kind of seeds, You have so many ideas, It's hard if you say yes but mean no.
	女： 十二收花种， 靠哥得发财， 哥却与人另外栽。	F: Let's collect the last kind of seeds, Depending on you we can make a fortune, But you plant flowers with someone else.

716

男：
初想结对比山厚，
今轻如纸被风刮。

M:
We wanted to develop intimate relationship,
But now it's as light as a piece of paper.

女：
为种名花妹才来，
怕郎分岔不重情。

F:
I come here for planting rare flowers,
Fear you have many other choices.

717

男：
收尽十二名花种，
十二名花种收罢。

M:
We've collected all twelve kinds of seeds already,
We've collected twelve kinds of seeds completely.

女：
十二花种全收来，
十二花种全收罢。

F:
We've collected all twelve kinds of seeds already,
We've collected twelve kinds of seeds completely.

十一、道公收魂回家
XI Concluding Ceremony

718 男：
得了花种咱启程，
得了花种回头走。

M:
After we get the seeds we start to leave,
After we get the seeds we start to return.

女：
得了花种咱启程，
哪天又见好情郎。

F:
After we get the seeds we start to leave,
Someday I'll meet my love again.

719 男：
得了好种回故地，
切莫眼黑驻他乡。

M:
We've got the good seeds we'll go back,
Don't indulge in an alien land.

女：
得了咱回家，
我俩欲回屋。

F:
After we get the seeds we'd go back,
We're about to go back home.

720 男：
到屋招魂宰灰鸡，
又宰乌鸡来招命。

M:
Kill the rooster to recall the souls,
Kill the rooster to recall the spirits.

女：
到屋招魂宰灰鸡，
又宰乌鸡来招命。

F:
Kill the rooster to recall the souls,
Kill the rooster to recall the spirits.

721

男：
百二条禄命来齐，
好魂全回咱们家。

M:
All of 120 lives are gathering,
The good souls will all return.

女：
百二条禄命来齐，
我俩安好胜从前。

F:
All of 120 lives are gathering,
We're better than before in body and mind.

722

男：
道公禄命收来尽，
我俩安好胜从前。

M:
The priest recall all the spirits,
We're better than before.

女：
拜谢道公收灵魂，
各人安好胜从前。

F:
We express our gratitude to the priest,
For everyone is better than before.

723

男：
俩丁邀道公就餐，
俩伊邀麽公饮酒。

M:
Two boys invite the priest to dinner,
Two girls invite the master for drinks,

女：
请哥与道公上座，
妹身做仆人斟酒。

F:
You and the priest please have a seat,
I fill the glass for you as a servant.

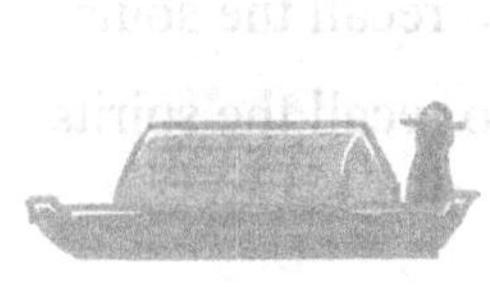

十二、辞别
Ⅻ Bidding Farewell

724

男： 喝酒了咱别， 喝茶了辞退。	**M:** After drinking wine, I bid farewell, After drinking tea, I bid farewell.
女： 喝酒了咱别， 喝茶了辞退。	**F:** After drinking wine, I bid farewell, After drinking tea, I bid farewell.

725

男： 辞别妹辞别， 下回逢再歌。	**M:** I'd say good bye to you, Sing again when we meet next time.
女： 别了另路花， 别了他乡情。	**F:** I'd say good bye to the flowers, I'd say good bye to my love to go faraway.

十二、辞别
XII Bidding Farewell

1224 男：　M:
喝酒了咱别，　After drinking wine, I bid farewell.
喝茶了咱别，　After drinking tea, I bid farewell.

女：　F:
喝酒了咱别，　After drinking wine, I bid farewell.
喝茶了咱别。　After drinking tea, I bid farewell.

1225 男：　M:
辞别你咱别，　I'd say good bye to you.
下回再唱歌。　Sing again when we meet next time.

女：　F:
别了花儿了，　I'd say good bye to the flowers.
别了尕妹花。　I'd say good bye to my love to go faraway.

浪花歌
Romantic Lyrics

收集：方国弟
汉译：黄建忠　方国弟
英译：覃　丹　李　涵

一、邀请歌

I Songs of Invitation①

此歌为未婚男青年歌手连唱

Single men sing:

1	傍晚哥出游， 闲游到夜深。	At dusk I go out for fun, Not till midnight I'd not return.
2	不玩山村静悄悄， 不游亭榭多荒凉。	Too quiet is the village if no one plays, Too lonely would be the pavilion if no one stays.
3	今夜景色好， 天阔满星光。	So beautiful it's tonight, Stars are twinkling bright.
4	今夜有凤降人间， 哥吃夜饭不安然。	There would come some girls fair, My excitement I could hardly forbear.
5	水进田鱼跃， 客来哥心欢， 犹如亮鱼下滩游。	Fish jumps as water flows into the paddy, My heart dances as girls come into the village, As fish plays down the stream happily.
6	河里鱼穿梭， 哪滩合意才驻下。	Fish swims back and forth, Only stops where it thinks worth.

① There are three kinds of invitation songs. One is sung by the single men only. The second is sung by all men. The third is sung during singing antiphonal songs, while the women stop singing suddenly, the men will sing this song until the women go on again.

7 今哥岔路去下棋，
突见飞来双喜鹊，
晓它是否落穷寨？

I took a side path to play chess,
Only to find there come two larks,
Will they stay at our poor village?

8 哥在河岸下棋子，
突见鱼跃水坝间，
突见好花[①]到村头。

By the river I play chess,
Only to see a fish jump about the river,
And a fair girl happens to enter.

9 哥出阳台晒麦子，
突见杜鹃飞过来，
是否落在贫瘠处？

I dry the wheat on the veranda,
Only to see the cuckoo fly over.
This poor place will it enter?

10 若落哥欲找，
若栖哥欲寻。

I'll try to seek for it if it stays,
I'll try to find it out if it stays.

11 今日无雨是阴天，
何人进寨撑阳伞，
打着雨伞到山庄。

It's a sunny day today,
Who is holding an umbrella,
And under it enters the village?

12 进村想来找，
入寨想来寻。

I want to meet her in the village,
I want to find her among the villagers.

13 哥来上家耍，
下家闻笑声。

I'm visiting the neighbor,
From next door comes laughter.

14 哥来旁家玩，
笑从篱孔穿过来。

I'm visiting the neighbor,
Through the hedge comes laughter.

15 闻到陌生音，
是客或家人？
主家或异地？

The voice I heard is so unfamiliar.
Is it a guest or a family member?
Is it the neighbor or a stranger?

---

①意指姑娘。

16
哥靠篱孔来窥视，
哥从篱缝偷偷瞧。

I peer through a hole in the hedge,
I peep through a chink in the hedge.

17
不是同寨姑娘面，
却是异乡妹露头。

It isn't a girl of this village,
But a girl from some other part.

18
早来或刚到？
刚来或返回？

How long has she arrived?
Newly arrival or ready to depart?

19
既然客从异地来，
偏到穷村来投宿。

A strange girl has come here,
To pay a visit to this poor community.

20
上村瓦房三十户，
下寨坯房五十家，
为何投穷处？

There're so many tile-roofed houses,
And brick buildings in the villages nearby,
Why do you stay at a hamlet?

21
哥家辅竹凳子脏，
请妹坐前抽好袍。

Dirty the bamboo chair may be,
Please mind your dress ere sitting.

22
今夜竹床睡不安，
去睡砖屋才暖和。

Uncomfortable the bamboo may feel,
It'd be better to stay at a bricked house.

23
请妹少夜莫忙睡，
请娘舍夜不入眠。

Please don't go to bed so early,
Please stay up all night with me.

24
请妹窗前赏月光，
请出晒台赏夜雾。

Let's enjoy the moonlight before window,
Let's enjoy the mist on the veranda.

25
不赏雾将散，
不赏月将落。

If no one enjoys the moon will fall,
And the mist will disappear after all.

26
恳求房中杨莓柱，
恳求家中父和母，
请催异地妹对歌。

The waxberry pillar lofty,
And the parents dear,
Would you urge the girl to sing with me?

27 恳求房中红栗柱，
恳求家中老大哥，
请催异地妹对歌。

The chestnut pillar lofty,
And the elder-brother my peer,
Would you urge the girl to sing with me?

28 恳求房中柏花柱，
恳请家里老大嫂，
开导异乡妹对歌。

The marigold pillar lofty,
And the sister-in-law so dear,
Would you urge the girl to sing with me?

29 恳求房中枫木柱，
恳求家中老大姐，
请催异乡妹对歌。

The maple pillar lofty,
And the elder-sister my dear,
Would you urge the girl to respond to my song?

30 恳求房中央木柱，
恳求家中伯母娘，
请催异乡妹对歌。

The central pillar lofty,
And the aunts so dear,
Would you urge the girl to respond to my song?

31 恳求房中蜜蒙柱，
恳求家中小姑娘，
恳请远方女对歌。

The Mimeng[①] pillar in the house,
And the little girl of the family,
Would you urge the girl to respond to my song?

32 红心李果甩过来，
异地贵女把歌抛。

Please throw over some red-pulp plums,
And respond to my song.

33 花斑李果甩过来，
唱匠乖女把歌抛。

Please throw over some spotted plums,
And respond to my song.

34 透黑李果甩过来，
唱匠金女把歌抛。

Please throw over some ripe plums,
And respond to my song.

35 青色李果甩过来，
闻名美女把歌抛。

Please throw over some bluish-green plums,
And respond to my song.

36 抛来，妹抛来，
哥驶船舟去接应。

Come on, do come along,
I'll pick you up with my boat.

① Name of a kind of tree.

37
去到百色南宁接，
去到皇帝城下候。

I'll pick you up in the city,
I'll wait for you in the capital.

38
哥请妹已久，
请妹亮嗓把歌对。

I've waited for you so long.
Would you please respond to my song?

39
鸦鸟快开口，
凤眼快睁开。

Birds, please open your mouths.
Phoenix, please open your eyes.

40
凤待哪时才起飞？
麒麟哪刻方启程？

Phoenix, when will you rise to the sky?
Kylin, when will you start your journey?

41
请妹吐出口中果，
请妹咳出喉中梨，
请娘亮嗓对山歌。

Dear girl, please stop eating
The fruit in your mouth,
Please sing songs with me.

42
哥笨用笨歌来还，
郎傻用傻歌来对。

Please respond to my earnest song,
Though I'm clumsy at singing.

43
不对多对少，
对上两句也就行。

It doesn't matter how much you'll sing,
With your song my heart would be rising.

44
请到芦苇根，
请到金竹节，
请到妹自身。

We could sing at the reeds,
Or at the bamboo bush,
Would you please just show yourself?

45
请妹盘通好主意，
快将山歌对上来。

Please think about what to sing,
I can't wait to hear your song.

46
烧柴哥讨一把灰，
哥也空讨玩笑话，
不怕摘花连巅掐。

I'd burn wood to get some ash,
I'd sing to get your response,
Though I'm clumsy at singing.

47
烧柴哥讨一枚炭，
哥也空讨搓麻绳，
不怕抓死妹鞋跟。

I'd burn some wood to get charcoal,
I'd sing to get your response,
I desire to make a family match with you.

48	生火烧空锅， 不烧冷灰飞满屋， 烧来铜锅要熔化。	A dilemma to burn the empty pot, Home will be cold without fire, But the pot will melt if I set the fire.
49	只借山歌来交往， 只借山歌来交流。	Let's make friends by singing songs, Let's communicate by singing songs.
50	相逢凭借对回歌， 别怕哥缠一辈子。	We meet by singing songs only, Don't be afraid of being stuck with me.
51	凭借相逢会次面， 攀亲永远万不能。	We can meet here by chance, But we won't make a family match.
52	本穷篱笆二度围， 哥穷礼节请鲜花， 十分不配也耐答。	Poor as my house, surrounded by two hedges, Without much sense of manners, I dare invite you, So please sing though we aren't well-matched.
53	哥处穷礼请娘妹， 请妹更穷甜蜜语。	I'm poor in manners and sweet words, To invite you to sing with me.
54	来到哥处穷道理， 请妹颈根要拉长。	As poor as I'm in manners, It's so kind of you to stand me.
55	妹莫嫌弃那么多， 忍耐亮花把歌对。	Don't reject me too much, Please open your mouth and sing.
56	请妹莫想那么多， 请娘亮花把歌答。	Don't think too much beforehand, Please open your mouth and sing.
57	田埂还有高低坎， 不答若嫌哥补肩①。	Paddy ridges may be high or low, Please sing if you don't mind I'm poor.

①补肩，穿着肩上缝补的破衣服。

58 田埂还有长和短，
不答若嫌不同辈。

Paddy ridges may be short or long,
Please sing if you don't mind I'm older.

59 穿烂哥远离，
身脏吾隔远。

In rags, I keep far away from you,
In dirty clothes, I stay away from you.

60 别怕玷污妹绫罗，
别怕晦染妹绸缎，
回去它还如故鲜。

Don't worry about your silk suits,
Don't worry about your satin dress,
They'll be fresh just as when you come.

61 天旱拜庙求雨水，
彼此相求莫推脱。

As praying in the temple for some rain,
Let's sing together without hesitation.

62 请妹颈根长，
亮嗓来对歌。

Would you please make a start?
Open your mouth and sing.

63 怨哥蠢才是傻瓜，
才来唱歌解忧愁。

I'm really not smart,
Singing to remove my anxiety.

64 只想对歌讨交往，
别怕同家共一屋。

I sing to make friends with you,
Not afraid to stay under the same roof.

65 指望果熟想讨吃，
无奈为人就唱歌。

Though I hope for the ripe fruits,
I must firstly sing songs.

66 山间鸟凤还结对，
郎只讨歌来交流。

I know birds in hills pair up,
I sing to you only to make friends.

67 天星追求伴月行，
哥也空讨一季花。

Stars want to accompany the moon,
I want to sing songs with you.

男唱
Men sing:

1	咱随水獭印， 跟踪河鱼影， 续行昨夜山歌路。	Following the footprints of otter, And the shadow of fish, Let's go on singing songs.
2	来咱接唱昨夜歌， 来咱再叙昨夜情。	Let's continue last night's song, Let's continue last night's feelings.
3	接唱使歌更丰厚， 接叙让情更密切。	Relay makes the song still richer, And the feelings more intimate.
4	再让花开更美丽， 再让花蕊更柔和。	Relay makes the flower more pretty, And the flower buds more tenderly.
5	再让花朵更娇艳， 再让花蕾更夺目。	Relay makes the flower more lovely, And the flower buds more charming.
6	歌交一夜情未厚， 歌交数晚意更深。	Singing songs can deepen our feeling, Love will be more dearly after nights' singing.
7	请妹吐出口中果， 请妹咳出喉中梨， 请妹高声接山歌。	Dear girl, Please stop eating The fruit in your mouth, Please sing songs with me.
8	凤待何时才起飞？ 麒麟哪刻才启程？	Phoenix, when will you rise to the sky? Kylin, when will you start the journey?

9 请妹开口快接歌，
请妹亮嗓快吟唱。

Dear girl, please open your mouth,
And sing songs with me.

10 对歌莫犹豫，
误过良机不回来。

Don't hesitate to sing with me,
Such golden opportunity shouldn't be missed.

11 哥处穷礼请娘妹，
请妹更穷甜蜜语。

I'm poor in manners and sweet words,
To invite you to sing with me.

12 身在哥处穷道理，
请妹颈根要拉长。

As poor as I'm in manners,
It's so kind of you to stand me.

13 请妹柔音来回歌，
再让花蕾更夺目。

Please answer my song with your soft voice,
Please continue singing with your sweet voice.

14 渡河不达人讥笑，
歌唱不完人非议。

Whoever gives up halfway will be laughed at,
Whoever stops singing will be talked about.

15 田头地角人议论，
那时我俩难得受。

If they talk about us in public,
It'd be hard for us to stand.

对歌当中，对方突然停顿，许久，主方插唱此段歌，至对方答歌为止。
During singing antiphonal songs, while the women stop singing suddenly, the men will sing this song until the women go on again.

1	为何妹为啥？ 为啥顿声不歌唱？	Why? Dear girl, can you tell me? Why do you stop singing?
2	为何丢哥独自唱？ 为啥弃吾独自歌？	Why do you let me sing alone? Why do you leave me and sing alone?
3	妹念屋里什么事？ 娘惦家中什么情？	Do you miss your household? Do you miss your family?
4	念屋明晚回去到， 惦家次晚得露头。	Go back tomorrow night, If you miss your home and family.
5	今夜竹楼睡不安， 明晚到家才慢眠。	You may not sleep well here tonight, So sleep soundly at home tomorrow.
6	怕妹念只勾尾鸭， 怕妹念家旧情侣， 才得弃哥不流连。	I wonder if you're missing your husband, Or your old lover at home, So you leave me without hesitation.
7	再说念屋里也好， 今夜强忍对回歌。	Though you're missing your home, Please sing songs with me tonight.
8	哥也全凭这一宵， 不是依人得凭靠。	I expect so much of tonight, Since I can't depend on any others.

9

连紧吃蔗口才甜，
连环唱歌才迷人。

Sugarcane is sweeter to enjoy fully,
Songs are more charming to sing continuously.

10

睡着妹快醒，
睡醒妹快歌，
请妹把歌连起来。

Dear girl, please stay awake,
And sing your song,
Please respond to my song.

11

女：
妹还拍飞蛾，
妹还拍蚊子，
妹还卡歌词。

F:
I have to flap the moths,
And drive away mosquitoes,
I can't come up with ready words.

12

男：
妹不拍飞蛾，
妹不拍蚊子，
妹不卡歌词。

M:
Don't flap the moths,
Nor drive away mosquitoes,
Please come up with ready words.

13

女：
为妹穷歌不成人，
十分愧对情郎君。

F:
I'm short of words in singing,
I'm ashamed of facing you.

14

男：
讲多也成多，
请妹接歌往前行。

M:
It's no use talking too much,
Would you please sing with me?

二、浪花歌
II Song of Romance

1

男：	M:
咋办呀阿妹， 让哥怎样好。	Hey, my dear girl, How should I start?
女：	F:
雨落闻滴声， 开嗓闻佳音， 突闻歌师唱。	Pitter-patter can be heard when it rains, Sweet voice is heard when I'm about to sing, Is you who are singing.

2

男：	M:
哥该怎么办？ 有口难还妹的歌。	What should I do, dear girl? I find it hard to respond to your song.
女：	F:
请哥慢思索， 大凡交往得对歌。	You can take time to find words, Since we need singing to make friends.

3

男：	M:
晚餐哥未毕， 未洗漱揩手， 谁来与哥寻开心？	I haven't finished my dinner, I haven't washed up, Who will make fun with me?
女：	F:
晚餐哥早毕， 早洗漱揩手， 妹来与哥寻开心。	You've finished your dinner, You've washed up, I'll make fun with you.

4

男：
晚餐哥未毕，
未洗漱抽烟，
谁来流连找阿哥？

M:
I haven't finished my dinner,
I haven't washed up and smoked,
Who would like to play with me?

女：
晚餐哥早毕，
早洗漱抽烟，
妹才流连找阿哥。

F:
You've finished your dinner,
You've washed up and smoked,
I'd like to play with you.

5

男：
晚餐哥未毕，
未漱口品茶，
谁来睁眼对山歌？

M:
I haven't finished my dinner,
I haven't drinked some tea,
Who will sing songs with me?

女：
晚餐哥早毕，
早漱口品茶，
妹才睁眼来唱歌。

F:
You've finished your dinner,
You've drinked some tea,
I'll sing songs with you.

6

男：
晚餐哥未毕，
未洗漱吐痰，
谁来与哥摆歌台？

M:
I haven't finished my dinner,
I haven't washed up and cleared my throat,
Who will sing songs with me?

女：
晚餐哥早毕，
早洗漱吐痰，
妹才与哥摆歌台。

F:
You've finished your dinner,
You've washed up and cleared your throat,
I'll sing songs with you.

7

男：
楼脚什么惊？
阳台什么噪？
给哥睡不安。

M:
What are disturbed downstairs?
What are excited under the veranda?
That makes me very uneasy.

女：
楼脚鸡鸭惊，
台下牛马噪，
在不安对歌。

F:
Chickens and ducks are disturbed downstairs,
Cows and horses are excited under the veranda,
Let's sing songs though uneasy.

8 **男：**
城中什么在喧哗？
让哥胆战心头慌。

M:
What is roaring in the town?
That makes me tremble with fear.

女：
城中小犬在喧闹，
哥莫胆战心头慌。

F:
Little dog is roaring in the town,
Please don't tremble with fear.

9 **男：**
哥肚泛如油，
吾心涝如水。

M:
Something is upsurging in my heart,
Something is upsurging in my mind.

女：
哥肚泛成歌，
郎心歌海荡。

F:
Songs are upsurging in your heart,
Songs are upsurging in your mind.

10 **男：**
荡成水欲流，
结成冰欲化。

M:
My heart turns into water to flow,
My mind turns into ice to melt.

女：
荡成歌欲对，
花绽想投缘。

F:
Your heart turns into songs to sing,
Blooming flower wants to form ties with you.

11 **男：**
风吹纳凉全身抖，
哥不敢开口。

M:
I want some cool but feeling chilled,
I daren't open my mouth.

女：
歌声飘来妹耳悦，
郎哥爱开口。

F:
Sound of song makes me so pleased,
You seem love singing too.

12 **男：**
懒开口取风，
懒开腔纳凉。

M:
I don't want to open my mouth,
Lest I may catch wind and cold.

女：
勤开口取风，
勤开腔纳凉。

F:
Please often open your mouth,
You'll only feel nice and cool.

13

男：
怕开口对歌，
怕开腔对唱。

M:
I'm afraid to open my mouth,
To sing songs with you.

女：
勤开口对歌，
勤开腔对唱。

F:
Please often open your mouth,
To sing songs with me.

14

男：
今是什么夜？
忧心睡不着。

M:
What's wrong with tonight?
I'm too anxious to sleep.

女：
十宜今夜好，
点灯没有芯也亮。

F:
Tonight is good for everything,
Even the lamp can light without wick.

15

男：
老人睡不着会咒，
同龄睡不安会骂。

M:
Both the old and the young
Will curse if can't fall asleep.

女：
老人难眠想听歌，
同龄难眠想听唱。

F:
Both the old and the young
Like listening to songs if can't fall asleep.

16

男：
骂来哥脸臊，
那时愧对乖阿妹。

M:
Cursing will make me
Ashamed of facing you.

女：
听歌人人夸，
咱也开心又欢喜。

F:
Songs will make people pleased,
And that will make us thrilled.

17

男：
风吹椿芽叶，
花从哪方邀？
歌从何处请？

M:
Wind stirs toona sinensis leaves,
Where can we invite the flower?
Where can we invite the song?

女：
风吹椿芽叶，
花从此处开，
歌从这方请。

F:
Wind stirs toona sinensis leaves,
We can invite the flower here,
We can invite the song there.

18

男：
歌声吱喳起，
从晒台飘来，
谁来请哥对山歌？

M:
The sound of singing
Began from the veranda,
Who would invite me to sing?

女：
歌声响吱喳，
从晒台发出，
是妹请哥来对唱。

F:
The sound of singing
Would begin from the veranda,
I invite you to sing.

19

男：
请鸭鸭想散，
请鹅鹅就惊，
真诚开台哥欲对。

M:
Ducks disperse if invited,
Geese are scared if invited,
But I'll sing if you're sincere.

女：
请鸭鸭想散，
请鹅鹅就惊，
真诚让哥把歌对。

F:
Ducks won't disperse if invited,
Geese won't be scared if invited,
I'm sincere to invite you to sing.

20

男：
想对山歌三两句，
不知唱得成不成？

M:
I'll sing two or three lines,
Well or not though I still wonder.

女：
歌如甘蔗甜，
比晾葱柔软，
歌声比花美。

F:
Your singing is sweeter than sugarcane,
Softer than green onion,
And lovelier than flowers.

21

男：
请哥哥乱应，
发誓还没讲。

M:
You invite me to sing,
But we haven't made an oath.

女：
妹请给哥应，
发誓一起讲。

F:
I invite you to sing,
Together let's make the oath.

22

男：
请妹窗外问月亮，
请出晒台问阳光。

M:
Have you asked the moon outside the window,
And the sunshine on the veranda?

女：
妹早出窗问月亮，
早出晒台问阳光。

F:
I've asked the moon outside the window,
And the sunshine on the veranda.

23

男：
阳光准才歌，
月许才能唱。

M:
We can sing if the sun permits,
We can sing if the moon permits.

女：
日也准妹歌，
月也许妹唱。

F:
The sun has permitted us to sing,
The moon has permitted us to sing.

24

男：
请妹回家先问婆，
请妹回家先问公。

M:
Have you asked your mother-in-law,
And your father-in-law?

女：
妹早回家问家婆，
妹早回家问叔公。

F:
I've asked my mother-in-law,
And my father-in-law.

25	男： 叔公准才歌， 婆给来才唱。	M: You can sing if your father-in-law permits, You can sing if your mother-in-law permits.
	女： 叔给妹来歌， 婆让妹来唱。	F: My father-in-law has permitted me to sing, My mother-in-law has permitted me to sing.
26	男： 请妹回家问夫君， 请妹回家先问婆。	M: Have you asked your husband, And your mother-in-law?
	女： 妹早回家问夫君， 吾早回家先问婆。	F: I've asked my husband, And my mother-in-law.
27	男： 婆让来才歌， 夫给来再唱。	M: You can sing if your mother-in-law permits, You can sing if your husband permits.
	女： 婆让妹来歌， 夫给妹来唱。	F: My mother-in-law has permitted me to sing, My husband has permitted me to sing.
	换位：	**Reverse:**
28	女： 请哥回房问爱妻， 请哥回家问姨太。	F: Have you asked permission From your wife and your concubine?
	男： 哥早回家问爱妻， 吾早回家问姨太。	M: I've asked permission From my wife and my concubine.

29	女： 姨让来才歌， 妻给来再唱。	M: You can sing if your wife permits, You can sing if your concubine permits.
	男： 姨也让来唱， 妻也给来歌。	F: My wife has permitted me to sing, My concubine has permitted me to sing.
	还原：	**Recovery:**
30	男： 坡是什么坡？ 坡有什么林？	M: What kind of slope is this? What are there on the slope?
	女： 坡本是山坡， 坡本属密林。	F: It used to be a hill slope, There used to be forests on it.
31	男： 坡长什么荆？ 为何偏要和哥唱？	M: What grows on the slope now? Why would you sing songs with me?
	女： 坡本长荆棘， 才得和哥对山歌。	F: Only brambles grow on the slope, So I can sing songs here with you.
32	男： 今日赶街来得夜， 到坳口漆黑。	M: I went to the fair late today, It's turning dark when arriving.
	女： 今日赶街哥来早， 早到山坳口。	F: You went to the fair early today, And got to the col at dusk.

33 男：
坳顶没篝火，
给哥独身怎么办？

M:
No bonfires at col top,
How should I go on as a single man?

女：
坳顶有篝火，
哥早会盘算。

F:
There are bonfires at the col top,
You've planned everything beforehand.

34 男：
想走怕丛林，
想回怕虎把路拦。

M:
I want to leave but fear the jungle,
There may be tiger blocking the way.

女：
想走不怕林，
想回没虎来拦路。

F:
If you want to leave,
No jungle or tiger would block your way.

35 男：
哥想借火光，
有光借火把，
让哥借光好探路。

M:
I want to borrow a torch,
Can you lend me your torch,
To explore my way at night?

女：
哪来有火光？
无光穷火把，
哪来给哥亮过路？

F:
Where have you seen the light?
I have no light and torch,
How can I help you at night?

36 男：
妹有竹火把，
照亮几里路。

M:
You have the bamboo for torch,
To light up miles of way.

女：
无凉竹火把，
亮不到一尺。

F:
I have no bamboo for torch,
To light up even one inch of way.

37

男：
毛竹做火把，
亮走几山弄。

M:
The torch made of Mao bamboo
Can illuminate several hills.

女：
无毛竹火把，
亮不到半步。

F:
I have no Mao bamboo torch,
To light up even half a step.

38

男：
今吾赶路途程远，
到妹村已黑。

M:
I've travelled a long way today,
It's turning dark when reaching your village.

女：
今哥赶路来得早，
早到妹山村。

F:
You've started off early today,
You've got to my village already.

39

男：
下村三十家瓦房，
上寨五十座砖屋，
异乡哥身不投宿。

M:
There're so many tile-roofed houses,
And bricked buildings in the village,
But I don't want to stay at any of them.

女：
下村三十家瓦房，
上寨五十座砖屋，
异乡哥身想投宿。

F:
There're so many tile-roofed houses,
And bricked buildings in the village,
You'd like to stay one of them.

40

男：
村近不想留，
远寨不想去。

M:
I won't stay at the next village,
Nor at the village far away.

女：
近村哥想留，
寨远哥想去。

F:
You'd like to stay at the next village,
Or at the village far away.

41

男：
偏进妹村来，
投宿到妹寨。

M:
I'll come to your village,
And want to stay at it.

女：
若哥不嫌就进来，
若哥不嫌就驾到。

F:
You can come to my village,
If you don't mind staying.

42

男：
妹村卵石来垫脚，
妹寨岩石来铺路。

M:
The streets in your village
Are paved with gravel and slabs.

女：
妹村垫脚无卵石，
妹寨铺路穷石板。

F:
The streets in my village
Aren't paved with gravel and slabs.

43

男：
天上还有星相连，
山高还有人开路。

M:
Far in the sky, stars link together,
High as the mountain, someone made the path.

女：
天上还有星相连，
高山哪有人开路。

F:
Far in the sky, stars link together,
High at the mountain, none had made the path.

44

男：
哥才有路走进来，
吾才沿道行至此。

M:
I come to your village,
By following a well-made road.

女：
妹村草路长满荆，
十分刺眼忍耐来。

F:
The road is overgrown with grass and thorn,
You must overcome them to come along.

45

男：
哥来失礼不会夸，
不如他人晓乡情。

M:
Poor in manners and flattering,
I'm innocent about the ways of the world.

女：
哥来知书又达理，
精明乖巧谁能比。

F:
Well-educated and reasonable,
You're the cleverest in the world.

46

男：
榕叶杂麻叶，
寨中妹有郎，
为何来跟哥对唱？

M:
Banyan leaves mix with hemp leaves,
You already have a lover in the village,
Why would you sing with me?

女：
榕叶杂麻叶，
寨中妹无郎，
才来找哥把歌唱。

F:
Banyan leaves mix with hemp leaves,
I have no lover in the village,
So I'd like to sing with you.

47

男：
园中菜不摘，
倒反下田里，
来挖苦野菜。

M:
Why not pick vegetables in your garden,
But go to the field,
To dig some wild vegetables?

女：
有园穷种来播撒，
才下到田里，
来挖野菜吃。

F:
No seeds to grow vegetables in my garden,
So I go to the field,
To dig some wild vegetables.

48

男：
野菜吃很苦，
田里菜更涩。

M:
The wild vegetables are bitter,
The field vegetables are astringent.

女：
野菜吃很甜，
田里菜很嫩。

F:
The wild vegetables are sweet,
The field vegetables are fresh.

49 男：
园中妹有红杆菜，
为何还来路边捡？

M:
There're purslanes in your garden,
Why do you pick them by the road?

女：
园中妹无红杆菜，
才得来到路边捡。

F:
No purslanes grow in my garden,
So I pick them by the road.

50 男：
十菜怎比红杆菜？
十郎怎比村郎贵？

M:
Ten vegetables can't compare with purslane,
Ten boys can't compare with your lover.

女：
十菜难比红杆菜，
十郎难比郎哥贵。

F:
Ten vegetables can't compare with purslane,
Ten boys can't compare with you.

51 男：
山鸡啄家鸡，
家鸡散上山，
今夜变成抢家花。

M:
The pheasant pecked at the chicken,
Which dispersed up to the hills,
Tonight I've come to rob a flower.

女：
山鸡没有啄家鸡，
家鸡没有散上山，
更没来抢哪家花。

F:
The pheasant didn't peck at the chicken,
And none dispersed up to the hill,
You haven't come to rob any flower.

52 男：
山鸡啄家鸡，
家鸡散进林，
今夜变成抢同庚。

M:
The pheasant pecked at the chicken,
Which dispersed into the forest,
Tonight I've come to rob my peer.

女：
山鸡也没啄家鸡，
山鸡没有散进林，
也没来抢同契庚。

F:
The pheasant didn't peck at the chicken,
And none dispersed into the forest,
You haven't come to rob your peer.

53

男：
山鸡啄家鸡，
家鸡散上坡，
今夜来冒犯朋友。

M:
The pheasant pecked at the chicken,
Which dispersed up to the slope,
Tonight I've offended your friends.

女：
山鸡也没啄家鸡，
家鸡也不散上坡，
更没冒犯朋友情。

F:
The pheasant didn't peck at the chicken,
And none dispersed up to the slope,
You haven't offended my friends.

54

男：
入林哥冒犯，
冒犯到山神。

M:
I've offended the mountain-god,
As I went into the forest.

女：
入林没冒犯，
没冒犯山神。

F:
You haven't offended the mountain-god,
As you went into the forest.

55

男：
进村冒犯人，
冒犯到同龄。

M:
I've offended the peers,
As I went into your village.

女：
没有冒犯人，
也没错同龄。

F:
You haven't offended the peers,
As you come into my village.

56

男：
一错山神庙，
二错土地公，
三错耄耋诸郡主。

M:
I've offended the Mountain-God,
The God of Earth,
The eldly and respected Region Lords.

女：
一不错神庙，
不错土地公，
不错耄耋诸郡主。

F:
You haven't offended the Mountain-God,
The God of Earth,
The eldly and respected Region Lords.

57 男：
四错家中父和母，
五错寨里老长辈。

M:
I've offended your parents,
And the elders in your village.

女：
四不错家中父母，
五不错寨里长辈。

F:
You haven't offended my parents,
And the elders in my village.

58 男：
六错众多同辈人，
七错全寨众朋友。

M:
I've offended many peers,
And friends in your village.

女：
六不错众多同辈，
七不错全寨朋友。

F:
You haven't offended any peers,
And friends in my village.

59 男：
八错阿妹好情侣，
九错阿妹好情人。

M:
I've offended your husband,
And offended your lover.

女：
八不错妹好情侣，
九不错妹好情人。

F:
You haven't offended my husband,
Nor offended my lover.

60 男：
十错上村和下寨，
错犯众天下。

M:
I've offended the villagers,
Nearby and far away.

女：
十不错犯上下村，
不怕错犯众天下。

F:
You haven't offended the villagers,
Nearby and far away.

61 男：
错不错别人，
专错妹情郎。

M:
I haven't offended any others,
But I should offend your lover.

女：
没错任何人，
没错哪位情郎君。

F:
You haven't offended anyone,
And none of my lover.

62

男：
风吹檀香叶，
歌从何处来？
歌从哪方请？

M:
Wind stirs the leaves of algum tree,
Where does the songs come from?
Where can I invite the songs?

女：
风吹檀香叶，
歌从此处来。
歌从这方请。

F:
Wind stirs the leaves of algum tree,
The songs come from this direction,
The songs can be invited this way.

63

男：
反来请异乡土人，
反来请异地汉郎，
反来请呆哥陌路。

M:
Why invite a rustic stranger?
Why invite a sturdy stranger?
Why invite a clumsy man like me?

女：
非请侬家后生哥，
交异乡俊郎，
真诚连枝异地花。

F:
I'd like to invite a young Zhuang,
I'd like to invite a handsome stranger,
And sincerely I want to tie knot with him.

换位： **Reverse:**

64

女：
反来邀鬓发土女，
反来邀长发汉妇，
要啥山歌来对唱？

F:
Why invite a rustic elder woman?
Why invite a woman who can't sing?
What songs should I sing with you?

男：
诚邀异乡侬家妹，
邀异地美女，
真诚邀妹对山歌。

M:
I sincerely invite a Zhuang girl,
I sincerely invite a pretty stranger,
To sing antiphonal songs with me.

	还原：	Recovery：
65	男： 反来邀请四方田， 反来请朵田间花， 哪个来邀哥对唱？	M: Why invite the square fields? Why invite the flowers on the land? Who would invite me to sing?
	女： 不是邀请四方田， 不是去请田间花， 真诚邀哥把歌唱。	F: I don't invite the square fields, Nor invite the flowers on it, I sincerely invite you to sing.
66	男： 咋来请到远方客？ 拿啥好歌来相对？	M: Why invite a stranger? What songs should I sing with you?
	女： 真诚请到远方客， 让哥拿好歌相对。	F: Sincerely I'd invite a stranger like you, To sing lovely songs with me.
67	男： 妹请第一度， 哥突然心惊， 唱不依人美名扬。	M: For the first time you invite me, I was trembling with fear, Since I can't sing well as some others.
	女： 同请第一度， 哥心莫要惊， 哥早扬名人知晓。	F: For the first time I invite you, Don't be trembling with fear, You've been famous for singing long ago.
68	男： 唯哥穷理不知书， 对歌更不如人乖。	M: Poor in manners and cultivation, I'm poor in singing too.
	女： 阿哥知书又达理， 对歌真是乖不过。	F: Good in manners and cultivation, You're good in singing too.

69

男：
吾处喝雨水人笨，
哥处喝雾水嘴蠢，
不知何样是道理？

M:
Drinking rainwater and mist
Makes me clumsy and inarticulate,
I'm poor in manners and cultivation.

女：
哥饮井水显精灵，
哥饮甘泉人乖巧，
句句说到情理中。

F:
Drinking from the well of inspiration
Makes you clever and capable,
Every word you sing is reasonable.

70

男：
妹请第二度，
哥主意未通，
穷词穷理不识事。

M:
For the second time you invite me,
I haven't come up with the songs,
Since I'm poor in manners and words.

女：
同请第二度，
主意哥早有，
今夜妹才得沾光。

F:
For the second time I invite you,
You've come up with the songs,
To sing with me tonight.

71

男：
若哥有翅就飞走，
奈何是人难得算。

M:
I'd fly away if I have wings,
But it's a pity that I'm not a bird.

女：
哥似天鹅飞得高，
妹才回头托喜福。

F:
You can fly high as a swan,
So I can sing songs with you tonight.

72

男：
妹请第三度，
哥想请教妹两句。

M:
For the third time you invite me,
I have something to ask you.

女：
同请第三度，
不知哥问妹啥事？

F:
For the third time I invite you,
What do you want to ask me?

73

男：
哥还盘算没有通，
怕妹错路来恭请。

女：
请哥快点盘算好，
非得与妹唱一宿。

M:
I'm still wondering if I'm
The right person you want to invite.

F:
Don't bother about it anymore,
Please sing songs with me tonight.

74

男：
妹请第四度，
哥也焦急在心中，
哪来好歌同妹唱。

女：
同请第四度，
哥也早喜在心头，
我俩初次对山歌。

M:
For the fourth time you invite me,
I feel too anxious to come up
With good words to sing with you.

F:
For the fourth time I invite you,
You seem to be glad,
To sing songs with me too.

75

男：
怕人多嘴三两句，
到时我俩都难堪。

女：
此话哥莫愁，
两手抚心只管唱。

M:
I fear the gossip about us,
Which will make us embarrassed.

F:
Don't bother about that,
We sing with pure purpose.

76

男：
嫩鸟下地怕乌鸦，
似掠下田怕枪炮。

女：
妹想把鸭放进田，
有枪无弹莫胆怯。

M:
Little birds fear crow while standing,
Fear gunfire while flying onto the field.

F:
I put the ducks into the field,
Since the gun with no bullets.

77

男：
妹请第五度，
哥想说再会，
怕妹划船丢篙杆。

M:
For the fifth time you invite me,
I want to say goodbye to you,
Fearing you drop paddling pole while rafting.

女：
同请第五度，
不知哥说啥，
见水嬉戏想去游。

F:
For the fifth time I invite you,
I can't understand what you mean,
I just want to play with the stream.

78

男：
怕妹丢竹篙一旁，
那时开心不到头。

M:
If you drop the paddling pole aside,
Our happiness will end halfway.

女：
同渡海深志不移，
非乘纸船达彼岸。

F:
Determining to cross the sea with you,
I won't stop until we reach our goal.

79

男：
怕妹丢篙下深潭，
到时咱俩空欢喜。

M:
If you drop the pole into the pool,
Our happiness will be over.

女：
海深百丈妹还泗，
怕哥无心自松懈。

F:
I dive into the sea though it's rough,
So you can't relax in your efforts.

80

男：
妹请第六度，
哥却白奔无名气，
连来不如他人情。

M:
For the sixth time you invite me,
I wonder if I'm flogging a dead horse,
Since our relation isn't so close.

女：
同请第六度，
奔波非要出名气，
连来一定要留名。

F:
For the sixth time I invite you,
All you gain would deserve your efforts,
Our relation will become closer.

81

男： 夜雾日出通天变， 南蛇哪能变蛟龙？	**M:** Night mist disappears at the rise of the sun, How can a snake become a dragon?
女： 雨后日出变青天， 连来情意胜别人。	**F:** Sky turns blue with sunshine after the rain, Our relation will be more intimate than others.

82

男： 妹请第七度， 悯怜鸡鸭去觅虫， 边吃边瞧天上鹰。	**M:** For the seventh time you invite me, I'm like a chicken or duck, Under constant threat of the eagle.
女： 同请第七度， 犹如鸭鹅攀水坝， 共同往前闯逆流。	**F:** For the seventh time I invite you, We're like the duck and goose, Making their way upstream in climbing the dam.

83

男： 乌站山怕鹰， 鱼游水怕网， 月爬怕雾遮。	**M:** Crow fears eagle while standing, Fish fears fishing net while swimming, The moon fears fog while up climbing.
女： 关鸭鹰不拿， 关鸡鹰不抓， 我俩开心莫要怯。	**F:** Eagle won't seize the duck in a cage, Eagle won't catch the chicken in a cage, Let's follow our hearts without fear.

84

男： 妹请第八度， 他人烤暖早共台， 我俩来连不抵值。	**M:** For the eighth time you invite me, You've lived with someone else, It's no need to develop our relationship.
女： 同请第八度， 哪得烤暖共阳台， 妹也空望花而已。	**F:** For the eighth time I invite you, I haven't lived with anybody else, I'm still looking for the right suitor.

85

男：
别人早连才珍贵，
种蒲哪能结黄瓜？

M:
Treasuring old friends like you,
How can I become your new friend?

女：
他人早连才是乖，
妹来陪人赏月光。

F:
Other people have made friends,
I've been but an onlooker.

86

男：
他田进水得三番，
哥才初来会首次，
连来怕得罪他人。

M:
Others have watered the fields three times,
I've come here for the first time,
Being your friend may annoy others.

女：
旱田哪有人作主，
在哪有水上到田，
别怕得罪任何人。

F:
No one cares about my dry field,
No one has watered it,
You won't annoy anyone.

87

男：
妹请第九度，
他人早日吃扁米，
我俩留名来不得。

M:
For the ninth time you invite me,
Someone has already taken your meal.
How can I take a share from them?

女：
同请第九度，
相逢讨得空玩笑，
再说哪能掐芽尖。

F:
For the ninth time I invite you,
We can only make fun with each other,
But can't we become permanent lovers.

88

男：
扁米九月才有吃，
不是平常有摆卖。

M:
Bianmi is available only in September,
We can't buy it the other time.

女：
相逢讨歌唱一时，
想连一世哪里能。

F:
We can sing songs when once we meet,
But can't associate with each other forever.

89

男：	M:
妹请第十度， 犹如萤光园中闪， 反让他人瞧刺眼。	For the tenth time you invite me, I'm like the light of firefly in garden, Offending the others' eyes.
女：	F:
同请第十度， 犹如萤虫游山间， 相逢见花也白看。	For the ninth time I invite you, You're like the firefly flies in mountain, Having no interests in the flowers.

90

男：	M:
山中凤凰早结伴， 几时轮到哥享情？	Phoenixes have paired up in mountain, When can I get your love?
女：	F:
妹只借歌作交往， 几时依人情深厚？	I sing to make friends only, Not knowing when we become closer.

91

男：	M:
妹请十一度， 哥突然想起， 生怕遭人瞧刺眼。	For the eleventh time you invite me, I'm still wondering whether I'm the thorn in others' eyes.
女：	F:
同请十一度， 不知哥叹啥， 有心尽快诉出来。	For the eleventh time I invite you, I don't know why should you bother, Just go ahead if you want to.

92

男：	M:
日晴还怕天转阴， 到时交往不抵值。	I worry sunny day may turn gray, Our relationship may soon be put away.
女：	F:
日晴别忧天变阴， 怕哥无心急死人。	Don't worry sunny day to turn gray, What needs to worry is your hesitation.

93

男：	**M:**
天旱田峒被淹没， 下雨都被火烧山。	Field is drowned though it's drought, Mountain is fired though it rains.
女：	**F:**
天旱水淹田别怕， 火烧我俩一起救。	Not scared with the abnormal phenomena, Let's fight with them together.

94

男：	**M:**
妹请十二度， 阿哥急坏在心里， 我俩重情不结缘。	For the twelfth time you invite me, I'm still more anxious, We can't be together though admiring.
女：	**F:**
同请十二度， 哥应高兴又喜欢， 相逢必定结情缘。	For the twelfth time I invite you, You should be glad rather than anxious, We may certainly love each other.

95

男：	**M:**
蛇还脱麟能变身， 老牛变鹿想不得。	Snake can change itself by shedding skin, But a buffalo can never change into a deer.
女：	**F:**
有心不惧锅边走， 老牛还能攀山崖。	You can walk at pan edge if intend to, As old buffalo can climb up the cliff.

96

男：	**M:**
请妹还是返回家， 请娘还是回家好。	Dear girl, please go back your home, You'd better go back to your family.
女：	**F:**
唯妹缺舍无家归， 才来和哥对山歌。	I have no home to go back, So I sing songs with you.

97 男：
回去睡下醒醒眼，
明早去哪也容易。

M:
Go back to sleep to clear your head,
Tomorrow you can go wherever you want.

女：
去睡一会眼睛花，
与哥对歌好不过。

F:
Sleeping a while makes me dizzy,
To sing with you I feel easy.

98 男：
若妹不回又不走，
让哥该是如何好。

M:
If you don't go back home,
I feel troubled what to do.

女：
妹本不回也不散，
让哥领唱一套歌。

F:
I don't have to go back home,
Please lead me to sing a round.

99 男：
拿啥山歌来对妹？
唱啥山歌给妹听？

M:
What song should I sing with you?
What song should I sing for you?

女：
歌在嗓喉里，
放声它自来。

F:
Songs stay in your throat,
It'll come out if you want to.

100 男：
歌声连连起，
檬长叶连叶，
给哥开哪叶才是？

M:
Songs link up in chains,
As lemon leaves grow in branches,
What song should I sing for you?

女：
歌声连连起，
檬长叶连叶，
随哥开哪叶都行。

F:
Songs link up in chains,
As lemon leaves grow in branches.
You can start with any one.

101

男：
哪句唱在先？
哪句放在后？
哪句才合妹心情？

M:
Which words should be the first?
Which words are to follow?
Which song will be to your desire?

女：
这句唱在先，
该句放在后，
句句都合妹心情。

F:
These words should be the first.
Those words are to follow.
Whatever you sing will meet my desire.

102

男：
风吹左右刮，
何人来催吾对歌？

M:
Wind blows back and forth,
Who would urge me to sing songs?

女：
风直少横吹，
妹请郎哥来对唱。

F:
Wind blows back and forth,
I ask you to sing antiphonal songs.

103

男[①]：
犬仔初猎未精明，
獐印牛印不分辨。

M[①]:
Little dog isn't smart in first hunting,
It can't tell the footprints of deer from cattle.

女：
灵犬猎物早精明，
獐印牛印早分开。

F:
Talented dog is so smart in hunting,
It can tell the footprints of deer from cattle.

104

男：
犹如犬仔学打猎，
不会对山吼，
不会过山坳。

M:
As little dog can't hunt,
I can't sing over mountains,
I can't cross the cols.

女：
犹如大犬早会猎，
早会翻山吼，
早会过山坳。

F:
Like big dog skilled in hunting,
You're skilled in singing over mountains,
You're skilled in crossing cols.

---

① 103 到 106 节只能由未婚男女对唱。

① Stanzas 103 to 106 can be sung by unmarried young men and women only.

105

男：
不会吼过山，
不会起音随阿妹。

M:
I can't sing over mountains,
I can't sing to follow you.

女：
早会吼过山，
早会起音教阿妹。

F:
You can sing over mountains,
You can sing to enlighten me.

106

男：
三年不抓笔手僵，
五年不骑马眼花，
久不出声把歌忘。

M:
Hands stiff if not holding pen for three years,
Eyes dizzy if not riding horse for five years,
Songs forgotten if not singing for certain time.

女：
遍郡哥都吃过饭，
早就老练闻天下，
时时有歌在心头。

F:
You've visited many places,
And been well-known for singing,
You can sing whenever you desire.

换位： **Reverse:**

107

女：
三年不抓针手僵，
久不抓纺车花眼，
很久不唱忘掉歌。

F:
Hands stiff if not using needle for three years,
Eyes dizzy if not spinning for a long time,
Songs forgotten for not singing too long.

男：
妹拿织四二布梳，
早熟织布巧工艺，
随时开腔歌出口。

M:
You're skilled in spinning,
You can spin all kinds of cloth,
You can sing whenever you want.

还原：	Recovery：

108

男： 鹰住山忘树， 鸡进圈忘笼， 哥到大庄忘记歌。	M: Eagle forgets trees while in mountain, Chicken forgets cage while in hen-house, I forget songs while in big village.
女： 鹰住山惦树， 鸡进圈惦笼， 哥到穷村记得歌。	F: Eagle misses trees while in mountain, Chicken misses cage while in hen-house, You remember songs while in poor village.

109

男： 猴吃多树果忘枝， 鱼吃多滩水忘潭， 拿啥来和妹开心？	M: Monkey forgets branches while eating fruits, Fish forgets pool while drinking water, How can I offer to make you happy?
女： 猴吃多树果记枝， 鱼吃多滩水记潭， 唱歌来对妹开心。	F: Monkey remembers branches while eating fruits, Fish remembers pool while drinking water, Singing with me will make me happy.

110

男： 让哥怎么办？ 哥该如何好？ 要啥当歌来对妹？	M: What should I do? Where should I begin? What can I sing to please you?
女： 歌有三筒黑芝麻， 歌有八筒芝麻籽， 拿它当歌对阿妹。	F: Your songs are like three tubes of black sesame, Your songs equal to eight tubes of sesame seeds, You can sing them with me.

111

男： 歌哥放在饭桌上， 歌哥放在酒桌间。	M: I've put songs on dinning table, I've put songs on wine table.
女： 歌哥在喉嗓， 歌哥藏肚里。	F: You've put songs in your throat, You've put songs in your chest.

112
男：
歌放席桌不得携，
歌放书桌旁没带。

M:
I haven't brought the songs on dinning table,
And the songs on reading table.

女：
歌放席桌记得携，
歌放书桌记得带。

F:
You've brought the songs on dinning table,
And the songs on reading table.

113
男：
歌放地棚不肯来，
歌放田棚不肯跟。

M:
The songs in the shed wouldn't come,
The songs in the field wouldn't follow.

女：
歌放地棚也跟来，
歌放田棚随身到。

F:
The songs in the shed are to come,
The songs in the field would follow.

114
男：
歌去练马已忘记，
歌去驯牛已迭光。

M:
I've forgotten songs while training horse,
I've lost songs while training buffalo.

女：
歌去练马没忘记，
歌去驯牛没有迭。

F:
You haven't forgotten songs while training horse,
You haven't lost songs while training buffalo.

115
男：
迭不迭何方，
偏迭水坝口。

M:
The songs lost nowhere,
But the mouth of dam.

女：
迭不迭何方，
捡得在河坝。

F:
Wherever the songs lost,
They're picked up at the dam.

116
男：
水卷到深潭，
拿啥来和妹开心？

M:
Songs are inhaled into deep pond,
What can I sing with you?

女：
水旋卷不着，
才有歌和妹开心。

F:
Songs aren't inhaled into deep pond,
You can sing them with me.

换位：	Reverse：
117 女： 歌妹放在菜篮里， 妹妈中餐当菜吃。	F: I've put the songs in basket, My mother has eaten them for lunch.
男： 歌妹放在菜篮里， 妹妈中餐捡得它。	M: You've put the songs in basket, Your mother has picked them up at lunch.
118 女： 歌妹放在碗柜下， 妈到晌午当菜吃。	F: I've put the songs under cupboard, My mother has eaten them at noon.
男： 歌妹放在碗柜下， 妈到晌午帮妹收。	M: You've put the songs under cupboard, Your mother has picked them up at noon.
119 女： 歌妹放在竹楼下， 妈到晚餐吃完了。	F: I've put the songs in bamboo building, My mother has eaten them for dinner.
男： 歌妹放在竹楼下， 妈到晚餐帮妹留。	M: You've put the songs in bamboo building, Your mother has picked them up at dinner.
120 女： 歌妹放在晒台上， 鸡刮迭下晒台脚。	F: I've put the songs on veranda, The chicken has kicked them away.
男： 歌妹放在晒台上， 鸡刮晒台迭不远。	M: You've put the song on veranda, The chicken hasn't kicked them far away.

还原：	Recovery:

121

男： 迭不迭何处， 迭路被牛踩。	M: The songs lost nowhere, But under the feet of buffalo.
女： 迭不迭何处， 路上被捡得。	F: Wherever the songs lost, They're picked up on the road.

122

男： 哥来爬陡走山路， 海深莫测无船舟。	M: No ship to cross deep sea, I have to climb the steep mountain.
女： 妹住一世也无悔， 哥来一时莫怨烦。	F: I never regret living here for a lifetime, Don't complain for staying a short time.

123

男： 砍柴拼往麻风林， 蚁蛰脚板步难行。	M: I cleave a path to Jatropha forest, But can't walk since ants sting my soles.
女： 蚂蚁叮别愁， 箭射心头才惊怯。	F: Don't worry about the ants, More terrifying is the arrow.

124

男： 让哥怎么办？ 去哪要歌来对妹？	M: What should I do now? Where can I get songs to sing with you?
女： 请哥慢思量， 想好歌自来。	F: Just take your time to consider, You'll come up with songs to sing with me.

125

男：
哥从底脚来，
遇上磐石坡。

M:
I come from the lower class,
And come across a rock slope.

女：
哥从底脚来，
少遇磐石坡。

F:
You come from the lower class,
And don't come across a rock slope.

126

男：
碰上理石娘，
来遇造歌女。

M:
I come across a pretty girl,
Who is good at singing.

女：
少遇理石娘，
不遇造歌女。

F:
You come across a girl,
Who isn't good at singing.

127

男：
该遇却不遇，
偏遇铁矿娘，
却遇阿妹造歌女。

M:
Really out of my expectation,
I should meet with a girl,
Who outweighs me at singing.

女：
矢的不对接，
少遇铁石娘，
却遇妹是穷歌女。

F:
Really out of your expectation,
You should meet with me,
Who is poor in singing.

128

男：
该遇却不遇，
偏遇黑矿娘，
却遇乖妹造歌女。

M:
Really out of my expectation,
I should meet with a pretty girl,
Who outweighs me at singing.

女：
该遇却不遇，
不遇黑矿娘，
却遇丑妹无歌女。

F:
Really out of your expectation,
You should meet with a plain girl,
Who is poor in singing.

129

男：
本遇却不遇，
偏遇红石娘，
偏遇造歌千金女。

女：
本遇却不遇，
难遇红石娘，
难遇造歌千金女。

M:
Really out of my expectation,
I should meet with a rich girl,
Who outweighs me at singing.

F:
Really out of your expectation,
You didn't meet with a rich girl,
But one who is poor in singing.

130

男：
本遇却不遇，
偏遇晶矿娘，
却遇靓妹造歌女。

女：
本遇却不遇，
难遇晶矿娘，
难遇造歌女。

M:
Really out of my expectation,
I should meet a song creator,
Who outweighs me at singing.

F:
Really out of your expectation,
You didn't meet a song creator,
But a girl poor in singing.

131

男：
矢的不对接，
偏遇花石娘，
遇对乖妹造歌女。

女：
矢的不对接，
难遇花石娘，
难遇有女造山歌。

M:
Really out of my expectation,
I should meet with a smart girl,
Who outweighs me at singing.

F:
Really out of your expectation,
You didn't meet with a smart girl,
But one who is poor in singing.

132

男：
该遇却不遇，
偏遇青石娘，
却遇扬名造歌女。

女：
该遇却不遇，
难遇青石娘，
难遇扬名造歌女。

M:
Really out of my expectation,
I should meet with a famous girl,
Who outweighs me at singing.

F:
Really out of your expectation,
You didn't meet with a famous girl,
But one who is poor in singing.

133

男：	M:
行路哥赞路，	I praise the roads walking on the roads,
行路哥赞道，	I praise the street while on the street,
赞初升红日。	I praise the rising sun.
女：	F:
行路同赞路，	I praise the roads walking on the roads,
行路同赞道，	I praise the street while on the street,
随哥同赞新太阳。	Let's praise the rising sun together.

134

男：	M:
吵烦屋下三岔路，	Bring trouble to the fork roads,
吵烦寨下环山道。	And the ring roads.
女：	F:
不烦屋下三岔路，	Bring no trouble to the fork roads,
不烦寨下环山道。	And the ring roads.

135

男：	M:
赞弯田环坡，	I praise the curved fields encircling the hill,
赞曲田绕寨。	And the curved fields encircling village.
女：	F:
同赞弯田环山坡，	I praise the curved fields encircling the hill,
同赞曲田绕村寨。	And the curved fields encircling village.

136

男：	M:
哥来问妹一话语，	Let me ask you a word,
哥来问妹一道题。	Let me ask you a question.
女：	F:
不知哥问哪一句？	What word would you like to ask?
不晓还问哪一题？	What question would you like to ask?

137

男：
什么环坡当弯田？
何是曲田绕山庄？

M:
What's like the curved fields encircling the hill?
What's like the curved fields encircling village?

女：
河流环坡像弯田，
路为曲田绕山庄。

F:
The river is like the curved fields encircling hill,
The road is like the curved fields encircling village.

138

男：
三十岭折叠，
什么过中间？
想到解给哥一句。

M:
There are so many mountains,
What link them together?
Please tell me if you know the answer.

女：
三十岭折叠，
山路过中间，
想到妹乱答。

F:
There are so many mountains,
The roads link them together,
I don't know if the answer proper.

139

男：
三十路折叠，
什么过中间？
记得妹快说。

M:
There are so many roads,
What hinders them now and again?
Please tell me if you remember.

女：
三十路折叠，
河流过中间，
记得妹就说。

F:
There are so many roads,
The rivers hinder them now and again,
I give the answer since I remember.

140

男：
三十河折叠，
什么过中间？
请阿妹解给。

M:
There are so many rivers,
What link the roads together?
Please tell me the answer.

女：
三十河折叠，
桥梁跨中间，
哥请到妹乱解答。

F:
There are so many rivers,
The bridges link the roads together,
Maybe I give the wrong answer.

141

男：
三十桥折叠，
什么过中间？
不知妹还记得起？

M:
There are so many bridges,
What go thru under the bridges?
Do you still remember?

女：
三十桥折叠，
船舟过中间，
不知哥看中不中？

F:
There are so many bridges,
The boats go thru under the bridges,
Is it the right answer?

142

男：
三十船折叠，
什么过中间？
记得再答哥一题。

M:
There are so many boats,
What push them back and forth?
Please tell me if you remember.

女：
三十船折叠，
摇浆在中间，
是否称心不称心？

F:
There are so many boats,
The oars push them back and forth,
Are you satisfied with the answer?

143

男：
哥从底脚来，
来碰猴吃果。

M:
I come from the lower class,
With a vain hope to see monkey eating fruits.

女：
哥从底脚来，
难碰猴吃果。

F:
You come from the lower class,
Hard for you to see monkey eating fruits.

144 男：
碰水獭溺鱼，
碰到异地花。

M:
With a vain hope to see otter killing fish,
And a strange flower.

女：
没水獭溺鱼，
难碰异地花。

F:
You don't come across an otter killing fish,
And a strange flower.

145 男：
来碰马打滚，
碰童孩挑水。

M:
With a vain hope to see horse rolling on ground,
And a little child carrying water.

女：
少碰马打滚，
少遇童挑水。

F:
Hard for you to see horse rolling on ground,
Or little child carrying water.

146 男：
吵烦水井供人喝，
吵烦清池供浴游。

M:
Bring trouble to the well to supply water,
And the pool for people to wash.

女：
少烦水井供人饮，
少烦清池供人浴。

F:
Bring no trouble to the well to supply water,
And the pool for people to wash.

147 男：
井水供饮食，
有乖妹浆衣。

M:
The well supplies people with water,
A smart girl starches clothes beside it.

女：
井水供饮食，
缺乖妹浆衣。

F:
The well supplies people with water,
No clever girl starches clothes beside it.

148

男：	**M:**
丁喝脸嫩白，	After drinking, man's face turns fairer,
伊喝面红绯。	Woman's face turns crimson.
女：	**F:**
丁喝脸白嫩，	After drinking, man's face turns fairer,
伊喝面红绯。	Woman's face turns crimson.

149

男：	**M:**
官喝官理事，	Officials fulfill their duties well drinking from it,
皇喝皇治国。	The emperor governs the country well.
女：	**F:**
官喝来理事，	Officials fulfill their duties well drinking from it,
皇喝来治国。	The emperor governs the country well.

150

男：	**M:**
童喝童聪明，	The children become clever,
人人上京去读书。	And have further study in the capital city.
女：	**F:**
童喝童聪明，	The children become clever,
一同上京去读书。	And have further study in the capital city.

151

男：	**M:**
翁喝翁长寿，	Old men live longer drinking the water,
咱饮咱安康。	We live more healthy with the water.
女：	**F:**
翁喝翁长寿，	Old men live longer drinking the water,
咱饮共安康。	We live more healthy with the water.

152

男：
客喝不想归，
姻喝不想回。

M:
The water makes guests and friends
Not want to go back.

女：
姻喝不想回，
甘愿攀契待一辈。

F:
The friends don't want to go back,
Willing to claim kinship to stay a lifetime.

153

男：
鱼水两头挑，
花歌两头担。

M:
Fish and water are carried on two ends,
Songs and flowers are carried by a shoulder-pole.

女：
两头穷鱼水，
花歌空两头。

F:
There aren't fish and water on either end,
There aren't songs and flowers on shoulder-pole.

154

男：
水桶拿什么来遮？
鱼桶用什么来盖？

M:
What's to cover the water bucket?
What's to cover the fish bucket?

女：
水桶一头树枝遮，
鱼桶那头水草盖。

F:
Water bucket is covered by tree branches,
Fish bucket is covered by waterweeds.

155

男：
哥从底脚来，
遇八面山峰。

M:
I come from the lower class,
To see a huge mountain.

女：
哥从底脚来，
少遇八面山。

F:
You come from the lower class,
But can't see a huge mountain.

156

男：	**M:**
来哥再问妹两语，	Let me ask you more words,
来哥再盘妹两题。	Let me ask you more questions.
女：	**F:**
不知哥要问妹啥？	What words would you like to ask?
不知哥要问哪样？	What questions would you like to ask?

157

男：	**M:**
八面妹要哪面应，	The mountain is so huge,
山峰妹要哪峰来。	Which side have you come from?
女：	**F:**
八面妹要左面应，	The mountain is so huge,
山峦妹要右峰来。	I've come from the left side.

158

男：	**M:**
何做八面对眼前？	What looks huge before us?
何做山峰面对面？	What are face to face?
女：	**F:**
神庙八面对眼前，	The temple looks huge before us,
神宇当峰面对面。	The temples are face to face①.

159

男：	**M:**
神庙名什么？	What's the name of the temple?
神宇何姓氏？	What's the name of the god?
女：	**F:**
神庙是姓梁，	The temple's surname is Liang,
神公是李氏。	The god's surname is Li.

① In Zhuang's village, there is one temple at either end. Traditionally, these two temples are built face to face.

160

男：
神庙拿啥子来遮？
神公拿什么来盖？

M:
What to cover the temple?
What to cover the god?

女：
神庙拿绿绸来遮，
神公拿花缎来盖。

F:
The temple is covered by green silk,
The god is covered by colored satin.

161

男：
神庙吃什么当餐，
神公吃什么当饭？

M:
What does the temple have as food?
What does the god have as food?

女：
神庙吃荤味当餐，
神公吃香火当饭。

F:
The temple has meats as food,
The god has burning incense as food.

162

男：
吵烦神庙佑方圆，
吵烦神公佑村寨。

M:
Bring trouble to the neighborhood temple,
And the god to bless the village.

女：
不烦神庙佑方圆，
不烦神公佑村寨。

F:
Bring no trouble to the neighborhood temple,
Or the god to bless the village.

163

男：
佑三千瓦房，
佑五万砖屋，
佑天下兴旺。

M:
Bless all the tile-roofed houses,
And bricked buildings,
Bless the world prosperous.

女：
同佑三千大瓦房，
同佑砖屋五万座，
同佑天下齐兴旺。

F:
Bless all the tile-roofed houses,
And bricked buildings,
Bless the world prosperous.

164

男：	**M:**
佑子孙繁衍，	Bless children for growing up quickly,
佑老人长寿，	The elder to live longer,
佑我俩安康。	And us both for health.
女：	**F:**
同佑子孙得繁衍，	Bless children for growing up quickly,
同佑老人得长寿，	The elder to live longer,
同佑我俩得安康。	And us both for health.

165

男：	**M:**
佑左侧猪犬，	Bless dogs and pigs on the left,
佑右侧鸡鸭。	And ducks and chicken on the right.
女：	**F:**
同佑左侧猪犬兴，	Bless dogs and pigs on the left,
同佑右侧鸡鸭旺。	And ducks and chicken on the right.

166

男：	**M:**
佑米粮满仓，	Bless the barns filled with grains,
佑金钱满柜。	And the money-lockers filled with money.
女：	**F:**
同佑米粮堆满仓，	Bless the barns filled with rice,
同佑金钱装满柜。	And the money-lockers filled with money.

167

男：	**M:**
佑鸡鸭满舍，	Bless the sheds full of ducks and chicken,
佑牛马满栏。	And the stables full of horses and buffaloes.
女：	**F:**
鸡鸭共满舍，	Bless the sheds full of ducks and chicken,
牛马同满栏。	And the stables full of horses and buffaloes.

168 男：
吵烦庙旁老神树，
吵烦村头老古榕。

M:
Bring trouble to the sacred tree beside temple,
And the old banyan tree at village entrance.

女：
不烦庙旁老神树，
不烦村头老古榕。

F:
Bring no trouble to the sacred tree beside temple,
Or the old banyan tree at village entrance.

169 男：
烦枝荣柠檬树，
烦叶茂柑橘林。

M:
Bring trouble to the flourished lemon tree,
And the orange grove with rich leaves.

女：
不烦枝荣柠檬树，
不烦叶茂柑橘林。

F:
Bring no trouble to the flourished lemon tree,
Or the orange grove with rich leaves.

170 男：
进寨哥赞寨，
进寨赞山村，
进村赞父老。

M:
I praise the village,
And the senior villagers,
When getting into the village.

女：
进寨同赞寨，
共同赞山村，
进村同赞众父老。

F:
We praise the village,
And the senior villagers,
When getting into the village.

171 男：
吵烦三千大瓦房，
吵烦砖屋五万座，
让哥流浪汉投宿。

M:
Bring trouble to the tile-roofed houses,
And the bricked buildings,
To accommodate a wanderer like me.

女：
不烦三千户瓦房，
不烦茅屋五万座，
若哥不嫌就投宿。

F:
Bring no trouble to the tile-roofed houses,
Nor to the bricked buildings,
Please stay up if you don't mind.

172

男：	**M:**
烦到河上风雨桥，	Bring trouble to the wind-rain bridge,
烦到亭榭共一殿。	And the pavilion.
女：	**F:**
不烦河上风雨桥，	Bring no trouble to the wind-rain bridge,
不烦到亭燕殿堂。	Nor to the pavilion.

173

男：	**M:**
烦到屋前李果树，	Bring trouble to the plum tree before house,
烦到窗外莎树梢。	And the grapefruit tree outside the window.
女：	**F:**
不烦到李树台阶，	Bring no trouble to the steps under plum tree,
不烦到桐树神台。	Nor to the altar beside tung tree.

174

男：	**M:**
烦到喂猪坪地头，	Bring trouble to the fields and the gates,
烦到喂鸡大门口。	Where pigs and chicken are fed.
女：	**F:**
不烦到寨道喂猪，	Bring no trouble to the roads and the steps,
不烦到台阶喂鸡。	Where pigs and chicken are fed.

175

男：	**M:**
何过楼脚不留痕？	What passes the pavilion without sound?
何过台下不留印？	What passes the pavilion without trace?
女：	**F:**
陈雾过亭榭无声，	Mist passes the pavilion without sound,
台风过亭浅无印。	Typhoon passes the pavilion without trace.

176 男：
烦到鸭笼编得密，
烦到养鸡金竹笼，
烦到牛栏白花木。

M:
Bring trouble to the firmly-made duck shed,
The bamboo hencoop,
And the wooden cattle pen.

女：
不烦鸭笼编得巧，
不烦养鸡金竹笼，
不烦牛栏白花木。

F:
Bring no trouble to the firmly-made duck shed,
And the bamboo hencoop,
Nor to the wooden cattle pen.

177 男：
何在楼脚穿铁鞋？
何在屋下穿破裙？

M:
What wears iron shoes downstairs?
What wears broken skirt downstairs?

女：
犁在楼脚穿铁鞋，
耙在屋下穿破裙。

F:
Plough wears iron shoes downstairs,
Harrow wears broken skirt downstairs.

178 男：
何在楼脚陪伴牛？
何在楼下陪伴鸡？

M:
What accompany cattle downstairs?
What accompany chicken downstairs?

女：
石墩伴牛住楼脚，
牛屎伴鸡在楼下。

F:
Stone seat accompanies cattle downstairs,
Bullshit accompanies chicken downstairs.

179 男：
何在楼脚戴冠帽？
何在园中撑雨伞？

M:
What wears a cap downstairs?
What holds umbrella in the yard?

女：
鸡罩戴冠在楼脚，
棕树园中撑雨伞。

F:
Chicken cover wears a cap downstairs,
Palm tree holds umbrella in the yard.

180

男：	M:
烦到米臼黑杉木，	Bring trouble to the fir-made rice mortar,
烦到谷槽灰杉做，	The fir-made rice manger,
烦到木梯七台阶。	And the seven-step wooden ladder.
女：	F:
不烦米臼黑杉木，	Bring no trouble to the fir-made rice mortar,
不烦谷槽灰杉做，	And the fir-made rice manger,
不烦木梯七台阶。	Nor to the seven-step wooden ladder.

181

男：	M:
烦到晒杆晾布衣，	Bring trouble to the poles drying clothes,
烦到阳台晒谷粮。	And the veranda drying grains.
女：	F:
不烦晒杆晾布衣，	Bring no trouble to the poles drying clothes,
不烦阳台晒谷粮。	Or to the veranda to dry grains.

182

男：	M:
黑衣晒篱梢，	Insolate the black clothes on fence,
蓝衣晒阳台，	The blue clothes on veranda.
妹去夫家还是在？	Will you stay here or go back home?
女：	F:
黑衣晒篱梢，	Insolate the black clothes on fence,
蓝衣晒阳台，	The blue clothes on veranda.
妹无夫家还留守。	I'll stay here since I have no husband.

183

男：	M:
若在借机想交往，	I want to make friends with you,
晓她是否还念情？	But will you accept my admiration?
女：	F:
妹本惦哥不断时，	I'm missing you all the time,
怕哥忘妹想她人。	But you may forget me very soon.

184 男：
进门哥赞门，
进门赞正堂。

M:
I praise the gate and the parlor,
When I come in the household.

女：
进门同赞门，
共同赞正堂。

F:
I praise the gate and the parlor,
When I come in the household.

185 男：
门框三天架，
门扇九天合，
边合边书画，
真是巧匠造门神。

M:
Doorframes are set in three days,
Door sheets are set in nine days,
Designs are drawn at the same time,
The door-gods are made by skillful craftsman.

女：
门框三天架，
门扇九天合，
边合边书画，
来日发财托鸿福。

F:
Doorframes are set in three days,
Door sheets are set in nine days,
Designs are drawn at the same time,
The door-gods will bring good fortune.

186 男：
门板画凤凰会飞，
门脚雕麒麟会行。

M:
Phoenix drew on door sheets can fly,
Kylin crafted on door-feet can walk.

女：
门板画凤凰会飞，
门脚雕麒麟同行。

F:
Phoenix drew on door sheets can fly,
Kylin crafted on door-feet can walk.

187 男：
进门哥赞门，
进门赞对联。

M:
I praise the gate and the couplet,
When I come into the household.

女：
进门同赞门，
进门赞对联。

F:
I praise the gate and the couplet,
When I come into the homestead.

188

男：
对联是谁书？
神符是谁画？

M:
Who wrote the couplet?
Who drew the hierogram?

女：
对联道公书，
神符师公画。

F:
The priest wrote the couplet,
The master drew the hierogram.

189

男：
对联怎么写？
请妹巧嘴念出来。

M:
How to read the couplet?
Can you read it out?

女：
田堂地土写左边，
文武秀才是右联。
不知是否合哥意？

F:
Tian Tang Di Tu on the left,
Wen Wu Xiao Cai on the right.
Do you think the couplet nice?

190

男：
扰到大门红对联，
扰到龛台黄神符。

M:
Sorry to bother the red couplet on the door,
And the yellow hierogram on the shrine.

女：
同扰大门红对联，
同扰龛台黄神符。

F:
Sorry to bother the red couplet on the door,
And the yellow hierogram on the shrine.

191

男：
进屋哥赞家，
进家赞祖先。

M:
I praise house and the ancestors,
When I come into the hall.

女：
进屋同赞家，
共同赞祖先。

F:
We praise home and the ancestors,
When we come into the hall.

192 男：
扰到台右列祖宗，
扰到台左圣母娘。

M:
Sorry to bother the ancestors on the left,
And the Mother God on the right of shrine.

女：
同扰台右列祖宗，
同扰台左圣母娘。

F:
Sorry to bother the ancestors on the left,
And the Mother God on the right of shrine.

193 男：
扰到米筒盛得平，
扰到流连绕上天。

M:
Sorry to bother the censer,
And the incense winding up to the sky.

女：
同扰米筒盛得平，
同扰流连绕上天。

F:
Sorry to bother the censer,
And the incense winding up to the sky.

194 男：
何为米筒盛得平，
何做流连绕上天？

M:
Why is the rice tube precise?
Why does the incense wind up to the sky?

女：
米筒盛平为香炉，
香霭流连绕上天。

F:
The rice tube is traditionally precise,
Incense brings fragrance to the sky.

195 男：
石上何发芽？
什么原地长？

M:
What sprouts on the stone?
What grows up from the original place?

女：
香炉石上萌，
香火原地长。

F:
Censer sprouts on the stone,
Incense grows up from the original place.

196

男：
何穿棉袄到年头？
何穿长袍一辈子？

M:
What wears padded jacket all year?
What wears long gown all life?

女：
利是穿袄到年头，
对联穿袍一辈子。

F:
Lucky money wears padded jacket all year,
Couplet wears long gown all life.

197

男：
何在龛前吃乌果？
何在楼上当明镜？

M:
What eats black fruit[①] before altar?
What looks like round mirror upstairs?

女：
油灯龛前吃黑果，
楼上蜘网像镜圆。

F:
Oil lamp eats black fruit before altar,
Spider web looks like round mirror upstairs.

198

男：
打扰房中杨莓柱，
打扰家中父和母，
让异地哥来讨宿。

M:
Sorry to bother the waxberry pillar,
And the parents at home,
To allow a stranger to stay put.

女：
少扰房中杨莓柱，
少扰家中老父母，
同是异乡来讨宿。

F:
You haven't bothered the waxberry pillar,
Or the parents at home,
It's usual for a stranger to stay put.

199

男：
打扰房中红栗柱，
打扰家中好大哥，
让异地哥来讨宿。

M:
Sorry to bother the chestnut pillar,
And the elder-brother at home,
To allow a stranger to stay put.

女：
少扰房中红栗柱，
少扰家中好大哥，
同是异乡来讨宿。

F:
You haven't bothered the chestnut pillar,
Or the elder-brother at home,
It's usual for a stranger to stay put.

---

① Black fruit can make teeth black. Zhuang people used to consider black teeth pretty.

200

男：
打扰房中紫杉柱，
打扰家中好大姐，
让异乡哥来借宿。

M:
Sorry to bother the yew pillar,
And the elder-sister at home,
To allow a stranger to stay up.

女：
少扰房中紫杉柱，
少扰家中好大姐，
同是异乡来借宿。

F:
You haven't bothered the yew pillar,
Or the elder-sister at home,
It's usual for a stranger to stay put.

201

男：
打扰房中白花柱，
打扰家中好大嫂，
让异乡哥来借宿。

M:
Sorry to bother the tung pillar,
And the sister-in-law at home,
To allow a stranger to stay up.

女：
少扰房中白花柱，
少扰家中好大嫂，
同是异乡来借宿。

F:
You haven't bothered the tung pillar,
Or the sister-in-law at home,
It's usual for a stranger to stay put.

202

男：
打扰屋中冬瓜柱，
打扰聪明小孩童，
哪天赔还重恩情。

M:
Sorry to bother the big pillar,
And the little smart children,
I'll repay their favor one day.

女：
少扰屋中冬瓜柱，
少扰聪明小孩童，
哪天共还重恩情。

F:
You haven't bothered the big pillar,
Or the little smart children,
Let's repay their favor one day.

203

男：
打扰四脚木板凳，
客来会接待。

M:
Sorry to bother the benches,
Which provide service to guests.

女：
少扰四脚木凳子，
客来同招待。

F:
It doesn't bother the benches,
For they would provide service to all guests.

204

男：
打扰火边水烟筒，
好客来自待。

M:
Sorry to bother the water pipe by fire,
For it offer me a smoke.

女：
不扰火边水烟筒，
好客来同待。

F:
It doesn't bother the water pipe by fire,
For it'd offer smoke to all guests.

205

男：
何嘴对嘴笑起来？
什么着火哭出声？

M:
What will laugh while in mouth?
What will cry if on fire?

女：
烟筒对嘴笑起来，
烟头着火哭出声。

F:
Water pipe will laugh while in mouth,
Cigarette butt will cry if on fire.

206

男：
打扰那块四方田，
打扰那朵中间花，
打扰外围护栏杆。

M:
Sorry to bother the square field,
The flower in the middle,
And the fence outside.

女：
少扰那块四方田，
少扰那朵中间花，
少扰外围护栏杆。

F:
You haven't bothered the square field,
The flower in the middle,
Or the fence outside.

207

男：
何是那块四方田？
何是花朵绽中间？
请妹解给哥。

M:
What's the square field?
What's the flower in the middle?
Can you tell me?

女：
火边像块四方田，
火堆像花绽中间，
不知是否合哥意？

F:
The square field is the fireplace,
The fire is the flower in the middle,
Does the answer meet your inquiry?

208 男：
打扰弄场无茅草，
打扰高山无树林。

M:
Sorry to bother the ground with no grass,
And the mountain with no trees.

女：
少扰弄场无茅草，
少扰高山无树林。

F:
You haven't bothered the ground with no grass,
Or the mountain with no trees.

209 男：
何做弄场无茅草？
何做高山无树林？

M:
What's the ground with no grass?
What's the mountain with no trees?

女：
火灶当弄无茅草，
锅底当山无树林。

F:
Hearth is the ground with no grass,
Pan's bottom is the mountain with no trees.

210 男：
打扰火旁泥鳅鱼，
打扰炉边老黄鳝。

M:
Sorry to bother the loach by fire,
And the eel by stove.

女：
少扰火旁泥鳅鱼，
少扰炉边老黄鳝。

F:
You haven't bothered the loach by fire,
Nor the eel by stove.

211 男：
何当火旁泥鳅鱼？
何当炉边老黄鳝？

M:
What's like the loach by fire?
What's like the eel by stove?

女：
火蔸盖灰像泥鳅，
炉边火钳像黄鳝。

F:
Upheaval ashes are like the loach，
Fire tongs look like eels.

212

男：
打扰卷睡小婴儿，
打扰灶口那匹骡。

M:
Sorry to bother the baby curled up sleeping,
And the mule by the kitchen range.

女：
少扰卷睡小婴儿，
少扰灶口那匹骡。

F:
You haven't bothered the baby curled up sleeping,
Or the mule by the kitchen range.

213

男：
何做婴儿卷着睡？
何做骡子守灶旁？

M:
What's like baby curled up sleeping?
What's like mule guarding kitchen range.

女：
猫做婴儿卷着睡，
酒壶当骡守灶旁。

F:
The cat is like baby curled up sleeping,
Wine jug is like mule guarding kitchen range.

214

男：
打扰平口炒菜锅，
打扰火灶三脚卯。

M:
Sorry to bother the pan,
And the trivet.

女：
少扰平口炒菜锅，
少扰火灶三脚卯。

F:
You haven't bothered the pan,
And the trivet.

215

男：
何在锅口长尾巴？
何在缸口长出角？

M:
What makes a tail on the pan?
What makes a horn on the water tank?

女：
锅铲长尾架锅边，
水瓢长角露缸口。

F:
Pancake turner makes a tail on the pan.
Baler makes a horn on the water tank.

216

男：	**M:**
打扰悬挂马蜂窝，	Sorry to bother the hanging hornets' nest,
打扰悬吊黄蜂巢。	And the hanging wasps' nest.
女：	**F:**
少扰悬挂马蜂窝，	You haven't bothered the hanging hornets' nest,
少扰悬吊黄蜂巢。	Nor the hanging wasps' nest.

217

男：	**M:**
何做悬挂马蜂窝？	What's like the hanging hornets' nest?
何做悬吊黄蜂巢？	What's like the hanging wasps' nest?
女：	**F:**
盐罐悬似马蜂窝，	Salt shaker hangs like hornets' nest,
油坛吊像黄蜂巢。	Oil jar hangs like wasps' nest.

218

男：	**M:**
什么白像铅？	What's as white as lead?
什么耀像银？	What's dazzling as silver?
成吃种不长。	They're eatable but can't be grown.
女：	**F:**
油粒白像铅，	Lard is white as lead,
盐粒耀像银，	Salt is dazzling as silver,
成吃种不长。	They're eatable but can't be grown.

219

男：	**M:**
什么来放菜会死？	What will make vegetable die?
什么放多菜会蔫？	What will make vegetable droop?
女：	**F:**
盐巴来放菜会死，	Salt will make vegetable die,
油来放多菜会蔫。	Lard will make vegetable droop.

220

男： 打扰房屋四柱家， 打扰房舍四角楼。	M: Sorry to bother the four-pillar house, And the quadrangular building.
女： 少扰房屋四柱家， 少扰房舍四角楼。	F: You haven't bothered the four-pillar house, Or the quadrangular building.

221

男： 何做房屋四柱家？ 何做房间四角楼？	M: What's like the four-pillar house? What's like the quadrangular building?
女： 碗柜像屋四柱家， 又像房舍四角楼。	F: Cupboard is like the four-pillar house, And the quadrangular building too.

222

男： 谢谢妹嘴巧， 谜意多深会揭底。	M: Thanks for your smart tongue, To speak out answers to all riddles.
女： 笨嘴莫要谢， 不知是否对一题？	F: Don't thank for my stupid mouth, Did I give the proper answer?

223

男： 谢妹得歌甜心里， 谢得蜜语暖心房。	M: Thanks for your songs and sweet words, I feel warm in my heart.
女： 望是不合就别要， 要去我俩坏名声。	F: Don't take them if they're wrong answers, Or it'll ruin our reputation.

224

男： 不谢却妹嘴金贵， 死里卖力去顶债。	M: You have noble mouth for songs, I'd try my best to popularize them.
女： 差歌不成夸， 俗语不成谢。	F: Poor songs and common words Aren't worth praises and thanks.

225 男：
天下唯妹是巧嘴，
死里卖牛去赎回。

M:
You have smooth tongue,
It's worth millions of thanks.

女：
谢来妹丑脸，
谢多妹害羞。

F:
Too much thanks will
Make me shy and coy.

226 男：
不谢却妹言语精，
谜寓深远解得准。

M:
Thanks for your clever tongue,
To answer the riddles correctly.

女：
谢来阿哥费乖嘴，
谢来损哥费甜言。

F:
Too much thanks will
Waste your words and time.

227 男：
怨哥知理也不多，
谢把两句来敷衍。

M:
As poor as I'm in manners,
I can't say more to thank you.

女：
少谢人说乖，
谢多人说笨。

F:
It's smart to say a little,
Saying too much may seem silly.

228 男：
扰到花碗黑亮筷，
扰到茶盆画凤凰。

M:
Sorry to bother printed bowls and chopsticks,
And the phoenix-patterned tea trays.

女：
少扰花碗黑亮筷，
少扰茶盆画凤凰。

F:
You haven't bothered the bowls or chopsticks,
Nor the phoenix-patterned tea trays.

229 男：
扰到饭桌早晚用，
扰到酒桌待贵宾。

M:
Sorry to bother the daily-used dinning table,
And the entertaining dinner table.

女：
少扰饭桌早晚用，
少扰酒桌待贵宾。

F:
You haven't bothered the daily-used dinning table,
Nor the entertaining dinner table.

230

男：
扰到卧室四四方，
扰到床铺有四角。

M:
Sorry to bother the square bedroom,
And the square bed.

女：
少扰卧室四四方，
少扰床铺有四角。

F:
You haven't bothered the square bedroom,
Nor the square bed.

231

男：
扰到蚊帐架房中，
扰到门帘挂房门。

M:
Sorry to bother the bed-net hanging in room,
And the curtain hanging on door.

女：
少扰蚊帐架房中，
少扰门帘挂房门。

F:
You haven't bothered the bed-net hanging in room,
Nor the curtain hanging on door.

232

男：
扰到木柜装土布，
扰到对箱装丝绸。

M:
Sorry to bother the wooden cabinet and cases,
Which are packed with cloth and silk.

女：
少扰木柜装土布，
少扰对箱装丝绸。

F:
You haven't bothered the cabinet or cases,
Which are packed with cloth and silk.

233

男：
扰到席垫绿花花，
扰到棉被画凤凰。

M:
Sorry to bother the green mat,
And the phoenix-patterned quilt.

女：
少扰席垫绿花花，
少扰棉被画凤凰。

F:
You haven't bothered the green mat,
Or the phoenix-patterned quilt.

234

男：
辞别妹再见，
下回得来再慢算。

M:
I have to say goodbye, dear girl,
Let's sing when I come next time.

女：
辞别先莫说，
如猪进园难回头。

F:
Don't say goodbye now,
It's hard for you to come again.

235 男：
有诚下回来才歌，
有心下趟来再唱。

M:
We'll sing next time for sure,
If you are sincere.

女：
下回有下回的歌，
下趟也有下趟唱。

F:
Next time we'd have other songs,
Next time we'd have other singing.

236 男：
日后我俩常来往，
哪时来对歌都行。

M:
Let's keep in touch from now on,
So we can sing whenever you want.

女：
此时面对面还假，
几时待后得相会？

F:
You're kidding while facing me,
How can I believe you in the future?

237 男：
来哥嘱咐黑头巾，
怕妹用心不抵值。

M:
Let me tell the black headband,
I'm afraid that I'll disappoint you.

女：
妹也惦记黑头巾，
才下决心与哥唱。

F:
I'm thinking about your headband too,
So I determine to sing with you.

238 男：
来哥嘱咐红头巾，
辞去会郎多么好。

M:
Let me tell the red headband,
It's better for you to find another man.

女：
妹只想念红头巾，
为了重情才跟哥。

F:
I miss your red headband only,
For admiration I'll sing with you.

239 男：
来哥嘱咐花头巾，
若妹重情就守候。

M:
Let me tell the colored headband,
Please wait if you take love seriously.

女：
妹只想念花头巾，
才来守候与哥唱。

F:
I miss your colored headband only,
So here I am to sing with you.

240

男：
对歌有啥好？
对歌有何用？

M:
What are the benefit and use
To sing antiphonal songs?

女：
妹笨求歌来解忧，
妹蠢求唱解忧愁。

F:
Singing songs can release
My worry and sorrow.

241

男：
陪土还得地，
陪土还得花，
陪田还得粮。

M:
You get field and flower,
If accompany the soil.
You get food if accompany the field.

女：
陪土同得地，
陪土同得花，
陪田同得粮。

F:
I get field and flower,
If accompany the soil.
I get food if accompany the field.

242

男：
陪哥空空白费眠，
情缘一样得不到。

M:
You get nothing but sleeplessness,
If you accompany me.

女：
陪哥得歌来开心，
陪哥得诗化愁意。

F:
I get songs and poetics to enjoy,
While I accompany you.

243

男：
陪哥不得手镯戴，
陪哥不得赶街钱。

M:
You get no bracelet and money,
If you accompany me.

女：
陪哥只盼得疼爱，
不求得钱去赶街。

F:
I accompany you for love,
But not money to go to fair.

244 男：
陪哥不得缘和情，
哪得留名依他人。

M:
You get no love if accompany me,
Since our relation can't be closer.

女：
陪哥指望有情缘，
愿得留名像他人。

F:
I accompany you for love,
Hoping our relation can be closer.

245 男：
反来白误织布工，
反来白误纳鞋活。

M:
You may delay spinning cloth
And making shoes.

女：
宁愿不抓织布机，
宁愿少鞋不去纳。

F:
I would rather not hold loom,
Or make some shoes.

246 男：
反来不理弃家务，
反来不顾弃家活。

M:
You may neglect doing housework,
You may neglect caring your family.

女：
家务时时做，
对歌不乱逢。

F:
I do housework every day,
But can only sing on very few occasions.

247 男：
凤凰初春来结对，
怕妹来连不抵值。

M:
Phoenixes pair up in early spring,
But I'm afraid I don't deserve your attention.

女：
凤凰结对在山中，
我俩对歌为了情。

F:
Phoenixes pair up in mountain,
We sing songs for affection.

248 男：
若妹不回又不走，
让哥该是如何好？

M:
If you don't go back home,
What should I do with you?

女：
妹本不走也不回，
让哥带妹一套歌。

F:
I wouldn't go back home,
Will you lead me sing a round.

249

男： 妹处不敢先， 哥处哥才领。	**M:** I'd take the lead only in my turn, But dare not do so in your turn.
女： 妹处请哥先， 此处让哥领。	**F:** I ask you to take the lead, When it comes to my turn.

250

男： 初一吏有旨， 带歌女子必牵头。	**M:** The official has an order on first day①, Woman should take the lead in singing.
女： 初一皇有旨， 带歌男子先开路。	**F:** The emperor issues decree on first day, Man should take the lead in singing.

换位： **Reverse:**

251

女： 芥菜萌城脚， 带歌女子必牵头。	**F:** Mustard sprouts at the foot of wall, Woman should take the lead in singing.
男： 芥菜萌城脚， 带歌男子先开路。	**M:** Mustard sprouts at the foot of wall, Man should take the lead in singing.

还原： **Recovery:**

252

男： 这样妹听哥， 咱丢栓担下河水。	**M:** Please listen to me, dear girl, Let's drop the carrying-pole into the river.
女： 这样一起来， 跟丢栓担下河水。	**F:** Now let's do it together, Drop the carrying-pole into the river.

① "First day" here refers to the first day of lunar month in China. The followings are the same.

253

男：	**M:**
栓担沉哥先，	If the carrying-pole sinks I'd take the lead,
若它漂流妹先行。	If it drifts you should lead the song.
女：	**F:**
栓担沉妹先，	If it sinks I'd take the lead,
若它漂流哥先行。	If it drifts you should lead the singing.

254

男：	**M:**
这样咱再来，	Let's do it another way,
来咱水里丢石头。	Let's drop the stone into the river.
女：	**F:**
这样一起来，	Let's do it together,
跟哥水里丢石头。	Drop the stone into the river.

255

男：	**M:**
石沉妹先带，	If the stone sinks you take the lead,
若它浮起哥先领。	If it drifts I'd lead the singing.
女：	**F:**
石沉哥先带，	If it sinks you take the lead,
若它浮起妹才领。	If it drifts I'd lead the song.

256

男：	**M:**
这样咱再来，	Let's do it another way,
来咱丢黑石下水。	Let's drop the black stone into the river.
女：	**F:**
这样一起来，	Let's do it together,
跟哥丢黑石下水。	Drop the black stone into the river.

257

男：	**M:**
黑石沉妹先，	If the black stone sinks you take the lead,
若它浮起哥就领。	If it drifts I'd lead the singing.
女：	**F:**
黑石沉哥先，	If it sinks you take the lead,
若它浮起妹才领。	If it drifts I'd lead the song.

258

男：
这样咱再来，
来咱丢红石下水。

M:
Let's do it another way,
Let's drop the red stone into the river.

女：
这样一起来，
跟哥丢红石下水。

F:
Let's do it together,
Drop the red stone into the river.

259

男：
红石沉妹先，
若它浮起哥走前。

M:
If the red stone sinks you take the lead,
If it drifts I'd lead the singing.

女：
红石沉哥先，
如果它浮妹走前。

F:
If it sinks you take the lead,
If it drifts I'd lead the song.

260

男：
这样咱再来，
来咱丢晶石下水。

M:
Let's do it another way,
Let's drop the crystal into the river.

女：
这样一起来，
跟哥丢晶石下水。

F:
Let's do it together,
Drop the crystal into the river.

261

男：
晶石沉妹先，
若它浮起哥走前。

M:
If the crystal sinks you take the lead,
If it drifts I'd lead the singing.

女：
晶石沉哥先，
若它浮起妹走前。

F:
If it sinks you take the lead,
If it drifts I'd lead the song.

262

男：
这样咱再来，
来咱丢红纸下水。

M:
Let's do it another way,
Let's drop the red paper into the river.

女：
这样一起来，
一起丢红纸下水。

F:
Let's do it together,
Drop the red paper into the river.

263

男：
红纸沉哥先，
它若漂妹前。

M:
If the red paper sinks I'd take the lead,
If it drifts you should lead the singing.

女：
红纸沉妹先，
它若漂哥前。

F:
If it sinks I'd take the lead,
If it drifts you should lead the song.

264

男：
这样咱再来，
来咱丢白纸下水。

M:
Let's do it still another way,
Let's drop the white paper into the river.

女：
这样一起来，
跟哥丢白纸下水。

F:
Let's do it together,
Drop the white paper into the river.

265

男：
白纸沉哥先，
它若浮妹前。

M:
If the white paper sinks I'd take the lead,
If it drifts you take the lead in singing.

女：
白纸沉妹先，
若它漂流哥就前。

F:
If it sinks I'd take the lead,
If it drifts you should lead the song.

266

男：
若它不沉又不漂，
让哥怎样做才好。

M:
If it doesn't sink or drift,
What then should I do?

女：
若它不沉又不漂，
请哥领唱莫推脱。

F:
If it doesn't sink or drift,
You shouldn't decline to take the lead.

267

男：
棉竹三百根，
檀木百二叶，
让哥开哪叶才是？

M:
I can sing so many songs,
So many songs I can sing,
Which one should I sing to start with?

女：
棉竹三百根，
檀木百二叶，
哥开哪叶都可以。

F:
You can sing so many songs,
So many songs you can sing,
You can choose any to start with.

268

男：
侧耳听微风，
回面听风响，
且听笨哥道。

M:
Giving ear to the breeze,
Catching the sound of it,
Then please listen to my singing.

女：
侧耳听微风，
回面听风响，
听哥来教唱。

F:
Giving ear to the breeze,
Catching it in resonance,
I wait for you to start singing.

269

男：
听听鸭即散，
听听鹅即惊，
听听婴学话。

M:
After listening to my singing,
Ducks and geese may feel amazed,
Baby can even repeat it.

女：
听听鸭即散，
听听鹅即惊，
听哥精灵带歌路。

F:
After listening to your singing,
Ducks and geese may feel amazed,
Still I wait for you to start singing.

270

男：
听听哥回答，
听听哥回应。

M:
Listen to my song,
Listen to my answer.

女：
带歌莫拖延，
稍下时光不复返。

F:
Don't waste time any more,
It'll fly away and never come back.

271

男：
扎筘比梳先，
轻头超妹前。

M:
Tie up the reed before combing,
Let me take the lead ahead of you.

女：
扎筘比梳先，
诚实在妹前。

F:
Tie up the reed before combing,
You are honester than me.

272

男：
扎筘比梭先，
寡人在妹前。

M:
Tie up the reed before shuttling,
Let me take the lead ahead of you.

女：
扎筘比梭先，
开心在妹前。

F:
Tie up the reed before shuttling,
You are happier than me.

273

男：
扎筘比筏先，
大胆超越妹乖嘴。

M:
Tie up the reed before rafting,
Let me take the lead ahead of you.

女：
扎筘比筏先，
哥精比妹前。

F:
Tie up the reed before rafting,
You are smarter than me.

274

男：
妹请哥乱对，
诺言还没讲。

M:
You invite me to sing,
But we haven't made an oath.

女：
妹请让哥对，
诺言同未讲。

F:
I invite you to sing,
Neither has made an oath.

275

男： 咱杀乌鸡把血喝， 杀灰鸡诅咒， 我俩断言走缸边。	M: Kill the black rooster for the blood, With which to make the oath, We're determined to sing along.
女： 跟哥杀乌鸡吃血， 杀灰鸡诅咒， 我俩断言走缸边。	F: Kill the black rooster to have blood, With the blood we make the oath, We're determined to sing along.

276

男： 随哥半路莫退缩， 跟哥半途莫撤回。	M: Don't you give up halfway, If singing with me.
女： 跟哥半路不退缩， 跟哥半途不撤回。	F: I won't give up halfway, Once singing with you.

277

男： 半道别丢哥伴露， 半道丢哥伴夜雾。	M: Don't leave me halfway With dew and fog and loneliness.
女： 半道不丢哥伴露， 决不丢哥伴夜雾。	F: I won't leave you halfway With dew and fog and loneliness.

278

男： 过河不到岸人笑， 对歌不尽头人议。	M: Who does things halfway will be laughed at, Who can't finish singing will be talked about.
女： 对歌催情情更浓， 浇花绽放才罢休。	F: Singing can promote feelings of love, We'll sing until the flowers bloom.

279 男：
道尽诺言方起步，
定好诺言往前行。

女：
道尽诺言同起步，
定好诺言共前行。

M:
Let's begin singing now,
Now that the oath is made.

F:
Let's begin singing then,
Now that the oath is done.

280 男：
千错刻在头，
大胆越妹巧嘴先，
大胆超越美声前。

女：
风吹栗树叶，
初一皇有旨，
带歌男先女随唱。

M:
Carving my mistakes on my head,
I boldly sing ahead of you,
Despite your smart tongue and sweet voice.

F:
Wind stirs the chestnut leaves,
The emperor issues decree on first day,
Man should take the lead in singing.

281 男：
哥不常外出，
何是歌路未精通，
若哥领错请纠正。

女：
阿哥吃遍全郡饭，
每样世面都见过，
妹若不配只管说。

M:
I seldom go out to visit the world,
And I'm poor in singing,
Please correct me if I sing it wrong.

F:
You've visited many places,
And know the ways of the world,
Please tell me if I don't deserve you.

282 男：
如此妹听好，
哥将歌开路。

女：
妹早就恭听，
听师带歌路。

M:
So please listen to my song,
I'll take the lead in singing.

F:
I'm listening to your song,
Please lead me to singing.

三、请宵夜
Ⅲ Night's Snack

请宵夜歌
Inviting for Night's Snack

1

女：
来妹说阿哥两声，
来妹讲郎兄两句。

F:
There's something I want to say,
Something I'd like you to hear.

男：
巧嘴对哥说什么，
甜言盘郎什么话？

M:
What sweet words do you want to say,
With your clever tongue and lips?

2

女：
请哥歇气喝杯茶，
请郎停歌吃碗饭。

F:
Please rest here and drink some tea,
Have a dinner and go on singing.

男：
多谢了阿妹，
多谢异地连情人。

M:
Thousands of thanks, lovely girl,
For the generosity to a outsider like me.

3

女：
饭后再唱歌，
吃饱再继续。

F:
Only after dinner shall we restart,
We won't go on till you dine enough.

男：
阿哥才刚吃，
吃罢妹才到。

M:
I've finished my dinner already,
Just before you invited me.

4

女：
哥吃妹不见，
郎吃娘不知。

F:
I don't see when you eat,
I don't know what you have.

男：
先吃不答谢，
吃多未叮咛。

M:
I started eating without acknowledging,
And helped myself to all the cuisines.

5

女：
现咱共餐才是真，
我俩同桌才算实。

F:
It feels right when we share a meal,
It feels true when together we sit.

男：
现共一餐思念多，
依人同世才抵值。

M:
A dinner makes me fall for you,
Never depart is what I want.

6

女：
相会共餐遇回把，
不怕跟踪一世人。

F:
Rarely have the chance to share a meal,
I don't afraid of following you.

男：
一世共餐才是行，
现同一日有啥用。

M:
With you I wish to share every meal,
A meal today is far from enough.

7

女：
给妹共餐作纪念，
妹同一回当痛爱。

F:
This dinner is worth to be memorized,
I'll keep it in my heart all the life.

男：
这样请妹先进桌，
哥坐跟后也是礼。

M:
Take a seat first please,
I should sit after you with politeness.

8

女：
与人一世还愿意，
跟妹一时莫推诿。

F:
You stay with others the whole life,
Don't refuse our dinner for a while.

男：
讲多话有多，
稍下饭冷难咽下。

M:
Let's talk later as you like,
Or dishes will get cold in a while.

9

女：
请哥快进桌，
请多害羞妹难过。

F:
Please sit here by my side,
Many times of inviting makes me shy.

男：
阿哥为人蠢又差，
同桌生怕配不起。

M:
I'm clumsy and not so fine,
I don't deserve to sit by your side.

10

女：
请哥快进桌来坐，
才是我俩初相逢。

F:
Please come here and take a seat,
Let's formally enjoy our first meal.

男：
妹和伙计坐上席，
哥为愚人坐旁边。

M:
You ought to take the honor seats,
Clumsy people like me should take side seats.

11

女：
枉费请哥来进桌，
妹却害羞难得对。

F:
Trying hard to invite you here,
But I'm too shy to say a word.

男：
哥也跟妹同一桌，
父母不联姻难过。

M:
Now we're sitting at a same table,
Feeling sad parents didn't make us a couple.

12

女：
坐凳灰尘多，
坐桌无一样。

F:
The chairs are thick with dust,
And I can't offer you good dishes.

男：
坐凳凳干净，
美食佳肴满桌面。

M:
The chairs are clean and spotless,
And tables are full of dainty cuisines.

13

女：
在家吃肉又吃鱼，
到此瓜苗接待哥。

F:
At home you have fish and meat,
But here I offer pumpkin seedling only.

男：
在家无油吃芥菜，
来妹却吃酱炒肉。

M:
At home I have oilless mustard usually,
But here I have paste-fried-pork freely.

14

女：
来妹吃菜苗，
来此干菜无油煮，
回去浮肿脸发黄。

F:
We can offer you seedlings only,
Which are neither moist nor oily,
You'll get sick and become puffy.

男：
来妹得吃醋炒鸭，
吃姜炒滑鸡，
得吃酱炒瘦肉片。

M:
I've dined and wined to satiety,
Including vinegar-fried-duck, paste-fried-pork,
And ginger-fried-chicken.

15

女：
吃饭无人装，
吃菜无人催，
坐进桌来光聊天。

F:
No one provides you with services,
No one entreats you to dishes,
We chat only after we take seats.

男：
吃饭有人挠，
吃菜有人催，
边吃边与哥谈笑。

M:
Indeed you all serve me the best,
And warmly ask me to enjoy dishes,
We laugh and laugh in the feast.

16

女：
人世以饭来当餐，
请哥莫要挨肚饿。

F:
People all live by having food,
Don't starve yourself and eat more.

男：
人世吃饭来做本，
全都感谢好伙计。

M:
People all live by having food,
I'm so satisfied because of you all.

17

女：
饭菜吃不成咋好，
请哥忍耐填肚饱。

F:
Dishes are not abundant enough,
Please be tolerant and eat more.

谢宵夜歌
Thanks for Night Snack

1

男：
慢吃了阿妹，
跟后了伙计。

M:
Enjoy your feast, lovely girl,
Bon appetite, my buddies.

2

男：
饭要吃得快，
饱了漱口接喝茶，
饱后继续唱山歌。

M:
I finish my snack quickly,
Rinse my mouth and drink some tea,
And I'm getting ready to go on singing.

女：
饭都吃得快，
饱才漱口接喝茶，
一同继续唱山歌。

F:
We all finish the snack quickly,
Rinse the mouth and drink some tea,
Together let's restart the singing.

3

男：
来哥说妹一两句，
来哥道娘一两题。

M:
There're songs I want to sing,
And some questions I want to ask.

女：
柔嘴想说妹哪声，
巧嘴想道娘哪句。

F:
What songs do you want to sing?
What questions will you ask?

4

男：
今晚对妹真不起，
越想对娘真不住。

M:
Tonight I behave rude and impolite,
Please allow me to sincerely apologize.

女：
阿哥道理真太多，
真是精人会说话。

F:
You say too many platitudes,
Only astute man speaks like this.

5	男： 酒米不是空着来， 用牛去犁耙。	**M:** Rice wasn't from nowhere, You cultivated the farm with cows.
	女： 酒米并不空着来， 哥也用牛一起耙。	**F:** Rice wasn't from nowhere, You also cultivated the farm with us.
6	男： 酒米不是自己成， 父母每天做辛苦。	**M:** Rice wasn't grown by itself, It was grown by your parents.
	女： 酒米也不自己成， 哥亦每天做辛苦。	**F:** Rice wasn't grown by itself, You also worked hard with my parents.
7	男： 父母辛苦还没吃， 倒来敬给哥吃先。	**M:** Yet your parents didn't eat, But first you made a toast to me.
	女： 父母每餐共饭桌， 情郎难相会。	**F:** With parents I share every meal, Yet with you I have little chance.
8	男： 父母自耕田和地， 今成酒茶哥先吃。	**M:** Lands were farmed by your parents, But I'm the one drinking wine first.
	女： 哥亦一起耕田地， 今成酒茶少相逢。	**F:** You also farmed the lands with my parents, Now we hardly meet after the harvest.

9

男：	M:
以前忙工不来帮，	I seldom helped while you were busy,
今成酒茶才来到。	But come here while the tea is ready.
女：	F:
以前忙工哥来帮，	You helped a lot while we were busy,
今无酒茶来敬上。	But we cannot serve you with enough drinks.

10

男：	M:
九月开镰去收割，	Last September you harvested grains,
那时我俩却不知。	And we first met as strangers.
女：	F:
九月开镰去收割，	Last September we harvested grains,
哥拿箩筐去帮挑。	You carried baskets to give helping hands.

11

男：	M:
养鸭得吃蛋，	You raise ducks, it'll lay eggs,
养鸡听啼声，	You raise roosters, it'll crow,
养哥还恩赔不起。	But living with me you'll gain nothing.
女：	F:
养鸭不生蛋，	The ducks we raise don't lay eggs,
养鸡不啼鸣，	And the roosters don't crow,
养哥懂还父母恩。	But you'll repay parents while living with us.

12

男：	M:
哥来则坐到深夜，	I come and stay till midnight,
吃到来年灭了种。	Almost eat up grains reserved for next year.
女：	F:
坐桌只谈古话题，	You're talking only the whole time,
哥别禁斋把肚饿。	Don't starve yourself and get hungry.

13

男：
哥来吃了几仓粮，
哥来喝了几坛酒。

M:
The grains I eat can fill many barns,
The wine I drink can fill many jars.

女：
哥来没喝一口酒，
也没得吃半碗饭，
哪日坏了自身骨。

F:
You don't drink a drop of wine,
And don't have a bowl of rice,
Don't starve yourself and get ill.

14

男：
出去喝稀一阵子，
六月拿瓢紧一段。

M:
I work odd jobs and get low pay,
Living a poor life in the productive July.

女：
出去全年吃得好，
哪天享福真感谢。

F:
You work well and get high pay,
Together we may live a happy life.

15

男：
明年自操管家业，
耕田种地把失补。

M:
Next year I'll run my own affairs,
Plough and farm to improve my life.

女：
哪样都靠哥来帮，
哪样都靠郎照顾。

F:
You give us help in all aspects,
And treat us well with good cares.

16

男：
会吃不会道，
会坐不会夸，
吃多不会谢。

M:
I take a seat and enjoy many dishes,
But lack words to express my appreciations,
Thank you so much for your kindness.

女：
未吃就先赞，
未坐则先夸，
真是名人知礼节。

F:
You praise the meal before you eat,
And say compliments before you sit,
No doubt you're courteous indeed.

17

男：	M:
哥属蠢笨方，	I'm just a poor stupid guy,
哥属愚家族，	Whose family is in dechine,
不知柔言哪句谢。	It's hard to give your compliment a reply.
女：	F:
哥饮泉水很聪明，	Drinking spring water makes you clever,
哥饮井水更乖巧，	Drinking from a well makes you behave well,
哪句都会谢尽头。	No words can describe your kindness!

18

男：	M:
苦死阿哥穷道理，	I'm a clumsy guy who has poor manners,
谢妹未及终话头。	And not good with words to express thanks.
女：	F:
讲多也有多，	We've been flattering too much,
请哥接歌往前行。	Let's start a song and continue to sing.

19

男：	M:
那么妹听好，	It's my great honor, lovely girl,
哥就接起唱新歌。	Please listen to my new songs.
女：	F:
妹已早早听，	I'm listening with all ears,
听师连新歌。	And can't wait to hear your new songs.

四、换声歌
Ⅳ Alternative Songs

在对歌过程中，其中一方需要同伴轮换，对方有不同意和同意两种态度。同意轮换时所唱的歌通常为1—3首，新歌手轮换后唱4—8首。

In the process of antiphonal singing, if a new singer wants to replace the singer on one party, the singer of the other party has the right to agree or deny. Stanzas 1-3 are usually sung when the singers reach an agreement in changing partner; and stanzas 4-8 are usually sung between the new partners.

1

男:
想说妹两声，
来哥说给娘两句。

M:
There're some words I want to sing,
Something I'd like you to hear.

女:
巧嘴想说妹啥话，
甜嘴想说娘啥句？

F:
What words do you want to sing,
With your clever tongue and lips?

2

男:
哥想要伙计来当，
哥想让同班来换。

M:
May I let my buddy replace me?
Would you like to sing with him?

女:
韭菜如葱花，
同班也是歌。

F:
Leeks and green onion are quite alike,
Singing with your buddy is also fine.

3

男:
那么妹听好，
同班就亮歌。

M:
Thanks a lot and please listen,
My buddy is preparing to sing.

女:
妹早已听好，
听听歌师亮歌喉。

F:
I'm listening with all ears,
And waiting to hear his songs.

4

男：
心想换伙计两句，
不知阿妹能喜欢？

M:
I'm taking his place and ready to sing,
Would you like to sing with me?

女：
哪个唱都成，
但愿高兴一路歌。

F:
It's alright and never mind,
I hope we both enjoy the time.

5

男：
吾不惯出路，
歌路在哪不精通，
若哥带错妹提醒。

M:
I'm not used to leading a song,
And don't know where to begin with,
Please remind me if I sing wrong.

女：
哥早吃饭跨县郡，
哪样锻炼早成熟，
妹才借光头一次。

F:
You've left home early and visited many places,
And become mature with all experiences,
But it's my first time joining this conference.

6

男：
若哥不懂就指教，
若哥不通帮引导。

M:
Please tell me if I take the wrong lead,
Please guide me if I can't follow.

女：
这话哥莫愁，
俩手抱心带好歌。

F:
Don't you worry and take it easy,
Rest your heart and lead the song.

7

男：
那么十分好，
哥也借机来开心。

M:
As your wish, lovely girl,
Let's take the chance and start to sing.

女：
那么哥带路，
妹也好心随哥行。

F:
Just sing first and lead along,
I'll follow you with great happiness.

8

男： 那么妹听好， 哥将接着把歌唱。	**M:** So listen carefully please, I'll continue to sing the song.
女： 妹早已听好， 随歌师带路。	**F:** I'm listening carefully, And ready to follow your song.

如对方不愿更换时，则唱本段歌 1—5 首。

If one singer refuses to change partner, he/she will sing stanzas 1-5.

1

男： 来哥讲阿妹两句， 来我说情娘两声。	**M:** May I interrupt you for a while? There're some words I want to say.
女： 有意要讲妹啥话， 有心要说娘什么。	**F:** It's alright and never mind, What words do you want to say?

2

男： 心想要伙计来当， 心想要朋友来换。	**M:** May I change to another singer? My friend is willing to take my place.
女： 伙计有伙计的歌， 朋友有朋友的意。	**F:** Your friend can sing with others, I don't want him to take your place.

3

男： 伙计同欢更开怀， 朋友同乐更欢心。	**M:** Shared joy is double joy, More friends bring greater fun.
女： 为哥妹才来， 必须睁眼唱到底。	**F:** You're the reason why I'm here, I'll sing with you till the end.

4

男： 哥对伙计真不起， 哥对朋友很不住。	M: It's regretful that you refuse, I feel sorry for my friend.
女： 鸡不惯下水， 心不服月公， 妹对郎哥不死心。	F: Just as roosters won't swim, Matchmaker won't change my mind anyway, My feelings for you will never change.

5

男： 这样哥依从， 我俩继续唱下去。	M: As you wish, lovely girl, Let's continue to sing together.
女： 此话十分妙， 路有多长随哥行。	F: It sounds couldn't be better, I'll accompany you to sing along.

双方愿意更换对象时唱 1—3 首，更换后歌手接唱 4—9 首。

If both singers agree to change to a new partner, they would sing stanzas 1-3. The new singer will continue to sing stanzas 4-9.

1

男： 来哥说妹两句话， 来哥道娘话两题。	M: May I interrupt you for a while? There're some words I want to say.
女： 不知哥说妹啥句， 不知郎道娘啥语。	F: It's alright and never mind, What words do you want to say?

2

男： 哥想要伙计来当， 想要同班来替换。	M: May I change to another singer? A buddy is willing to take my place.
女： 妹也要伙计来当， 也要同班来替换。	F: I also want to change to another singer, A friend of mine will take my place.

3

男： 那么请听好， 同班要开腔。	**M:** Please listen carefully, My buddy is going to sing.
女： 那么亦听好， 同班开口跟对歌。	**F:** Please listen carefully, My friend will follow him to sing.

4

男： 心想换伙计两句， 怕不中意娘妹心。	**M:** Taking friend's place I'll start to sing, Fearing that I'm not your type.
女： 妹亦换伙计对歌， 怕不匹配也为难。	**F:** I'll also take friend's place to sing, Fearing that you're not satisfied.

5

男： 阿哥懂歌也不多， 带歌不精像别人。	**M:** Songs I know are limited, I lack experiences of leading a song.
女： 阿妹亦不懂山歌， 请哥有耐心才得。	**F:** Songs I know are also limited, Please be patient while hearing my song.

6

男： 若是偏差莫取笑， 若不到头别骂哥。	**M:** Don't laugh at me if I sing wrong, And don't scold me if I cannot go on.
女： 若妹不懂互相教， 若妹不通要指点。	**F:** Please teach me when I have problems, Guide me along if I cannot go on.

7

男：
哥出门不多，
什么是理还不知，
请妹吞声又忍气。

M:
I seldom leave home and go outside,
And know little about common rules,
Please tolerate while I'm singing.

女：
妹属蠢笨女，
一生未曾学唱歌，
请哥好心来帮教。

F:
I'm such a clumsy girl,
Who has never learnt about singing,
Please be patient to help me along.

8

男：
我俩说罢一起赶，
我俩讲好一起行。

M:
Let's stop talking and begin to sing,
Together we'll sing our new song.

女：
那么哥带去，
我俩接歌往下唱。

F:
Please sing first and lead the song,
Together we can continue along.

9

男：
那么妹听好，
吾将开歌路。

M:
Please listen to me carefully,
I'm about to lead the song.

女：
早日妹听好，
听哥为师带歌路。

F:
I'm listening with all ears,
And I'll follow you to sing along.

五、禁鸡鸣歌

V Overwhelming Rooster's Crow

1

男：
来呀，妹来呀，
妹来哥想说。

M:
Come on, dear girl, do come on,
There're some words I want to say.

女：
来呀，一起来，
不知哥说啥。

F:
Come on, let's go on,
What words do you want to say?

2

男：
马栏鸡拍翅，
又上牛栏拍，
鸡啼天快亮。

M:
Rooster flutters wings on the horses stall,
And flies to the cattle pen,
It crows for the near dawn.

女：
马栏鸡拍翅，
又上牛栏拍，
鸡啼天快亮。

F:
Rooster flutters wings on the horses stall,
And flies to the cattle pen,
It crows for the near dawn.

3

男：
凤散往山坡，
鸦散往树林。

M:
Phoenixes are flying back to mountains,
Crows are flying back to woods.

女：
凤亦散回坡，
鸦亦归树林。

F:
Phoenixes are flying back to mountains,
Crows are flying back to woods.

4

男：
来哥禁鸡不忙啼，
咱禁日头不忙起。

M:
Let me stop the roosters from crowing,
And stop the sun from rising.

女：
跟哥禁鸡莫忙啼，
跟郎禁日莫忙起。

F:
Let's stop the roosters from crowing,
And stop the sun from rising.

5

男：	M:
鸡啼第一声，	The rooster crows for the first time,
哥突心头惊，	Suddenly my heart aches,
想别而情还深厚。	I should leave but my heart refuses.
女：	F:
鸡啼第一声，	The rooster crows for the first time,
妹亦心头惊，	My heart also aches,
想别而情还深重。	I should let go but my heart refuses.

6

男：	M:
情意多好才相逢，	What a great fortune that we meet,
我俩开心还不够。	But our happy time has gone too fast.
女：	F:
情意几好才相逢，	What a great fortune that we meet,
妹亦开心还未够。	But our happy time has gone too fast.

7

男：	M:
几多与娘重情意，	I cherish the love we share,
生死与妹结良缘。	I'd like to marry you live or die.
女：	F:
执着与郎重情意，	I treasure the love we share,
决心与哥结良缘。	Thought of marrying you is in my mind.

8

男：	M:
话别急死在心中，	Anxiety fills my heart while saying goodbye,
怎么辞别异地情？	How can I leave my love far away?
女：	F:
话别妹也全身急，	I'm trembling while saying goodbye,
怎么离别异地郎？	How can I leave my lover far away?

9 男：
欲别树叶还丰厚，
怎么别情自孤立？

M:
Leaves are still flourishing on trees,
How can I leave without my love?

女：
欲别树叶还未卷，
怎么离别异地人？

F:
Leaves haven't fallen from trees,
How can I see off my love?

10 男：
鸡啼第二遍，
天边还黑怎么办，
哥也交情未尽头。

M:
The rooster crows for the second time,
What can I do before the sky lights up?
I hope the happiness will never end.

女：
鸡啼第二遍，
天边还黑怎么办，
一起交情未尽头。

F:
The rooster crows for the second time,
What can I do before the sky lights up?
I wish the happiness will never end.

11 男：
以前花幼不相见，
今花长高才相逢。

M:
We were strangers when buds bursted,
We meet till flowers are flourishing.

女：
以前还小不相见，
今花长高才相逢。

F:
We were strangers when buds bursted,
We meet till flowers are flourishing.

12 男：
想来是更急上急，
恨死摘要花枝梢。

M:
The more I think the worrier I become,
I'm thirsty to pick the flower on branch.

女：
想来也是急上急，
何人想摘花枝梢。

F:
The more I think the worrier I become,
Will you pick the flower on branch?

13

男： 我俩相交如初月， 想别心里却还亲。	**M:** Our love is as pure as the moonlight, We'll be apart but our hearts closer.
女： 我俩相交如初月， 想别心里却还亲。	**F:** Our love is as pure as the moonlight, We'll be apart but our hearts get closer.

14

男： 鸡啼第三遍， 我还问阿妹。	**M:** The rooster crows for the third time, There is something I want to ask.
女： 鸡啼第三遍， 哥问妹什么？	**F:** The rooster crows for the third time, What else do you want to ask?

15

男： 情缘相遇又相逢， 哥还想欢多一刻。	**M:** Fate makes us meet and fall in love, With you I hope to share more happiness.
女： 情缘相遇又相逢， 妹也想欢多一时。	**F:** Fate makes us meet and fall in love, With you I hope to share more happiness.

16

男： 凤凰麒麟结成双， 妹还日后不见面。	**M:** Phoenix and Kylin are in pairs, But I can't meet you after you leave.
女： 凤凰麒麟亦结双， 各自回家难相见。	**F:** Phoenix and Kylin are in pairs, But we can hardly meet after we separate.

17

男： 与人别论异乡哥， 别议异地郎。	**M:** Don't tell others about me, I'm not worth your mentioning.
女： 与人评哥心地好， 夸郎名师通礼哲。	**F:** I'll tell everyone you're a singing master, Who has been so nice and polite.

18	男： 论来哥脸红， 论来哥耳烫。	**M:** My face blushes at your overpraising, My ears are burning for your words.
	女： 评好面不红， 夸妙耳不烫。	**F:** Neither my face nor ears are blushing, There is no exaggeration in my words.
19	男： 鸡啼第四遍， 心中急又急， 天边半黑半明亮。	**M:** The rooster crows for the fourth time, Increasing anxieties grow in my heart, Half of the dark sky is getting bright.
	女： 鸡啼第四声， 心中一起急， 天边半黑半明亮。	**F:** The rooster crows for the fourth time. Increasing anxieties grow in my heart, Half of the dark sky is getting brighter.
20	男： 凤也将别回山中， 鸦也飞回树上巢。	**M:** Phoenixes are flying back to the mountains, Crows are returning to their nests on trees.
	女： 凤亦将别回去山， 鸦亦飞回树上巢。	**F:** Phoenixes are flying back to the mountains, Crows are returning to their nests on trees.
21	男： 燕子离别飞回窝， 龙也回泉去。	**M:** Swallows are flying back to their nests, Dragons are flying back to their caverns.
	女： 燕也将要飞回窝， 龙也回泉去。	**F:** Swallows are flying back to their nests, Dragons are flying back to their caverns.

22

男： 心想还聚多一刻， 却没福分真难办。	M: I'm willing to stay for a little longer, But don't have that good fortune.
女： 心亦想聚多一会， 没有福分也无法。	F: I'm willing to stay for a little longer, But don't have that good fortune.

23

男： 鸡啼第五道， 楼下牛马也惊愕， 我俩留名不到头。	M: The rooster crows for the fifth time, Which wakes up the cattle and horses downstairs, We can't be together any longer.
女： 鸡啼第五道， 楼脚牛马一起惊， 我俩扬名不到头。	F: The rooster crows for the fifth time, Which wakes up the cattle and horses downstairs, We can't be together any longer.

24

男： 凤凰将别飞回山， 我俩情还深咋办？	M: Phoenixes are flying back to the mountains, What can we do to keep our love?
女： 凤凰将别飞回山， 咱情还深咋个办？	F: Phoenixes are flying back to the mountains, What can we do to keep our love?

25

男： 让哥白爱一场空， 卵石拦坝水难留。	M: My love for you is all in vain, Water can't be stored by gravel dam.
女： 妹也白爱一场空， 卵石拦坝水难积。	F: My love for you is all in vain, Water can't be stored by gravel dam.

26

男：
人家有福成缘分，
金花银花并蒂连。

M:
Others are lucky to become couples,
Like twin lotus flowers growing on one stalk①.

女：
人家有福成姻缘，
金银花开配成双。

F:
Others are lucky to become couples,
Like twin lotus flowers growing on one stalk.

27

男：
是果爬上树去采，
是人空讨观其影。

M:
A fruit can be picked from the tree,
But you're human I see only your shadow.

女：
是果攀树去摘它，
是人空讨观其影。

F:
A fruit can be picked from the tree,
But you're human I see only your shadow.

28

男：
鸡啼第六道，
哥白劳碌却无名，
在也变成把人罪。

M:
The rooster crows for the sixth time.
I tried so hard but still failed,
I may offend others should I stay.

女：
鸡啼第六道，
妹身劳碌也无名，
留来也得罪人家。

F:
The rooster crows for the sixth time,
I tried so hard but still failed,
I may offend others should you stay.

29

男：
人家对歌化情缘，
哥对讨名还落空。

M:
Singing songs leads others to be couples,
We sing along but get nothing.

女：
人家对歌结姻缘，
妹讨名头也落空。

F:
Singing songs leads others to be couples,
We sing along but get nothing.

---

① The twin lotus flowers on one stalk: symbolize a devoted married couple, and the long-lasting and sincere love.

30

男：
鸡啼第七道，
思来全身发寒战，
花开再好也要别。

M:
The rooster crows for the seventh time,
I'm shivering to think of departing,
Even flourishing flowers will wither away.

女：
鸡啼第七道，
深思同感身发麻，
花开再好也要别。

F:
The rooster crows for the seventh time,
I'm shivering to think of departing,
Even flourishing flowers will wither away.

31

男：
鸡啼第八道，
日照晒台梢，
对歌多甜也离别。

M:
The rooster crows for the eighth time,
The sun is shining on the veranda,
We have to leave however we want to linger.

女：
鸡啼第八道，
日照晒台梢，
对歌多甜也离别。

F:
The rooster crows for the eighth time,
The sun is shining on the veranda,
We have to leave however we want to linger.

32

男：
鸡啼第九遍，
人家联姻请喜酒，
苦哥痛别异地花。

M:
The rooster crows for the ninth time,
Others set wine for their wedding feast,
It hurts to leave my love in distant place.

女：
鸡啼第九遍，
人家欢饮喜酒茶，
恨哥丢妹去他方。

F:
The rooster crows for the ninth time,
Others set tea for their wedding feast,
My heart hurts to see you off.

33 男：
鸡啼第十遍，
萤虫对月影，
怎舍离别异地情。

M:
The rooster crows for the tenth time,
You and I are like the moon and firefly,
I can't bear to leave my true love.

女：
鸡啼第十遍，
萤虫对月影，
妹讨赏花未满足。

F:
The rooster crows for the tenth time,
You and I are like the moon and firefly,
I haven't admired enough the flowers.

34 男：
真苦哥真苦，
真苦黑公鸡先啼。

M:
I'm feeling painful and lost,
The black rooster crows first.

女：
亦苦妹亦苦，
亦苦黑公鸡先啼。

F:
I'm feeling painful and lost,
The black rooster crows first.

35 男：
恨死嫩鸡啼得高，
恨死雄鸡啼得早。

M:
I hate chicks that crow loudly,
Also hate roosters that crow early.

女：
恨死嫩鸡啼得高，
恨死雄鸡啼得早。

F:
I hate chicks that crow loudly,
Also hate roosters that crow early.

36 男：
为啥瘟王不诅咒，
拖瘦公鸡去宰杀。

M:
Why doesn't the King of Plague cast a curse?
The sick rooster deserves to be killed.

女：
为啥瘟王不诅咒，
把瘦公鸡拉去杀。

F:
Why doesn't the King of Plague cast a curse?
The sick rooster deserves to be killed.

37

男：
用力举刀砍，
剁它分几截。

M:
I'll kill the rooster with a knife,
Then cut it into pieces.

女：
共挥刀去砍，
剁它分几截。

F:
Let's kill the rooster with the knife,
Then cut it into pieces.

38

男：
一截禁鸡莫忙啼，
一截禁日莫忙起。

M:
A cut stops the rooster from crowing,
Another cut stops the sun from rising.

女：
一截禁鸡莫忙啼，
一截禁日莫忙起。

F:
A cut stops the rooster from crowing,
Another cut stops the sun from rising.

39

男：
让日初升把头回，
我俩狂欢更开心。

M:
Force the rising sun to fall back,
So that we can enjoy more happy hours.

女：
让日初升把头回，
我俩狂欢更开心。

F:
Force the rising sun to fall back,
So that we can enjoy more happy hours.

40

男：
我俩交流那么久，
哥心不甘为歌亡。

M:
We sing along the whole night,
Only our song can keep me alive.

女：
我俩交流那么长，
妹心不死为郎哥。

F:
We sing along the whole night,
My love for you will never die.

41

男： 给哥石上栽果树， 何日依人得挂果？	M: I plant fruit trees on the rock, When can I see them graw fruits?
女： 让妹石上栽果树， 几时得吃像人家？	F: I plant fruit trees on the rock, When can I pick up their fruits?

42

男： 人家上山种密蒙， 哥种怎么不开花？	M: Mimengs planted by others are flourishing, Why do my Mimengs never bloom?
女： 妹亦上山种密蒙， 妹亦咋个不见花？	F: Mimengs planted by others are flourishing, Why do my Mimengs never bloom?

43

男： 哥命运不好， 种果不结白饿死。	M: I don't have a good fortune, My orchard bears no fruit and I'll be starved.
女： 妹命运亦不佳， 栽树无果不如人。	F: I don't have a good fortune, No fruit is produced on the trees I plant.

44

男： 独思琢磨心肠软， 饿吞苦水白看人。	M: Thinking of you makes me suffer, Bitter tears swallow my broken heart.
女： 独自深思心亦软， 同咽苦水白看人。	F: Thinking of you makes me suffer, Bitter tears swallow my broken heart.

六、瞌睡歌

Ⅵ Farewell to Sleepiness

1

男：
我俩来送眠两句，
来送瞌睡一两声。

M:
Let's sing together to dispel sleepiness,
Sing a song to send it away.

女：
跟哥送眠意两句，
随兄送瞌睡两声。

F:
Let's sing together to dispel sleepiness,
Sing a song to send it away.

2

男：
妹从内扫出，
哥从外扫去，
眠去远方不回头。

M:
You sweep it out from the rooms,
I sweep it out of the doors,
It'll be sent away and return no more.

女：
同在内扫出，
同在外扫去，
送眠去千里莫回。

F:
I sweep it out from the rooms,
You sweep it out of the door,
It'll be sent away and return no more.

3

男：
送去到岔路不返，
送去到大路不归。

M:
Send it to the fork and main road,
Then it won't find the way to return.

女：
亦送到岔路不回，
亦送到大路不归。

F:
Send it to the fork and main road,
Then it won't find the way to return.

4

男：
送去到河里喂鱼，
送去到田里施禾。

女：
亦送到河里喂鱼，
亦送到田里施禾。

M:
Send it to the river to feed fishes,
Send it to the field to grow grains.

F:
Send it the o river to feed fishes,
Send it to the field to grow grains.

5

男：
送到树梢喂乌鸦，
送到山顶喂老鹰。

女：
亦送到树梢喂鸦，
亦送到山顶喂鹰。

M:
Send it to treetop to feed crows,
Send it to mountain peak to feed eagles.

F:
Send it to treetop to feed crows,
Send it to mountain peak to feed eagles.

6

男：
送去到青天不来，
送到去绿云不返。

女：
亦送上青天不来，
亦送到绿云不返。

M:
Send it to the blue sky,
Send it into the white clouds.

F:
Send it to the blue sky,
Send it into the white clouds.

7

男：
送去上黄云不来，
给它去游荡异乡。

女：
亦送到黄云不来，
给它去游荡异乡。

M:
Send it into the floating clouds,
Which will carry it to foreign lands.

F:
Send it into the floating clouds,
Which will carry it to foreign lands.

8

男：
瞌睡送上天敬仙，
它去千年永不回。

M:
Make it a sacrifice to the gods,
Then it will never return.

女：
亦送到天上倍仙，
亦给去千年不回。

F:
Make it a sacrifice to the gods,
Then it will never come again.

9

男：
瞌睡送上天伴月，
送它去千年不归。

M:
Fly it to the moon,
Make it revolve round the moon forever.

女：
亦送上天伴月亮，
亦给去千年不归。

F:
Fly it to the moon,
Make it revolve round the moon forever.

10

男：
送去到三重天光，
送去到八重天青，
给它去千载不回。

M:
Send it to the heaven,
To the temples where gods live,
Make it stay there for thousands of years.

女：
亦送到三重天光，
亦送到八重天青，
亦送去千载不回。

F:
Send it to the heaven,
To the temples where the gods live,
Make it stay there for thousands of years.

11

男：
十夜不得睡，
眼还亮依旧。

M:
Even I stay awake for ten days,
My eyes will still be luminous.

女：
十夜亦不睡，
眼亦亮依旧。

F:
Even I don't sleep for ten days,
My eyes will still be luminous.

12 男：
眼比猫眼亮，
眼比鹰眼清。

M:
They're brighter than cat's eyes,
And more piercing than the eagle's.

女：
亦比猫眼亮，
亦比鹰眼清。

F:
They're brighter than cat's eyes,
And more piercing than the eagle's.

13 男：
眼还比鹰亮，
眼还如猫醒，
眼还清依旧。

M:
They're sharper than eagle's eyes,
Even clearer than the cat's.
And are also shining and gleaming.

女：
眼亦比鹰亮，
眼亦比猫醒，
眼亦清依旧。

F:
They're sharper than eagle's eyes,
even clearer than the cat's,
And are also shining and gleaming.

七、褒家里歌
Ⅶ Song of Household Affairs

1

男：
吾来褒家里两句，
来吾褒庭内两声。

M:
I want to sing a song to eulogize the household,
Sing a song to bless the family.

女：
跟哥褒家里两句，
随郎褒庭内两声。

F:
I want to sing a song to eulogize the household,
Sing a song to bless the family.

2

男：
褒家里安宁，
褒庭内兴旺。

M:
May the family members be harmonious,
May the family be more prosperous.

女：
亦褒给家人安宁，
亦褒给庭内兴旺。

F:
May the family members be harmonious,
May the family be more prosperous.

3

男：
褒给老人健康，
褒给小孩愉快。

M:
May the elders be healthy,
And children live happily.

女：
亦褒老人健康，
亦褒小孩愉快。

F:
May the elders be healthy,
And children live happily.

4

男：
儿孙也繁昌，
老人也长寿，
我俩给安康。

M:
May children have bright future,
Elders enjoy longevity,
And we both be well-off and happy.

女：
儿孙亦繁昌，
老人亦长寿，
我俩亦安康。

F:
May children have bright future,
Elders enjoy longevity,
And we both be well-off and happy.

5

男：
发病不求神也好，
咳嗽不服药自愈。

M:
May illness be healed without god's miracle,
And cough be cured without taking medicine.

女：
发病不求神亦好，
咳嗽不服药亦愈。

F:
May illness be healed without god's miracle,
And cough be cured without taking medicine.

6

男：
粮吃给满仓，
钱财给满柜。

M:
May the barns be filled with grains,
And money-lockers be filled with treasures.

女：
粮吃亦满仓，
钱财亦满柜。

F:
May the barns be filled with grains,
And money-lockers be filled with treasures.

7

男：
鸡鸭给满舍，
牛羊给满栏。

M:
May poultry sheds be full of chickens and ducks,
And stables be full of cattle and horses.

女：
鸡鸭亦满舍，
牛羊亦满栏。

F:
May poultry sheds be full of chickens and ducks,
And stables be full of cattle and horses.

8

男：	**M:**
黑猪给满栏，	May the pigpens be full of pigs,
花猪给满圈，	There'll be pigs of all colors,
白猪给满舍。	Including black, spotted, and white pigs.
女：	**F:**
黑猪亦满栏，	May the pigpens be full of pigs,
花猪亦满圈，	There'll be pigs of all colors,
白猪给满舍。	Including black, spotted, and white pigs.

9

男：	**M:**
养猪不喂糠也长，	May pigs grow well without feeding bran,
养马不喂草也壮，	Horses grow strong without feeding grass,
母家富裕过从前。	And the family be richer than ever before.
女：	**F:**
养猪不喂糠亦长，	May pigs grow well without feeding bran,
养马不喂草亦壮，	Horses grow strong without feeding grass,
母家亦富过从前。	And the family be richer than ever before.

10

男：	**M:**
女孩也通气，	May the girls be smart and fair,
男孩也聪明，	Boys be handsome and clever,
每人进城做生意。	And they will run their business in city.
女：	**F:**
女孩亦通气，	May the girls be smart and fair,
男孩亦聪明，	Boys be handsome and clever,
每人进城做生意。	And they will run their business in city.

11

男：
出门去找钱也利，
在家做生意也赢，
母家出名过从前。

M:
May family members earn money everywhere,
No matter at home or abroad,
And the family becomes more famous than ever.

女：
出门去找钱也得，
在家养猪鸡也肥，
母家富裕过从前。

F:
May family members earn money everywhere,
No matter at home or abroad,
And the family becomes more famous than ever.

12

男：
钱财进前门，
牛马进后院，
母家比从前喜。

M:
May money keeps rolling into the family,
Cattle and horses grow rapidly,
And the family be happier than before.

女：
银财也亦进前门，
牛马也亦进后院，
母家高兴过从前。

F:
May money keeps rolling into the family,
Cattle and horses grow rapidly,
And the family be happier than before.

13

男：
小孩也聪明伶俐，
个个进京城读书。

M:
May children distinguish themselves at school,
And can pursue further study in the capital city.

女：
小孩亦聪明伶俐，
每人亦进城读书。

F:
May children distinguish themselves at school,
And can pursue further study in the capital city.

14

男：
每句都褒齐，
每样都褒尽。

M:
We've sung to eulogize the family,
With everything well blessed.

女：
每句亦褒齐，
每样亦褒尽。

F:
We've sung to eulogize the family,
With everything well blessed.

八、吩咐歌
Ⅷ Song of Lingering

1

男：
来哥嘱家里两句，
来我道庭内两声。

M:
There's something I want to say,
Say some farewells to the family.

女：
跟哥嘱家里两句，
随郎道庭内两声。

F:
There's something I want to say,
Say some farewells to the family.

2

男：
慢在了右边祖公，
慢在了左边花王。

M:
Farewell, the ancestors on the left,
Farewell, Flora on the right.

女：
亦在了右边祖公，
亦在了左边花王。

F:
Farewell, the ancestors on the left,
Farewell, Flora on the right.

3

男：
慢在了量平米筒，
慢在了留练上天。

M:
Farewell, the rice measurer,
Farewell, the swirling incense.

女：
亦在了量平米筒，
亦在了留练上天。

F:
Farewell, the rice measurer,
Farewell, the swirling incense.

4 男：
慢在了神台对联，
慢在了龛上神符。

女：
亦在了神台对联，
亦在了龛上神符。

M:
Farewell, the altar and couplets,
Farewell, the hierogram on the shrine.

F:
Farewell, the altar and couplets,
Farewell, the hierogram on the shrine.

5 男：
慢在了杨莓柱头，
慢在了家里老人，
我俩异地子离退。

女：
亦在了杨莓柱头，
亦在了家里老人，
我亦异地子离退。

M:
Farewell, the waxberry pillar,
Farewell, dear parents,
We'll leave home and go afar.

F:
Farewell, waxberry pillar,
Farewell, dear parents,
We'll leave home and go afar.

6 男：
慢在了栗木柱头，
慢在了家里大哥，
我俩异地子离退。

女：
慢在了栗木柱头，
慢在了家里大哥，
我亦异地子离退。

M:
Farewell, chestnut pillar,
Farewell, dear elder brother,
We will leave home and go afar.

F:
Farewell, chestnut pillar,
Farewell, dear elder brother,
We'll leave home and go afar.

7 男：
慢在白花木柱头，
慢在了家里大嫂，
我俩异地子离退。

女：
亦在白花木柱头，
亦在了家里大嫂，
我亦异地子离退。

M:
Farewell, tung pillar,
Farewell, dear sister-in-law,
We'll leave home and go afar.

F:
Farewell, tung pillar,
Farewell, dear sister-in-law,
We'll leave home and go afar.

8

男：
慢在了黑杉柱头，
慢在了家里大姐，
我俩异地子辞退。

M:
Farewell, black cedar pillar,
Farewell, dear elder sister,
We'll leave home and go afar.

女：
亦在了黑杉柱头，
亦在了家里大姐，
我亦异地子辞退。

F:
Farewell, black cedar pillar,
Farewell, dear elder sister,
We'll leave home and go afar.

9

男：
慢在冬瓜木柱头，
慢在了聪明小孩，
哪日能还恩得起？

M:
Farewell, big pillar,
Farewell, smart kids,
When I can repay all your kindness.

女：
慢在冬瓜木柱头，
慢在了聪明小孩，
哪日能还恩得起？

F:
Farewell, big pillar,
Farewell, smart kids,
When I can repay all your kindness.

10

男：
慢在了柏木柱头，
慢在了隔壁伯母，
我俩异地子辞退。

M:
Farewell, cypress pillar,
Farewell, neighbor aunt,
We'll leave home and go afar.

女：
亦在了柏木柱头，
亦在了隔壁伯母，
我俩异地子辞退。

F:
Farewell, cypress pillar,
Farewell, neighboring aunt,
We'll leave home and go afar.

11

男：
慢在了矮桌用餐，
慢在了高桌喝酒。

M:
Farewell, the low table for regular meal,
Farewell, the high table for banquets.

女：
亦在了矮桌用餐，
亦在了高桌喝酒。

F:
Farewell, the low table for regular meal,
Farewell, the high table for banquets.

12

男：	**M:**
慢在了印花碗筷，	Farewell, the patterned bowls and chopsticks,
慢在了印凤茶盆。	Farewell, the phoenix-patterned tea trays.
女：	**F:**
亦在了印花碗筷，	Farewell, the patterned bowls and chopsticks,
亦在了印凤茶盆。	Farewell, the phoenix-patterned tea trays.

13

男：	**M:**
慢在了碗柜四方，	Farewell, the square cupboard,
慢在了楼房四角。	Farewell, the quadrangular building.
女：	**F:**
亦在了碗柜四方，	Farewell, the square cupboard,
亦在了楼房四角。	Farewell, the quadrangular building.

14

男：	**M:**
慢在了四方田块，	Farewell, the square fields,
慢在了中间朵花，	Farewell, the flowers on it,
我俩异地子辞退。	We'll leave home and go afar.
女：	**F:**
亦在了四方田块，	Farewell, the square fields,
亦在了中间朵花，	Farewell, the flowers on it,
我亦异地子辞退。	We'll leave home and go afar.

15

男：	**M:**
慢在了平口锅头，	Farewell, the frying pan,
慢在了三舌卯架。	Farewell, the trivet.
女：	**F:**
亦在了平口锅头，	Farewell, the frying pan,
亦在了三舌卯架。	Farewell, the trivet.

16

男：
慢在山弄无茅草，
慢在了无树的山。

女：
亦在山弄无茅草，
亦在了无树的山。

M:
Farewell, the hearth with no firewood,
Farewell, the mountain with no trees.

F:
Farewell, the hearth with no firewood,
Farewell, the mountain with no trees.

17

男：
慢在了火边烟筒，
好客来自待。

女：
亦在了火边烟筒，
好客来亦待。

M:
Farewell, the tobacco pipe by the fire,
Guests can use the pipe by themselves.

F:
Farewell, the tobacco pipe by the fire,
Guests can use the pipe by themselves.

18

男：
慢在了四脚板凳，
有客来自待。

女：
亦在了四脚板凳，
有客来亦待。

M:
Farewell, the benches,
Guests can take a seat by themselves.

F:
Farewell, the benches,
Guests can take a seat by themselves.

19

男：
出门哥谢门，
出门我谢堂。

女：
出门亦谢门，
出门亦谢堂。

M:
I thank the door and the parlor,
When I leave my home.

F:
I thank the door and the parlor,
When I leave my home.

20 男：
慢在门框三天做，
门板七天合，
边做边刻花，
慢在发财好门户。

M:
Doorframes are made in three days,
Door sheets are made in seven days,
Designs are carved at the same time,
Farewell, the door that can bring good fortune.

女：
亦在门框三天做，
门板七天合，
边做边刻花，
亦在发财好门户。

F:
Doorframes are made in three days,
Door sheets are made in seven days,
Designs are carved at the same time,
Farewell, the door that can bring good fortune.

21 男：
慢在门口红对联，
慢在门头黄神符。

M:
Farewell, the antithetical couplet on the door sheets,
Farewell, the yellow hierogram on the door head.

女：
亦在门口红对联，
亦在门头黄神符。

F:
Farewell, the antithetical couplet on the door sheets,
Farewell, the yellow hierogram on the door head.

22 男：
慢在竹竿晒衣被，
慢在阳台晒谷粮。

M:
Farewell, the bamboo pole for hanging clothes,
Farewell, the veranda for drying grains.

女：
亦在竹竿晒衣被，
亦在阳台晒谷粮。

F:
Farewell, the bamboo pole for hanging clothes,
Farewell, the veranda for drying grains.

九、离别下楼梯歌
Ⅸ Down the Stairs

1

男：	M:
慢在了七阶楼梯，	Walking down the last seven staircases,
想起鼻子已辛辣，	I can't help whimpering sadly,
怎么别异地情人？	How can I leave my lover in a distant place?
女：	F:
亦在了七阶楼梯，	Walking down the last seven staircases,
亦想鼻子真辛辣，	I can't help whimpering sadly,
亦怎别异地情人？	How can I leave my love in a distant place?

2

男：	M:
哥想下楼梯，	I'm about to walk down stairs,
见到好情人又退。	But I hold back while seeing you.
女：	F:
妹将下楼梯，	I'm about to go down stairs,
念到好情人亦退。	But I pause when thinking of you.

3

男：	M:
给哥怎么好，	What else can I do?
两手扶楼梯当棍。	I support myself by holding handrail.
女：	F:
亦不知咋好，	What else should I do?
脚软两手抱楼梯。	I can't stand upright without holding handrail.

4

男：
我俩几妙才相逢，
哥也来欢乐未够。

M:
It's a great fortune to meet you,
I'm not content with the joy so short.

女：
我亦几妙才相逢，
妹亦来欢乐未够。

F:
It's a great fortune to meet you,
I'm not content with the joy so brief.

5

男：
不别我道路遥远，
离下楼梯哥脚软。

M:
I have to go because journey is long,
I can hardly lift my feet near stairs.

女：
那哥莫忙去，
我俩交花到尽头。

F:
So just stay here instead,
Then we can have fun till the end.

6

男：
下第一阶梯，
哥突然心惊，
怎么离异地情人？

M:
Walking down the first staircase,
Suddenly my heart aches,
How can I leave my lover in a distant place?

女：
亦下第一阶，
妹亦突心惊，
怎让情人离别去？

F:
Walking down the first staircase,
Suddenly my heart aches,
How can I let my love go away?

7

男：
棵花几多好才逢，
认为得欢乐一辈？

M:
We meet while flowers are blooming,
Why can't the happiness can't last forever?

女：
棵花亦几多才逢，
认为亦欢乐一辈？

F:
We meet while flowers are blooming,
Why can't the happiness last forever?

8

男：	M:
下第二阶梯，	Walking down the second staircase,
阿哥急死在心中，	Anxiety is killing me,
怎别异地金贵情？	How can I leave my precise love?
女：	F:
亦下二阶梯，	Walking down the second staircase,
妹亦在内心着急，	Anxiety is killing me,
怎别异地好情郎？	How can I leave the man I love?

9

男：	M:
花别异地难相逢，	We can hardly meet if we are apart,
在哪得如今开心？	Where can I have such fun again?
女：	F:
花别去异地他乡，	You'll leave me and go afar,
哪日得来往相逢？	When can we see each other again?

10

男：	M:
下梯阶中间，	Walking down the third staircase,
自身急得两脚软。	My feet are too weak to support me.
女：	F:
亦下阶中间，	Following you down to the third staircase,
亦急在心实难言。	Tensions fill my heart but I can hardly say.

11

男：	M:
怎别棵花走出去，	How can I say goodbye and go away,
怎让花蕊自独居？	Leaving you alone at home all day?
女：	F:
怎么让棵花出去，	How can you just say goodbye and go away?
恨死许配共一家。	Why cannot in the same house we stay?

12

男：	**M:**
下第四阶梯，	Walking down the fourth staircase,
急得哥发愁，	Tension drives me crazy,
怎么能别好情侣？	How can I leave without you?
女：	**F:**
亦下第四阶，	Walking down the fourth staircase,
同急得发愁，	Tension drives me crazy,
怎让情侣离别去？	How can I just let you go?

13

男：	**M:**
哥还留恋异地花，	I'm still in love with my dear,
怎能离别独自行？	How can I start the journey alone?
女：	**F:**
棵花去异地难回，	We can hardly meet if you leave,
棵花去他乡难归。	It's hard to return if you go.

14

男：	**M:**
下第五阶梯，	Walking down the fifth staircase,
哥继往下踏，	I continue to move my steps,
怎别异地那朵花？	How to say goodbye to my love?
女：	**F:**
亦下第五阶，	Walking down the fifth staircase,
亦继往下踏，	I continue to move my steps,
何日与哥得重逢？	When can I meet my love again?

15

男：	**M:**
易别难重逢，	Departure is easier than reunion,
何时得如此开心？	When can I have such chance again?
女：	**F:**
易别难得回，	Departure is easier than reunion,
哪日如此得交心？	When can I open my heart again?

16

男： 下第六阶梯， 辛苦劳碌无名气， 皇帝在京却守寡。	M: Walking down the sixth staircase, I'm still lonely despite all the efforts, So what if I were the Emperor?
女： 亦下第六阶， 辛苦劳碌也落空， 认为沾缘得一时？	F: Walking down the sixth staircase, I get nothing despite all the efforts, Why doesn't fate give us more time?

17

男： 人家相连还享情， 哥来相连白白空。	M: Others gain their love from singing, The singing with you turns out nothing.
女： 人家来交有名气， 妹来将成又落空。	F: Others become famous from singing, I almost had it but still lose everything.

18

男： 下第七阶梯， 鼻酸眼泪流， 这回真别好情人。	M: Walking down the seventh staircase, My eyes are blurred with tears, Finally I have to leave my love.
女： 亦下第七阶， 妹亦如何好， 哥别眼泪流成海。	F: Walking down the seventh stair, What should I do to stop my tears, Tears for you converge to become an ocean.

19

男： 不别又不得， 想哭不成笑， 同在怕她丈夫骂。	M: There's no choice than saying goodbye, I'm unable to cry or force a smile, Fearing your husband may curse if I stay.
女： 同在又不得， 亦哭不成笑， 恨死埋头想去跟。	F: There's no choice than saying goodbye, I'm unable to cry or force a smile, How I wish I could follow your steps.

20 男：
慢在了杉木米臼，
慢在了桦木谷槽，
慢在了七阶楼梯。

M:
Farewell, the cedar wood rice mortar,
Farewell, the birch manger,
Farewell, all the seven staircases.

女：
慢在了杉木米臼，
慢在了桦木谷槽，
慢在了七阶楼梯。

F:
Farewell, the cedar wood rice mortar,
Farewell, the birch manger,
Farewell, all the seven staircases.

21 男：
梯脚长茅草，
篱脚长截草，
离去能否还得来？

M:
Grass are growing at the foot of staircase,
As well as the foot of fence.
Can I come again after I leave?

女：
梯脚长茅草，
篱脚长截草，
不知哥别还回来？

F:
Grass are growing at the foot of staircase,
As well as the foot of fence,
Will you come again after you leave?

22 男：
慢在了栗木鸭舍，
慢在了金竹鸡笼，
慢在白花木牛栏。

M:
Farewell, the chestnut wood duck shed,
Farewell, the bamboo hencoop,
Farewell, the cattle pen.

女：
慢在了栗木鸭舍，
慢在了金竹鸡笼，
慢在白花木牛栏。

F:
Farewell, the chestnut wood duck shed,
Farewell, the bamboo hencoop,
Farewell, the cattle pen.

23 男：
慢在了庭院喂猪，
慢在了门前喂鸡。

M:
Farewell, the courtyard that raise pigs,
Farewell, the doorway that feed chickens.

女：
慢在了庭院喂猪，
慢在了门前喂鸡。

F:
Farewell, the courtyard that raise pigs,
Farewell, the doorway that feed chickens.

24

男：	**M:**
慢在了门前李树，	Farewell, the plum tree by the front gate,
慢在窗前构叶木。	Farewell, the leaf wood by the window.
女：	**F:**
慢在了门口李树，	Farewell, the plum tree by the front gate,
慢在了窗前构叶。	Farewell, the leaf wood by the window.

25

男：	**M:**
慢在柠檬斑花叶，	Farewell, the lemon trees,
慢在叶尖柑果树。	Farewell, the orange trees.
女：	**F:**
慢在柠檬斑花叶，	Farewell, the lemon trees,
慢在叶尖柑果树。	Farewell, the orange trees.

26

男：	**M:**
慢在瓦房三十栋，	Farewell, hundreds of houses,
慢在砖房五十座，	Farewell, thousands of buildings,
我俩异地子辞别。	We two will be apart and live far away.
女：	**F:**
慢在瓦房三十栋，	Farewell, hundreds of houses,
慢在砖房五十座，	Farewell, thousands of buildings,
我俩异地子辞别。	We two will be apart and live far away.

27

男：	**M:**
慢在了亲朋好友，	Farewell, dear relatives,
慢在了伙计众人。	Farewell, dear friends.
女：	**F:**
慢在了亲朋好友，	Farewell, dear relatives,
慢在了伙计众人。	Farewell, dear friends.

28 男：
慢在了楼榭晒台，
慢在了凉亭金殿。

M:
Farewell, pavilions and verandas,
Farewell, golden pagodas.

女：
慢在了楼榭晒台，
慢在了凉亭金殿。

F:
Farewell, pavilions and verandas,
Farewell, golden pagodas.

29 男：
慢在了村头神树，
慢在了村口古榕。

M:
Farewell, the old holy banyan tree,
Which standing at the entrance of the village.

女：
慢在了村头神树，
慢在了村口古榕。

F:
Farewell, the old holy banyan tree,
Which standing at the entrance of the village.

30 男：
慢在佑民土地婆，
慢在护村土地公。

M:
Farewell, the earth god and goddess,
Who guards the village and villagers.

女：
慢在佑民土地婆，
慢在护村土地公。

F:
Farewell, the earth god and goddess,
Who guards the village and villagers.

31 男：
慢在饮泉众人喝，
慢在浆洗清水池。

M:
Farewell, the spring from which we drink,
Farewell, the pool in which we wash.

女：
慢在饮泉众人喝，
慢在浆洗清水池。

F:
Farewell, the spring from which we drink,
Farewell, the pool in which we wash.

32 男：
慢在了屋下岔路，
慢在了村下大道。

M:
Farewell, the fork roads below the house,
Farewell, the main streets crossing the village.

女：
慢在了屋下叉路，
慢在了村下大道。

F:
Farewell, the fork roads below the house,
Farewell, the main streets crossing the village.

十、分别歌

X Songs for Departure[①]

通常分别歌
Song for Usual Departure

1

男：	M:
暂别啦阿妹，	Goodbye for the time being, lovely girl,
下回哥得来再算。	I'll come for you next time.
女：	F:
话别哥慢讲，	Don't make a promise so casually,
猪进菜园难退回。	Pigs won't return from the garden easily.

2

男：	M:
含泪离别异地花，	Tears rush out while I'm leaving you,
难舍离别他乡情。	Painfully I wave off my love to go away.
女：	F:
花儿多妙才相逢，	How lucky we are to meet each other,
哥别红花慢点想。	Whether to leave, please think it over.

3

男：	M:
不别也有它道理，	We may be together according to tradition,
不是此时造出来。	Which wasn't set up at present time.
女：	F:
虽然也有它道理，	Although I know there's a tradition,
我俩难逢梨花开。	We can hardly reunite at pear blossom season.

① There are two kinds of departure songs. One can be sung by all people, but the other can only be sung between the lovers.

4

男：	**M:**
道理古代造出来， 男女暂别各一方。	The tradition was set up at ancient time, Lovers should experience a parting time.
女：	**F:**
道理古代也定有， 男女对歌把情连。	The tradition passed down from ancient time, Man and woman make a match by singing.

5

男：	**M:**
各人离别回自家， 各人离别回屋住。	The crowd is disappearing gradually, People are leaving for their home.
女：	**F:**
哥有家室就离去， 妹无屋居怎么办？	You can return to your wife freely, Where is the home I can go?

6

男：	**M:**
海水流去海， 海水归大洋， 不是相怨才离别。	Water will return to the sea, Water will flow to the ocean, They all depart without any hatred.
女：	**F:**
海水回海去， 海水归大洋， 多想眷恋向未来。	Water will return to the sea, Water will flow to the ocean, They still long for a common future.

7

男：	**M:**
海水离去海多好， 我俩异地话离别。	It's natural that water returns to the sea, Outsiders like us will be apart as well.
女：	**F:**
小溪下河一起流， 怎别他乡异地花？	Streams join together into river, Why do we have to depart from each other?

8

男：
妹别往左有福来，
哥别拿碗去讨饭。

M:
Leaving me you'll have a brighter future,
I have to earn a living by begging.

女：
哥别朝左有家住，
妹别流浪一辈人。

F:
Leaving me you can return home,
I have to roam about the whole life.

9

男：
妹别似水离河坝，
何日似今得相逢？

M:
You'll go as water leaves the dam,
When can we meet again like today?

女：
哥别似水下河滩，
妹想相逢难上难。

F:
You'll go as water runs into river,
I can hardly see you again.

10

男：
妹别呵护有公婆，
哥似猪崽上下窜。

M:
You'll be looked after by parents-in-law,
I'll be antsy like a piggy.

女：
哥离会妞相依偎，
妹别孤苦又伶仃。

F:
You'll be chased by other girls,
I'll be alone as I used to.

11

男：
妹别当家享金贵，
哥别卖力还挨骂。

M:
You'll marry someone with great fortune,
I'd better give up to avoid being scolded.

女：
哥别有家给哥去，
妹别不知怎么办？

F:
You have a home that can return,
What can I do if I leave you?

12

男：
妹别找亲来逗笑，
哥别连头抬不起。

女：
哥别痛惜有情人，
妹别苦水荡心头。

M:
You'll marry someone who makes you happy,
I feel too painful to raise my head.

F:
You'll find someone who loves you,
Bitterness lingers around my heart.

13

男：
妹别吃肉又吃鱼，
哥别瓜叶还没有。

女：
哥别吃香又喝辣，
妹别过节菜无油。

M:
You'll enjoy abundant dishes,
I can't even afford the cheapest vegetable.

F:
You'll enjoy excellent cuisines,
I have no oil to cook in festivals.

14

男：
哥别无亲心就忧，
妹别抱子乐心头。

女：
妹别无家心就忧，
哥别与亲多高兴。

M:
Without you I'm all alone,
You'll have kids by your side.

F:
Without you I become homeless,
Your family will live a happy life.

15

男：
来哥吩咐妹两句，
有心听郎道两声。

女：
俐嘴吩咐妹啥句？
有心听郎道啥题？

M:
I have some words to say,
Please listen to me patiently.

F:
What words will you say?
I'm listening to you carefully.

16

男：
别去莫恋糯饭不停口，
莫要贪尝多树果，
不知哪天挨毒死。

M:
Don't eat too much sticky rice,
Don't eat fruits from other trees,
Or you'll be poisoned one day.

女：
别去莫下街舂米，
小心品酒莫贪杯，
不懂哪天身体坏。

F:
Don't help other girls to pound rice,
Don't drink too much wine,
Or your health will be doomed.

17

男：
莫想朝廷太皇子，
莫忘家中田和地，
莫弃夫君勾他人。

M:
Don't follow those noble lords,
Don't forget the farmland at home,
Don't betray your husband and have affairs.

女：
莫念香嫩枫树叶，
莫念香甜蜜檬花，
莫丢贤妻恋别人。

F:
Don't be fascinated with young maple leaves,
Don't be hooked on sweet Mimeng flowers,
Don't dump your wife and seduce others.

18

男：
莫拿斧头忘记刀，
莫要发气恨丈夫，
瞒夫甜言迷他人。

M:
Don't pick up an axe and forget the knife,
Don't be angry about your husband,
Don't wheedle others behind his back.

女：
切莫出街去熬酒，
莫视自妻不起眼，
光记追踪找野鸡。

F:
Don't drink outside till midnight,
Don't look down upon your wife,
Don't chase street girls all night.

19

男： 哥讲妹记牢， 莫像簸箕抛米头。	**M:** Don't throw my advice out of mind, As cast chaff away on winnowing-pan.
女： 哥话妹记好， 犹如听仙来教诲。	**F:** Everything you said will remain in my mind, Just as I listen to oracles from gods.

20

男： 娘妹请慢在， 寄妹请慢留。	**M:** Farewell, lovely girl, Please don't see me off.
女： 慢走哥慢去， 日后念花就回来。	**F:** Please watch out on your way, Just come again whenever you miss me.

情人分别歌
Song for Lovers' Departure

1

女： 来妹讲阿哥一句， 来娘道郎兄一声。	**F:** There're some words I'd like to say, Something that I want you to hear.
男： 快嘴想说哥哪句， 巧嘴想道哥哪题？	**M:** What words would you like to say, With your clever tongue and lips?

2

女： 我俩痛心辞别花， 不死下次来慢算。	**F:** Unwillingly we have to say farewell, I'm dying to see you again.
男： 初升太阳红如火， 若妹连哥心还热， 为何辞别这么快？	**M:** The rising sun is as red as fire, If your heart still links with mine, Why do you say goodbye so easily?

3

女：
不别妹途路还远，
别来花情则还深。

F:
Though my home is far away,
My heart won't change anyway.

男：
有心走三天说近，
不亲隔壁还说远，
咱情多深还离别。

M:
With love three days' journey won't be afar,
Without it neighborhood would become aloof,
You'll still leave even we're in love.

4

女：
话别天突暗，
不舍离别异乡情，
怎舍离别异地花？

F:
Suddenly the sky gets dark,
I'm reluctant to leave my love,
How can I stand going off?

男：
话别哥心急，
不愿让情离别去，
怎让鲜花离别走？

M:
My heart is burning when we part,
I hate to let go of my love,
How can I stand to see you off?

5

女：
抬脚眼泪飚，
不舍情郎离别走，
怎让情妹自己在？

F:
Tears rush out as I walk away,
I can't bear to leave you away,
How can you let me go alone?

男：
话别不思餐，
怎让情妹辞别去，
死活留妹在一起。

M:
The farewell takes my appetite away,
How can you leave me away?
I'd rather die than to live alone.

6

女：
宁愿弃宝别仙家，
不愿离别重深情。

F:
I'd rather reject treasures from fairyland,
But don't want to say farewell to my love.

男：
宁少珍宝都不要，
不愿让情两分开。

M:
I'd rather throw precious jewels away,
But don't want to separate from my love.

7 女：
话别妹哭泣，
哭得流血泪，
怎别亲情投他方。

F:
I can’t help crying bitterly,
Tears of blood stream down my cheeks,
How can I go somewhere without you?

男：
话别妹莫哭，
但愿情意底子厚，
情在异地也还亲。

M:
Don’t you cry, my sweetheart,
If our love is deep enough,
It won’t change even we’re apart.

8 女：
糖比甘蔗甜，
不愿去做他人奴，
怎别娘妹好亲情？

F:
Candy is sweeter than sugarcane,
I want to marry no one but you,
How can I live without your love?

男：
人家吃糖早种蔗，
妹早会合去远方，
才来弃别割痛爱。

M:
Others had long got candy from sugarcane,
You will marry someone sooner or later,
Now you come to kill me with hopeless love.

9 女：
妹似山里藤缠树，
别哥偷在床头哭，
泪满枕头流成海。

F:
I love you like rattans winding the tree,
I’ve been crying before the goodbye,
Until pillow was wet through with tears.

男：
哥像陡壁独猴在，
别妹叹气断了餐，
昼夜无食也觉饱。

M:
I’m alone like a lonely monkey living on cliff,
I couldn’t eat at the thought of the goodbye,
I’ve lost all desires for food and drink.

10	女： 别情眼泪掉成潭， 别哥泪水汇成江， 认为相依得一世。	F: The tears I cried could form a lake, They ran continuously like the river, I used to think we could be together.
	男： 丢哥像丢石下河， 插秧结棉人家穿， 丢哥与别人当家。	M: You'll abondon me as throw stone into river, Farm and make dresses for the other, Abandoning me to be wife to another.
11	女： 我俩像李同一园， 恨死不得共一家。	F: We're like trees growing in a garden, How I wish we could live together.
	男： 我俩似李同一山， 恨死不得结夫妻。	M: We're like trees growing in a mountain, How I wish we could be a couple.
12	女： 别哥似棉别纺车， 别走像夫妻散离。	F: Leaving you is like pulling threads from spindle, It's difficult as a wife leaves her husband.
	男： 别妹像叶离开树， 别去早晚不见影。	M: You will go as leaves fall from a tree, Once leave, you will never return.
13	女： 不别河水还有多， 别走恋哥心不死。	F: With you, love is a river that never drys, Our departing not kill our love.
	男： 不别河水它还流， 别去恋妹心不开。	M: With you, love is a river that never drys, Our departing will take away my happiness.

14 女：
咱情贪吃季黄瓜，
怕哥贪吃别园果，
那时就不记得妹。

F:
We used to share secret fruit together,
If you eat fruits from other gardens,
You may forget me forever.

男：
哥不贪吃多季瓜，
也不贪吃别园果，
爱情一世记在心。

M:
I'm satisfied with the fruit we shared together,
And won't eat fruits from other gardens,
My love for you will last forever.

15 女：
请哥守花等娘妹，
莫让花瓣两头落。

F:
Please hold on and wait for me,
Don't let the flower of love fade away.

男：
妹也守好这朵花，
花在远方难约会。

M:
Please hold on to our love,
Though we have little chance to meet again.

16 女：
路上叶未枯，
哥念在心莫要忘。

F:
The leaves are not withered yet,
Don't ever forget our true love.

男：
路上叶未蔫，
妹也莫忘记心头。

M:
The leaves are not withered yet,
Don't ever forget our true love.

17 女：
慢在亲爱异地花，
慢在亲爱他乡情。

F:
Farewell, dear lover away from my hometown,
Farewell, my dearest lover.

男：
慢走亲爱异地花，
慢行亲爱异乡情。

M:
Farewell, dear love away from my hometown,
Farewell, my dearest love.

十一、叮咛歌
Ⅺ Wish and Response

勤耕田地
Farming

1

男：
未别想嘱妹两句，
有心听郎道两声。

M:
I'll say a few words for farewell,
Please listen patiently.

女：
未别想嘱妹啥句，
有心想道娘啥句。

F:
What words will you say?
I'll listen carefully.

2

男：
回去别打扮出街，
莫要浪荡逛街上，
莫要与人贪风流。

M:
Don't dress up to go out,
Don't flaunt yourself in the streets,
Don't play around and flirt with others.

女：
阿妹三年不出街，
哪去浪荡逛街上，
几时风流像阿哥？

F:
Years I have neither hanged out,
Nor flaunted myself in the streets,
I'm not a dissolute person like you.

3

男：
起早背刀下田去，
起来扛锄上地头。

M:
Just get up early every day,
Take a hoe to work on the farm.

女：
妹属耕田种地命，
一年锄头不离身。

F:
Being a farmer is my destiny,
I'll work everyday with my hoe.

4

男：
莫让地长草，
莫让田丢荒。

M:
Don't let grass grow in the field,
Don't forsake the farmland.

女：
不怕地长草，
不怕田丢荒。

F:
Don't worry about grass in field,
I won't forsake the farmland.

5

男：
种地给开花，
耕田给长谷。

M:
If you do work hard enough,
You'll harvest flowers and grains.

女：
种地也开花，
耕田也长谷。

F:
I always work so hard,
I can harvest flowers and grains.

6

男：
得谷就酿酒等吾，
得花就备茶等哥。

M:
Make wine with grains, make tea with flowers,
Prepare them well and wait for me.

女：
得谷定酿酒等郎，
得花定备茶等哥。

F:
Make wine with grains, make tea with flowers,
I'll prepare them well and wait for you.

7

男：
将来有日办酒茶，
耐吩咐到异地哥。

M:
When wedding feast is prepared,
Please send me a message.

女：
将来有日办酒茶，
吩咐请哥来一次。

F:
When wedding feast is prepared,
I'll send you a message.

8

男：
给哥去喝酒一回，
再说情不浓也罢。

M:
Let's have a drink together,
Don't come along if you don't value the love.

女： 忍耐来穷处一回， 不成干女妹也罢。	**F:** My family is too poor to serve you, It's alright if you discard our love.

9

男： 给哥去喝酒一趟， 再说情不甜也可。	**M:** Being invited would satisfy me already, It's alright if you don't cherish our love.
女： 忍耐来穷处一回， 不怕跟踪一辈子。	**F:** If you don't mine my poor family, I'll follow you forever.

10

男： 哥嘱妹记好， 莫别去远就忘却。	**M:** Please keep my words in mind, Don't forget them after we seperate.
女： 哥嘱妹都记， 似有神仙来教诲。	**F:** I'll keep your words in mind, Just as I listen to gods' oracles.

11

男： 嘱罢哥想回， 嘱毕哥离去。	**M:** I've finished my words already, I have to go in a minute.
女： 哥嘱莫忙走， 吩咐莫忙离。	**F:** Don't leave me so quickly, Please stay here for a minute.

12

男： 慢在了异地的花， 慢在了他乡的情。	**M:** Farewell, my dearest girl, Farewell, my true love.
女： 慢走了异地的花， 日后念花又回来。	**F:** Farewell, my dear lover, Please come again when you miss me.

纺纱织布
Spinning and Weaving

1

男:	**M:**
未别吩咐妹两句，	To you I'll say a few words for farewell,
有心听郎嘱两声。	Please listen patiently.
女:	**F:**
未别想道妹啥句，	What words will you say to me?
有心想嘱娘啥声。	I'll listen carefully.

2

男:	**M:**
回去别打扮出街，	Don't dress up to go out,
别去街上展花枝，	Don't flaunt yourself in the streets,
别去与人贪风流。	Don't play around and flirt with others.
女:	**F:**
阿妹三年不出街，	For years I have neither hanged out,
哪去街上展花枝，	Nor flaunted myself in the streets,
几时风流像阿哥。	I'm not a dissolute person like you.

3

男:	**M:**
起早背刀上山坡，	Get up early, carry the chopper and hoe,
起来扛锄下地角。	And go to work in mountains and fields.
女:	**F:**
起来都背刀上山，	Every morning I cut woods in mountains,
起早都扛锄下地。	And work hard in the fields.

4

男：
念哥种棉多几片，
爱哥织布多几匹。

M:
If you miss me badly,
Plant more cotton and weave more cloth.

女：
念哥不得顾挖地，
哪有布匹在家里？

F:
I always miss you so badly,
And find it hard to plant cotton or weave cloth.

5

男：
有意织布多几个，
惦记舍分给一掐。

M:
You can weave cloth for many people,
I'm hoping you reserve me a pinch.

女：
哥早有妻织棉布，
早日有福到今天，
哪还盼妹送一寸？

F:
Your wife weaves cloth for you,
You always enjoy a happy life,
Do you really want my cloth?

6

男：
每岁分一套讨穿，
给哥讨得个脸面。

M:
Please give me a dress every year,
It's my honor to receive your present.

女：
哥早有人来裁衣，
妹送成刺人家眼。

F:
Your wife has made dresses for you,
She'll be angry if I do so.

7

男：
给哥外出讨装扮，
不怕忘妹好情缘。

M:
Your dress will make me look fabulous,
I won't forget your generosity.

女：
哥早外出得扮身，
几时等妹装模样？

F:
You've got many dresses to wear,
Do you really need my dresses?

8	男： 妹布三七织得紧， 三八织得厚， 布扎四十织得密。	M: The cloth you weave is gorgeous, Which is thick and solid, With it you can make nice clothes.
	女： 妹穷扎三七得紧， 妹穷三八织厚， 送去怕不配帅哥。	F: The cloth I weave is thin and flimsy, Which is too poor to make good gift, You deserve better than my clothes.
9	男： 若得一套讨欣赏， 犹如念异地情人。	M: If you can make a dress for me, I'll cherish it as I cherish you.
	女： 若哥有心恳情意， 哪日连情拜托缘。	F: If you want to win my love, Come and propose marriage before long.
10	男： 讨瞧巧手美工艺， 犹如深厚男女情， 再说不成妻也亲。	M: The excellent dresses indicate your ingenuity, Which are as wonderful as love, I love you even if we can't get married.
	女： 阿妹手艺很粗糙， 若成深厚男女情， 十分不成妻也值。	F: The dress I make is very shabby, If you really cherish it so much, I'll be satisfied even though we can't get married.
11	男： 若妹送针线给郎， 哥也死三身不忘。	M: Even a needle given by you, I'll cherish it till I die.
	女： 若哥惦念到娘妹， 妹死三身还亲昵。	F: If you sincerely love me, I'll cherish our love till I die.

12

男：
日出别让天变阴，
别让哥费心空回。

M:
Please ask the sun to light the sky,
Don't let my love be in vain.

女：
日出莫怕天变阴，
但愿哥守心等妹。

F:
The sun will illuminate the sky,
Please hold on and wait for me.

13

男：
哥嘱妹记好，
不要离去远又忘。

M:
Please remember what I say,
Don't forget them when away.

女：
这句哥别愁，
两手搂心在家等。

F:
Please don't be worried about it,
I'd be surely waiting for you.

14

男：
吩咐完哥去，
叮嘱了我回。

M:
I've finished my words already,
I have to take the journey home.

女：
吩咐完莫去，
叮嘱了莫回。

F:
Please don't go so quickly,
Stay with longer a little while.

15

男：
慢在了娘妹，
往后得来再慢算。

M:
Farewell, lovely girl,
I'll come back if I have chance.

女：
慢走哥慢去，
往后念花再回来。

F:
Farewell, my love,
Come again when you miss me.

切莫外遇
Free from Flirting

1

女:	**F:**
来妹讲阿哥两句,	There're some words I'd like to say,
来我道兄郎两声。	Something I want you to hear.
男:	**M:**
俐嘴想讲哥啥句,	What words would you like to say,
乖嘴想道兄啥声?	With your clever tongue and lips?

2

女:	**F:**
我俩将要话离别,	It's time for us to say goodbye,
不死下次来再算。	Hope we'll meet again some time in future.
男:	**M:**
太阳初升红似火,	The rising sun is as red as fire,
若妹连哥心还热,	If your heart still links with mine,
为何急别那么快?	Why do you say farewell so easily?

3

女:	**F:**
将别吩咐哥两句,	I'll say something for farewell before leaving,
有心听妹道两声。	Please listen to me carefully.
男:	**M:**
将别吩咐哥啥句,	What do you want to say to me?
有心要道郎啥声?	I'm listening carefully.

4

女：
离去赶街莫挎包，
莫与人家谈风流。

F:
Don't carry a bag to the market,
Don't hook up and flirt with others.

男：
人生如鸡被鹰叼，
谁不风流也是傻。

M:
Life is challenging as eagles capture chickens,
Only fools don't expect romance.

5

女：
起早随妻下田里，
莫要上山套野鸡。

F:
Get up early and work with your wife,
Don't catch wild chickens in mountains.

男：
心想压铁木做弓，
想打野鸡来养命。

M:
I'll make bow and arrow with wood,
To earn a living by shooting wild chickens.

6

女：
家有贤妻勤织布，
哥有福气享不完，
与妻养子创家业。

F:
Your wife is a hard-working woman,
You should cherish your good life,
To raise children and run businesses with her.

男：
不去肚子还挨饿，
不猎嘴巴还想吃，
开炮又怕白费弹。

M:
Giving up hunting I'll suffer from hunger,
I also want to taste the wild chicken's flavor,
But I'm afraid I'll waste the bullets.

7

女：
有米别撒喂野鸡，
返来骂家禽，
那时人怪妹不说。

F:
Don't waste your grains on wild chicken,
Don't return home to curse your domestic hen,
Don't blame me for not warning you.

男：
家鸡不孵才挨骂，
才想喂野鸡一次，
娘妹好心才来劝。

M:
Domestic hen is cursed because it didn't hatch,
So I want to feed wild chickens once,
But still thanks for your kindhearted advice.

8 女：
楼脚家鸡老在盼，
哥不撒米去喂它，
倒去坡上找野鸡。

F:
The domestic hen is waiting downstairs,
You don’t throw grains to feed her,
But spend time in seeking wild chickens.

男：
家鸡个别叮主人，
早晚饲喂白费米，
才去迷恋找野鸡。

M:
Domestic hen pecks its owner,
It’s a waste to feed her every day,
That’s why I’m hooked on wild chickens.

9 女：
坡上野鸡骨头硬，
怕哥吞咽挨卡喉，
哪天枯死都不知。

F:
The bones of wild chicken are so hard,
It’s too difficult for you to swallow,
You might be choked to death one day.

男：
坡上野鸡吃可口，
想找一餐记年月，
怕命不长废人生。

M:
Wild chicken tastes good indeed,
One bite can be remembered for years,
I want some memories in the short life.

10 女：
家鸡每天勤喂米，
野鸡不归喂老虎，
怕哥挨吃残剩物。

F:
You should feed domestic hen every day,
Wild chicken will be tiger’s food someday,
You may eat others’ leftover food one day.

男：
家鸡每天还喂米，
讨瞟野鸡一刹那，
才记心中忘不掉。

M:
I feed domestic hen every day,
But wild chicken is hard to be seen,
So it exists in my mind deeply.

11 女：
林中野鸡虽好看，
酱醋煮熟还臭腥，
家鸡好吃不用油。

F:
Although wild chicken looks beautiful,
It tastes rancid no matter how you cook,
Domestic hen is delicious and easy to cook.

男：
家里缺项鸡，
酱醋来炒吃不完，
野鸡不用油盐配。

M:
Domestic hen doesn’t taste good,
It’s hard to be swallowed even with ingredients,
But wild chicken tastes delicious without sauce.

12

女：
饲养家鸡好不过，
专赏野鸡更饥饿，
难养家中儿和女。

F:
Feeding domestic hen is good for your life,
Watching wild chicken can't fill up your stomach,
Not to mention raising your own children.

男：
人穷家鸡养不起，
早晚目睹野鸡游，
一世无妻一样过。

M:
I'm too poor to raise domestic hen,
If I can watch wild chicken every day,
I'd be satisfied though without a wife.

13

女：
家鸡还得享一世，
野鸡中看嘴不肥，
一年见一次不值。

F:
Domestic hen can accompany you for lifetime,
Wild chicken can be watched for a while,
Seeing it once a year is not worthy.

男：
人家流传野鸡甜，
只要救得一时饥，
一年一次也值得。

M:
All people say wild chicken is delicious,
If it can fend off hunger for a while,
One time in a year is also worthy.

14

女：
话毕妹将走，
嘱咐好妹回。

F:
I'll go since I've finished my words,
Hope you can take my advice.

男：
话毕莫忙走，
山歌还要继续唱。

M:
Don't go so quickly please,
Yet we haven't finished our songs.

15

女：
留步慢在异地花，
往后得来再慢算。

F:
Farewell, hold your steps,
Let's sing together next time.

男：
缓行慢走异地花，
往后念情再回来。

M:
Farewell, be cautious on the way,
Come again when you miss me.

约会重逢
Reunion Promise

1

男：
将别吩咐妹两句，
有心听哥道两声。

M:
I'll say a few words for farewell to you,
Please listen patiently.

女：
将别吩咐妹啥句，
有心想道娘啥话？

F:
What will you say to me I wonder?
I'll listen carefully.

2

男：
不得同家也就算，
一同喝水瞧倩影，
不得结缘也还亲。

M:
It doesn't matter we can't be a couple,
We meet and have a drink together,
Love remains even we can't get married.

女：
虽不同家也就算，
一同喝水赏明月，
只要郎哥还念亲。

F:
It doesn't matter we can't be a couple,
I have drink and enjoy the moon together,
Love remains if you're still missing me.

3

男：
爱妹似海水不枯，
怕妹分身割不得。

M:
My love is like a sea that never dries,
But you can't live in two families.

女：
念哥似水归龙潭，
只要相依讨得欢。

F:
My love is as deep as the dragon pool,
The time spent with you is marvelous.

4

男：
我俩因坡隔了坳，
坳口隔中间，
想妹不见人。

M:
We're blocked up by the hills,
Which lie between the places we live,
I wish we could meet at any time.

女：
有心别怕坡隔坳，
不怕隔中间，
只要有哥常惦念。

F:
True love won't be blocked up by hills,
Lovers can overcome any difficulties,
As long as you're stilling missing me.

5

男：
盼妹得来见一面，
想捎句话无处寻，
莫让日夜空相思。

M:
How I wish we could meet again,
But you're nowhere to be found,
I stay awake all night for missing you.

女：
我俩因住各一方，
若有哥话传去到，
妹就随后来相聚。

F:
Although we live in different places,
I'll come to you at any time,
As soon as you send me a message.

6

男：
念妹不见面发愁，
念情不见影心慌。

M:
All I want is meeting you again,
My heart breaks while I'm missing you.

女：
镜破端水来照面，
咱俩都一样。

F:
Mirror is broken, then I look into water,
My face is full of sadness like you.

7

男：
惦念就出街相见，
当作惦记我俩情。

M:
Let's have a date when you're missing me,
To review the romance we once shared.

女：
念哥就出街来找，
生怕人家白了眼。

F:
I'll meet you when I'm missing you,
Fearing that scandals would fly everywhere.

8

男：	**M:**
见面讨瞧靓倩影，	Just a glance at you is enough,
既不成妻也抵值。	I'd be satisfied even you aren't my wife.
女：	**F:**
见面讨瞧多一回，	Just a short appointment is enough,
既不成夫也亲热。	Love remains even you aren't my husband.

9

男：	**M:**
我情如山重，	Our love is as heavy as mountains,
深过日夜夫妻情。	And even deeper than spouse.
女：	**F:**
我俩情缘比海深，	Our love is as deep as the sea,
胜过从前祝英台。	And closer than Shanbo and Yingtai.

10

男：	**M:**
相逢甜言多珍贵，	The sweet words between us are precious,
好比孩童见母亲。	Just as the words between kids and mother.
女：	**F:**
相逢蜜语暖心窝，	The romantic whispers we share are fantastic,
好比与仙会银河。	Just as the meeting of lovers after long departure.

11

男：	**M:**
莫贪家务那么勤，	Don't work too hard at household affairs,
莫贪柴草那么多，	Don't cut too much firewood,
哪天瘦死也不抵。	It's useless if you get sick.
女：	**F:**
与哥抽剥隘烟丝，	I'd like to serve you a smoke of tobacco,
离哥做工心头懈，	Without you I can't focus on work,
不懂哪日丧性命。	I might die of carelessness someday.

12

男：
米粮够吃就得了，
莫要只管田和地，
莫丢我俩情和意。

M:
Planting grain sufficed for eating is enough,
Don't care about farm work too much,
Don't abandon our love away.

女：
不劳肚子却挨饿，
不做无食来糊口，
做来情意顾不及。

F:
Grain won't come itself without sowing seed,
I won't have food if I don't work,
There isn't enough time to maintain our love.

13

男：
风华正茂在三十，
五十以下好年景，
谁不风流是傻瓜。

M:
We're aged between thirties and fifties,
Which is the finest and glorious time,
Only fools don't expect a romance.

女：
同欢同乐在三十，
过了五十乐不起，
妹无依靠咋个办？

F:
We can play around in the thirties,
But can't afford chasing pleasure after fifties,
Who can I depend on at that time?

14

男：
搭肩三掰布，
那时子女挂前后，
妹想风流乐不起。

M:
Hanging baby carrier on your shoulders,
You'll carry babies at your back and front,
Then won't be able to have fun.

女：
念情莫要半路丢，
那时关照顾到底，
许妹相依讨开心。

F:
Don't give up our love so easily,
Please accompany me till the end,
I'd like to please you by your side.

15

男：
那时裤脚结黑果，
才来念情毁人生。

M:
Don't feel regret for wasting your life,
Until you're occupied by housework.

女：
要是裤脚结黑果，
也还顾情到末终。

F:
My love for you will never end,
Even I'm occupied by housework.

16

男：
哥讲妹记好，
不要远离就忘情。

M:
Please remember our vows,
Don't forget it when we're apart.

女：
哥话妹铭记，
怕哥要糠来诱鸡。

F:
I'll remember our vows,
Don't lure other hens with rice bran.

17

男：
留步慢在异地花，
留步慢在他乡情。

M:
Farewell, hold your steps, my dear love,
Farewell, hold your steps, away I'd go.

女：
缓行慢走异地花，
慢去慢回他乡情。

F:
Farewell, hold your steps, my lover,
Farewell, my dear lover, hope you bear me in mind.

15

男：

[illegible]

[illegible]

M:

Don't feel regret for wasting your life,

Until you're occupied by housework.

女：

[illegible]

[illegible]

F:

My love for you will never end,

Even I'm occupied by housework.

16

男：

[illegible]

[illegible]

M:

Please remember our vows

Don't forget it when we're apart.

女：

[illegible]

[illegible]

F:

I'll remember our vows,

Don't lure other hens with rice bran.

17

男：

[illegible]

[illegible]

M:

Farewell, hold your steps, my dear love,

Farewell, hold your steps, away I'd go.

女：

[illegible]

[illegible]

F:

Farewell, hold your steps, my love,

Farewell, my dear love, hope you bear me in mind.